Eight Hours

The Short Story Reinvented

Independent Book Publisher

Legend Press Ltd
13a Northwold Road, London, N16 7HL
info@legendpress.co.uk
www.legendpress.co.uk

Contents © Legend Press Ltd, the selection, and the following
contributors to the collection © Josie Henley-Einion, Hilary Lloyd,
E.C. Seaman, C L Raven, Kevin Chandler, Nick Tyler, Jackie
Blissett, Daniel Gothard 2008

Collection selected and edited by Emma Howard

British Library Cataloguing in Publication Data available.

ISBN 978-0-9551032-9-2

*All characters, other than those clearly in the public domain, and
place names, other than those well-established such as towns and
cities, are fictitious and any resemblance is purely coincidental.*

Set in Times
Printed by J. H. Haynes and Co. Ltd., Sparkford.

Cover designed by Gudrun Jobst
www.yellowoftheegg.co.uk

Legend Press
Independent Book Publisher

The Short Story Reinvented

Legend Press' unique short fiction series, 'The Short Story Reinvented', is designed for today's busy, but discerning, reader. Short fiction is a perfect answer in a world where everyone wants things to be easily accessible, sleek and tailored to fit their needs.

High-quality, thought-provoking short fiction can perfectly fill what before may have been an enforced gap of 'dead-time' in a daily routine. Dipping into short fiction on a commute or during a lunch break is not as daunting as delving into a thick novel when you know that you might soon be interrupted mid-chapter; yet the subject matter in this popular series is weighty and meaningful, providing something new to think about and feel inspired about for the rest of the day, week, month and year.

Legend Press receives hundreds of submissions for the collections, from all over the UK and around the world including the US, Norway, Italy, New Zealand and South Africa. The successful entries for each book are chosen so that the stories combine and contrast compellingly to make the most varied, yet at the same time the most cohesive, collection possible.

The other collections in the series are:
The Remarkable Everyday (ISBN 9780955103209)
and Seven Days (ISBN 9780955103230)

Contents

5am

Hush Little Baby

By Josie Henley-Einion

It's five. If I fall asleep now then I've got like two and a half hours till the alarm goes off. That should be enough. I'm sure I could cope. It's only Thursday, no PE. At least I'll have had some sleep. Not like last time when I couldn't drop off at all. Still I managed to survive the whole day, only nodded a bit in Maths. Not that anyone noticed.

I just need to fall asleep now. That's all.

Try counting sheep, she says. I've done sheep, cows, pigs, chickens, the whole bloody barnyard. Even started on zebras and hippos. She's full of shit. Thinks I'm watching too much TV, drinking too much coke, got too many hormones, god knows what. What does she know? Does she lie awake night after night? No, she snores like a warthog in a snoring competition. What am I supposed to say when she complains about me yawning at breakfast? Mother dear, I'm kept awake by that godawful racket you make like you're trying to drill a hole through the wall between us. Like yeah, that would go down well wouldn't it?

And if it's not her then it's something else. Twittering bloody birds outside the window, the cat licking his bits making slurping noises, rattling trains screeching over leaves on the line, helicopters chasing criminals and god knows what else. I swear I can hear the stars popping out, like ping ping ping. God I wish I could sleep.

My pillow is too hot. I lean up on my elbows and turn it over, sink gratefully into the cool soft fleshy fuzz. I drift. I've been trying to meditate, to calm my brain and think pleasant thoughts. Maybe if I just try not to think about anything, try to blank my mind, then it'll happen. I'll sleep.

I can't empty my mind. I try. I push all the thoughts over to one side and get a big empty space. But it fills again. Like water leaking through the gaps in a lock. Like a tiny squeak that you wouldn't normally notice but when everything else is quiet it takes over your whole brain. Like forcing all your old toys and games into a cupboard and it's door creaks and groans and suddenly springs open. Then you've got stuff flying over the room and you find a headless doll that you used to love and the last piece from a jigsaw that you've already thrown out and before you know it the room is full of crap again and I'm totally not managing to keep a blank mind at all.

The problem with trying not to think about something is that as soon as you tell yourself not to think about it, you're already thinking about it. I fill my head with other stuff. All day I fill my head. I read read read. I study study study. If I can think about anything else, anything at all then I can stop thinking about the thing that I don't want to think about.

My pillow is still hot. Turn it over. Turn it over again. Turn it over. Turnitover. I push the pillow off the bed and lie on the bare sheet. Cool sheet covering shiny mattress. Uncle Tom Cobbly gets up in a huff and stalks over to my desk where he perches like an Egyptian temple cat giving me the evil.

Calm calm try to be calm. Try to just breathe. Just breathe and nothing. Nothing else. Nothing in my head. Nothing.

I drift for some minutes.

Nothing. Nothing a big pile of nothing. Snap, my brain fires something in. Images, faces emerging. Push it away. Put it in the cupboard. Nothing. Eyes closed tight. Concentrate on nothing. Tight tight concentrate. Think nothing think nothing think nothink thinknothink. Ping, in comes another thought. Fire it out. Smash it down. Like a mallet on the moles in the arcade. Bang. Another thought. Bang. Another image. Bang! Like Lady Macbeth's dog. Out, out damned Spot!

It's no good. I turn over. I'm on my back. I can't not think.

11

I have to think something. Okay. Try another tactic. I'm floating. Imagine I'm floating. Drift away drift away floaty floaty float. I turn over onto my stomach. My arms out. I'm floating floaty light.

I imagine that I'm soaring over the village, over the school, the church, the river. All the people are under me, no one sees me but I see them. I see what they're doing and I see their thoughts in speech bubbles above their heads. The vicar is farting, thinking about his dog. Vera in the bakery is laying out cakes laced with poison, chuckling to herself about the greedy customers getting sick.

Children are walking to school, dancing and skipping. Thinking about their friends and their dinners. Feeding horses in the field and laughing at the angry geese. The old man is at the park gates, hiding. I'm floating, I'm floating like an angel. I'm a guardian angel looking down on them all.

There is Debbie, delightful, delicious Debbie. Swinging her bag as she walks over the bridge. Flouncing her hair like she does when she knows she's being watched. I'm watching, I'm watching. If only she knew, but she doesn't, and I make sure of that. We're friends, just friends. None of that monkey business, not for pure little me. Yeah, right. I swoop down lower and lower. I see her. I feel her. I breathe her. Then she looks up. She looks up my angel skirt.

Heart pounding, I gasp, grasping the covers. Did she see? Did she see? Didshesee?

Oh god now I'm never going to sleep. Why did I have to go and think about Debbie? Now I'm hot all over. Every night I say I'm not going to think about her. Every bloody night I spend the whole night not thinking about her. When am I going to get her out of my head?

I'm a fallen angel. I laugh. I laugh out loud. Cover my mouth hold my breath. Did she hear me? Did I wake her up? No. She stopped snoring but now she's turned over and it's started again. The wall vibrates like it's tissue paper stretched over a comb and Granddad is playing it at Christmas. And he's laughing and I'm opening my presents and everyone is happy. But it's not. It's just a wall and it's vibrating because it's too thin because this flat is crap because it's not our house and Granddad isn't here and it's all crap.

Why did we have to move to this godforsaken hole in the universe? Why couldn't we stay in the village? Mother dear, snoring mother, ugly fat noisy ugly mother sold the house, rented a shoebox flat in the stinking noisy fat ugly city. Why couldn't we stay in the village? Why can't I sleep?

Uncle Tom Cobbly creeps back onto the bed. He snuggles up next to my leg and I can feel his purr vibrating through my duvet. He doesn't stay annoyed with me for very long. I put my hand down to stroke him and he rubs against it for a few seconds but then bites my finger. Ow. Bad tempered old bag. Maybe he's not getting enough sleep either. Cats are supposed to be able to sleep sixteen hours a day, I read it on the internet. What's wrong, Uncle Tom, am I depriving you? Have you only had fourteen hours today?

I stare at the LED display on my clock. 05:09. I close my eyes and the digits are burnt into my retina. 05:09. I open my eyes. 05:09. I close my eyes. 05:09. I close my eyes tighter. 05:09 moves up and to the left. I move my eyes and 05:09 moves down again. 05:09 spins. 05:09 begins to fade. I open my eyes. 05:09. I close my eyes. 05:09 shines brightly, moves, spins. I open my eyes. 05:10. If I go to sleep now I'll have two hours and twenty minutes of sleep.

I need the loo. I need to go again. When did I go last? About three o'clock I think. Two hours ago. I shouldn't have had that handful of water. But I was thirsty. I get so thirsty at nights. So hot and lying awake all night makes me thirsty and I have to drink and I have to pee. I don't think I can sleep without peeing. But if I get up now for the toilet then I'll be wide awake when I get back. But I'm wide awake now. Sod it.

I get up. Uncle Tom flies off the bed again. I walk to the door. I bang into the wall. I've been here a few weeks and I still can't get used to the size of this box that we call my bedroom. I open the door. I take two steps. I open the bathroom door. I take one step. I sit on the toilet. I'm naked. I'm cold. Shivering. I need a pee. I can't go. I turn on the tap. Listen to the trickle of water. Lean on the sink. I go. It burns. Maybe I'm dehydrated. I take a sip of water from the tap as I stand. A tiny sip.

I step back to my room. I fall onto my bed. I drag the duvet over me. I grab my pillow from the floor. It's cool again. I put it over my head. Turn to the wall. Sleep. I've got to sleep. I really have to. Can't keep on like this.

When I was a kid and I couldn't sleep, Granddad used to sing to me. Hush little baby don't say a word. I wasn't a little baby but I liked the song. I think about it now. I think about his voice. I try to remember his voice. I try to remember his face before the stroke. It's difficult to remember because every time I think about Granddad I get the unwanted thoughts. The ones when he's ill and thin and his face is collapsed and he can't talk and he's in the care home and I was glad when he finally died because it was better for him.

Turn on my side. Press the pillow into my ear to keep out the noise. I wish I could press it all the way into my ear and through to my brain and muffle the thoughts. I don't want to think about it. I don't want to think about Granddad and I don't want to think about Debbie and I don't want to think about what Debbie said about Granddad and I don't want to think about what Mum said about Debbie.

Shut up! Shut up! Stop thinking about it! Stop it stop it stopit.

Hush little baby don't say a word. Granddad's gonna buy you a mocking bird. Sleep. God if I could just sleep. It wouldn't be so bad if I'd already left school. I could stay up all night reading, studying, whatever. If I could work to my own routine instead of this stupid set routine that we're all supposed to work to but it's artificial because in the old days people just worked when there was sunlight and slept when there wasn't. If I could work all summer and sleep all winter. If I was living in the North Pole. If there weren't any other people around. If I had some peace. If she would just stop snoring.

Bloody bloody hell! I throw the pillow off me again. It goes to the end of the bed. I sit up. I turn over. I lie on my side. Look at the clock. 05:14 blink 05:15 it changes. Blip blip.

I get this weird feeling that I'm being watched. Like the hairs prickling on the back of my neck. I turn around but there's only the wall. I sit up. Uncle Tom Cobbly is parked on the box at the bottom of the bed sitting upright but swaying as if he's hypnotised himself. Maybe he's trying to hypnotise me? Maybe he's saying, 'You are feeling sleeeepy. Goooo toooo sleeeep.'

Yes, yes and yes. In the greater scheme of things when there are people dying of starvation and they can't get clean water, one girl not being able to sleep at night is not really that significant. But for me it is. For me it takes over my whole body, my whole world. It stops me functioning properly and it makes me obsessed with minute details. It makes me start to think of things that I shouldn't be thinking about and it makes me imagine things that aren't there, or were never there or were they?

I'm going to be no good in school tomorrow. No good at all. I know I can't think straight when I've had no sleep. I can't think straight anyway. I think all bendy and wiggledy and all over the place, with sleep or without. What lessons have I got? Biology I know that. Double maths, computers. I got my bag ready but I can't remember seeing the biology book. I checked at two o'clock for the maths and computers books but can't remember seeing biology. I get up. I sit on the end of the bed. I pull my bag over. Sift through the books. Get

15

everything out one by one. Maths. Biology. Computers. Pencil case. Long ruler that doesn't fit in the pencil case. Chemistry, what's chemistry doing in there? I don't have chemistry on a Thursday. Take it out. English lit, Shakespeare bloody *Hamlet*. That's all. That's it. Don't need any more. Zip up the bag. Put it back. Lie back down. Get up again. Didn't see my snack. Check the pocket of the bag. There's the pack of oatcakes. Of course. I put them in there so they wouldn't get crushed. Put the bag back. Lie back down. Uncle Tom Cobbly steps cautiously onto the very bottom of the bed and begins to circle, purring and pricking the duvet.

Why do I have to study bloody Shakespeare? What's Shakespeare got to do with people living today? All that to be or not to be nonsense. It's got nothing to do with me. Nothing at all. I don't even know what to be or not to be means. What does it mean? Am I dead or alive? Is it better to be alive and miserable or dead and happy? Something like that. But that doesn't make sense at all. Or maybe it does. Maybe it's got everything to do with me. If they could just update it a bit. Put it on the internet. Youtube it. Then it would be interesting. Somebody said they'd done a graphic novel. So it's probably already on the internet. But in my school they're still working from battered textbooks with scribbles that are years old. Nothing fancy for us. No internet. Even in computers you can't go on the internet. Well you can, but every time you try to access something interesting you get blocked. At least I can use it at home. It's about the only good thing about this crappy place.

I read on the internet that there are multiple universes and that every possibility of what might happen in your life is happening to another you somewhere else in another dimension. So there's another me in another universe who's still living in the village and another Granddad who's still alive. It sounds like science fiction but there are researchers who say it's true. In physics they look at particles and they say

16

that the particles disappear and go into another dimension and then come back again, presumably because they didn't like it there. And they say this proves that these other universes exist. But it's a bit different isn't it, a tiny particle of light or a human being? I mean, maybe the researchers just blinked a bit and missed the particle. Maybe it didn't go anywhere after all. It could have got fed up with being watched and hidden somewhere. Particles of light are funny like that, just like cats. Uncle Tom used to hide when it was time to go out at night. Maybe the particles of light that the researchers were watching were actually cats in the other world. Maybe the research physicists were students who'd done a few too many drugs and they were hallucinating.

I read on the internet that people with sleep deprivation get hallucinations. You need to dream. People who can't dream get hallucinations because the brain is still dreaming even if you're awake. The hallucination is the dream. What would my hallucination be? Would I even know if I was hallucinating? Maybe this flat is my hallucination. Maybe this life is my hallucination. Maybe my Granddad is still alive and we still live in the old house in the village and I'll wake up and I've been dreaming all along. Yeah right.

I sometimes dream about Debbie. If she knew the dreams I've had about her then she probably wouldn't be my friend. I wonder if she'd have said that about my Granddad. I wonder if she'd have said that if she knew. Would she have said it differently? Would she have said, 'You're disgusting, just like your Granddad.'

Stop it! Stop thinking about it. Eyes shut tight I can't think about it. If I think about it then it's going to happen and I don't want it to happen. I don't want it and if I don't want it then I'm not like that. Isn't it right that it's a choice? That you don't have to be like that if you don't want to be? Debbie was lying anyway. She said her Gran told her but her Gran was lying. How does her Gran know anything about my Granddad and anyway if Granddad was like that I'd have known wouldn't I? Wouldn't I?

I have to block it. I have to study. I study history, theology, Latin. Good strong solid subjects. I study philosophy, psychology, biology. My Granddad would be proud. My Granddad would laugh and he would be proud and he'd hug me and tell me I'm a good girl. I would tell him all the things I've learned and I'd show him my certificates and my prizes and he'd be happy and proud.

I turn over. I'm hot. Uncle Tom sways like he's on a boat and he opens one eye but doesn't look up. I push the duvet off and lie naked. The corner of it hits Uncle Tom's ear and he flicks it but doesn't look up. I lie in the cool and I lie naked. I feel good. I feel so good. I feel cool. I feel like I'm floating. I feel brushed like something touched me. I can't see anyone but someone touched me. I can't do it. No I can't. I can't do it. I feel vulnerable. I feel exposed. I pull a sheet. Just a sheet. Now I'm wrapped up in a toga like a Roman. Like an angel. A guardian angel. I'm flying but the sheet slips. It's slipping slipping and the people below can see. I sit up. I'm shivering. I'm hot but I'm shivering. I pull the duvet and my pillow back. I bury myself inside. I'm hot but I'm scared and I'm buried inside.

Something touched me. Someone touched me. I felt it. It wasn't a dream. I was awake. I felt it. It wasn't Uncle Tom. He's still on the bottom of the bed. Someone touched me. Was it Granddad? Was he here because I was thinking about him? Did he come back? Was he here? I'm buried inside. If it was Granddad then I would smell his soap. I would smell his tobacco. If it was Granddad then he'd be there, then he'd be standing by my bed. If it was Granddad then I'd just need to put my head out and then I'd see him.

Should I put my head out? What if he's there? What if he's not there? I'm hot and I need to put my head out. I don't know if I can. I can't breathe under here but I can't put my head out.

What if I died under here? What if I suffocated? Would anyone notice? Would Mum get up without me? Would she find me before it was school time? Would it matter? What does school matter if you're dead? Would Debbie miss me? Would she ever think about me?

I'm hot. I have to put my head out. If I put my head out but don't open my eyes then I won't see whether Granddad is there or not. If I put my head out and just sniff the air then I'd know whether Granddad is there because I'd smell his scent. I'd smell his soap, his tobacco. If I put my head out I can breathe but nothing can get me if I don't open my eyes.

I'll do it. I'll put my head out. But I have to count. I'll count to three then I'll put my head out. I'll count to three. I'll do it. One, two, but what if Granddad touches me again? It's too hot. I have to get out of here for some air. One, two, I can do it. I know I can do it.

One, two, three, out! Breathe. Eyes tight shut. Under again, buried again, inside again in safe inside safe. Safe again. He wasn't there. I know he wasn't there because if he'd have been there I'd have known. I'd have sensed him if he was there, even though I was only out for one breath I'd have known.

But I'm not going to be able to sleep like this. I'm safe buried here in the duvet but I'm not going to sleep. I have to uncurl. My muscles snapped tight need to relax before I can sleep. I have to unfurl. Slowly I make my feet move downwards. Slowly I move my knees away from my chest. But I can't stretch right out. I can't put my feet to the bottom of the bed. The sheet is cooler there and it's nice but I can't put my feet to the bottom. When I was little I used to imagine monsters under the bed. They would grab at my feet if my feet were close to the bottom. They would put their hands over the sides of the bed and grab me. I would have to curl tight right in the middle of the mattress not close to any edge. If I was close to the edge then they would grab me, they would get me.

I'm not little now. I tell myself I'm not little and it's silly to think that. But at 05:19 in the morning when it's still dark and there's no one else around not even a dead Granddad guardian angel it's difficult to stretch your feet out to the bottom of the bed in case there are monsters.

Hush little baby don't say a word. I'm not little I'm fifteen. I'm a fifteen year old insomniac. I push the duvet off my head. It's not dark anymore anyway. It's getting light now. Grey light like an old black and white film about the war that Granddad used to watch. I breathe in the cool air. I lie on my back. And if that mocking bird won't sing, Granddad's gonna buy you a diamond ring.

I lie on my back. I smooth the duvet down. It's crinkly uncomfortable. I smooth it down on the top and then I put my hands under the duvet and smooth down the underside of the duvet. It's all smooth that's better. I put my hands under the duvet. I smooth down my ribs and they tingle. I smooth down my legs. I smooth down over my stomach. I think about Debbie. I shift my legs. The duvet moves. It moves against my body. I think about Debbie. Stop! I have to stop. I'm on a bed of nails. I'm hot and cold I have to stop. I can't do that I can't do it.

My pillow is hot. Turn it over. Turn it over again. Turn it over. Turnitover. Punch it pound it ugly fat stinking pillow punch it punchit. Stop snoring stopit stopit.

Uncle Tom Cobbly gets up and walks up the bed to me. He stands and looks at my face. He is so close that his whiskers almost touch me. He looks at me. I want to say I'm sorry. I want to stroke him and cuddle him but I can't. He turns his back on me and jumps off the bed, his feet pushing into the mattress and making me rock. Uncle Tom wanted to stay with Granddad in Granddad's house in the village. He is Granddad's cat and he didn't want to come with us to the city. He is bad tempered and old and sometimes I think he smells bad like pee.

He jumps up on my windowsill and checks outside. There aren't any birds out yet, Uncle. It's too early. He looks back at me. His eyes say, 'The early cat catches the bird.' He settles down on the edge of the windowsill, his tail falling over the edge. He purrs and his head drops forward rhythmically with each purr until his nose is touching his paws in front of him.

I have a map of my life like an old explorer's map. My life mapped out logically, drawn diagrammatically on parchment crumbling at the edges. Like Christopher Columbus with the known world and a vast area of unknown. Like an old explorer who might find Atlantis or the Garden of Eden. Like it might still be there it's all new, it's all unknown. A vast area with ripples for the sea and 'here be monsters'. My life.

He wasn't a monster. He couldn't have been. My Granddad was a lovely man. He loved me and he was lovely. He couldn't have been a monster. I don't believe it. Debbie was lying and her Gran was lying. It's totally not possible. If he was like that then he'd have tried it with me wouldn't he? Wouldn't he?

Mum never liked him. She didn't like me being with him. She was jealous. That was the only reason. She didn't like us being close because she was jealous of him. He wouldn't hurt anyone. He would never hurt anyone. My Granddad was special and he wouldn't hurt me or anyone else. What does Debbie's Gran know about my Granddad? What does Debbie's Gran know about anything anyway? She was probably just trying to wind me up. Would she wind me up about that? Isn't that a horrible thing to do, to tell someone their Granddad was a dirty old man and liked to touch children up? What did she expect me to do, laugh it off? Why can't a girl be close to her Granddad without people thinking it's suspicious? Why can't I love him, why is that unnatural?

I look at the clock. 05:23. If I go to sleep now I've got like two hours and a bit till the alarm goes off. Who am I kidding? I'm never going to get to sleep. Not while there's monsters under my bed and Debbie in my head.

I read on the internet that it's genetic. That some people think it's biology which means basically that I could inherit it from my Granddad. But that doesn't make sense to me. How would I inherit it from him? If it's boys that he preferred, if Debbie is telling the truth and not making it up, then how could I inherit that and yet prefer girls? I don't see how that can be. It doesn't make sense.

Was that a bird tweeting then? Was that a bloody bird? Oh for god's sake. Now I'm never going to sleep. If that's the dawn bloody chorus then I'll never get to sleep. You wouldn't think there'd be birds in the city, would you? But oh yes there are. Not as many varieties as we saw in the village, but it's like the noisiest ones come here to roost. Maybe the quieter ones are driven out by all the racket of the traffic. I don't know but whatever it is, there's still a whole load of pigeons, sparrows and house martins chirruping away up there and if I had a pellet gun I'd pop the lot of them.

Uncle Tom gets up and stares out of the window again. He scrabbles at the glass, making squeaky noises. He does that all the time. Mum says she'll give him a cloth and he can clean the windows. I pick up my slipper from the side of the bed and throw it at him. He scoots off under my desk and sits there glowering at me. Those bloody birds.

Why did we have to get the top flat anyway right under the roof? I know why, because she decided we needed to move quickly and she took the first one offered. Like we didn't have the money to hang around in Granddad's house. We could have done but she didn't want to. Why was she in such a hurry? What did she think would happen if we'd stayed?

Close my eyes. Tight shut tight. Seeing red on the inside of my eyelids. Seeing red. I throw my pillow at the wall. Stop snoring, stop bloody snoring! I'm so angry. I'm angry angry angry. I'm angry with Debbie for saying that and for saying it in front of Mum and for making a joke out of it. I'm angry with Mum for being angry with Debbie. I'm angry with Granddad for dying and leaving me alone. I'm angry with myself for being angry.

What is there left for me? How can I sleep? How can I stop this deluge every night? I need to zap my brain, stick electrodes in there and fry it all out. Take scissors to the antique map, cut out 'here be monsters'. Cut it all out. Like that's going to do any good because I know that it's going to fester and moulder and smoulder and grow back and take over the rest of me like disease. I should just kill myself right now before it gets any worse. If I did, would anyone bother? Would anyone miss me, really?

I don't think that Debbie would. I think she knows. I think she suspects something and that's why she said that. That's why she made that joke because she wanted to see how I'd react. Talking about my Granddad like that. She must have known that I'd be upset. She must have known I'd be angry. Even if she didn't realise that Mum would overhear she should have pretended it was a mistake instead of turning it into a joke. How did she think that Mum was going to react? God this is just impossible. I may as well get up and read. There's no point trying to sleep. But I've got to sleep. I've got to get at least some sleep. What time is it now? 05.31 still could get two hours before the alarm goes off. Nearly two hours. Just need to calm down and think about nothing.

And if that diamond ring turns brass, Granddad's gonna buy you a looking glass. I never knew what happened to the ring. Mum said it turned out to be fake but why did it disappear? You'd keep it even if it were only sentimental value. I totally think she sold it. I remember him showing it to me, opening the tiny velvet box and the diamond glinting in the sunlight like on a film or something. 'Your Grandma's ring.' And he told me one day it would be mine. Well it's gone now. Like everything else. Gone.

I loved the village. I loved playing in the park. I loved

going to the shop for sweets. I loved it when I was little. It got a bit boring more recently because there's nothing to do. Hanging around with the others isn't my thing. But I loved it growing up. We went to the park and played and walked through the park to the shops. As long as I was with other children Mum didn't mind because I didn't have to cross any roads. She didn't have to come with me like she came with me to other shops.

And if I stayed out playing too long, Granddad would come and get me. He always knew where to find me, even if I was hiding he'd find me. That was before the stroke and before he stopped being able to walk. Then we couldn't go through the park any more. Some kids said there was a man in the park. A dirty old man who showed them his bits. I never saw him. I wished I had. Debbie and me used to laugh about it. That strange mixture of fear and excitement that made you think you wanted to see it but also that you didn't want to see it. And if I'd seen it would I have laughed or would I have run away?

Maybe that's what Debbie meant about Granddad – that he was that man? Maybe I got the wrong end of the stick and I'd only thought she meant something else because I was thinking about me. And thinking about me and her. Like I think about me and her a lot. Well what am I supposed to think about while I'm lying here awake? I could think about Latin. *Amo amas amat*. I love you love she loves. Then I think about Debbie again.

God god god! Why can't I bloody sleep? Where's my pillow? I need my pillow. It's on the floor again. How did it get there? Pick up the pillow. Put it on the bed. Put myself on the bed. Put myself on the pillow. Sleep. You'd think it would be that simple. It's the only thing I can't force myself to do. I can force myself to eat when I feel sick. I can force myself to be quiet when I want to scream. I can force myself to walk away when I want to get close. I can force myself to smile when I want to attack. What is it that I want to do, that I need to do? What is it that stops me from sleeping? Maybe if I knew what it was that I wanted to do then I'd be able to block it like I block everything else. I'd sleep knowing what it was, blocking it like I block everything else.

I know it's got something to do with Debbie or I wouldn't keep thinking about her. I know. I know, I know what it is. I'm not stupid. I'm not a baby. I know all about sex and everything. But I don't understand how it is Debbie, bloody Debbie that I'm focusing on after all that's happened. What is my brain doing to me? I don't want to think about bloody Debbie. If I have to think about anyone in that way why can't I think about someone I don't have to see every day? Some famous pop star like Pink or someone. I can think Pink all I like and I don't have to talk to her and get embarrassed when I'm around her.

Uncle Tom Cobbly comes out from under the desk. He sneaks up to the side of the bed, thinking that I won't notice him, and sits there contemplating what to do next. Then he makes the decision and jumps up on me, coming forward and purring. Rubbing up against me and pricking the duvet with his claws again. His fur is in my face and his claws scrape my arm. He's being loving but he's hurting me. I stroke him and he rolls over in ecstasy. I tickle his belly. He bites my hand. Then he rubs against me. Mixed messages all the time from the grumpy old git. He gets up and nose-dives against my hand. Okay, that's enough, settle down now Uncle Tom. We both need to sleep. Get your paws off me, Uncle, you're hurting. Get off, I don't want it.

Uncle Tom Cobbly didn't want to leave the village any more than I did. He was happy chasing rats and hiding under hedges. Now he can't go out at all. He's stuck. It wouldn't have been quite so bad moving here if I was going to a new school. But mother dear in her wisdom decided that I should stay in the same school to do my GCSEs rather than switching schools so I still have to go back to the village kids every day. And they think I'm up myself because I've moved and they want to live in the city and they think it's cool but it bloody isn't because I can't go anywhere or do anything and I have to eat my breakfast on the bus and it's crap. So the irony is that I have all this resentment directed at me for no reason. I'd gladly swap with any of them if it meant I'd sleep.

Just let me sleep. I'll do anything if you just let me sleep. I'll be good I promise. I won't think about Debbie or any other girl. I won't think about anything like that. If I don't think about it then it can't happen. If I don't think about it then I'm not like that.

Granddad, if you can hear me, just remember that I never believed her. I never believed what she said for one minute. I wish you were here so you could tell me that it's all rubbish but I think it's rubbish anyway. I don't believe it at all. Not at all. Granddad, if you're here then please let me smell your soap, your tobacco, so I know you're here. Do something Granddad, make something happen so I know you're here. Make something fall or knock or do something like they do on the TV on the haunted shows. Make a light in the corner or a breeze or make it go colder. Granddad if you can hear me make something happen.

The silence is mocking me. A mocking bird. And if that mocking bird don't sing. What does a mocking bird sound like? Is it a twittering or more like a 'coo coo'? It's supposed to sound like a laugh isn't it? That's why it's called mocking bird. Mock me, mocking bird. Mock me like everyone else laughs at me so you may as well laugh too mocking bird. Were you laughing at me Granddad? Were you laughing at me all this time? No, I don't believe it. I don't believe it at all.

05:33 it's still only 05:33. That's impossible. It was ages ago that I looked at the clock and it was 05:31. What's going on? Have I fallen into a time warp? I wish I could. I wish I could stop time for a week or more and get all the sleep I need and then start it again and be bright and awake and ready for school. But what if I stopped time and then I couldn't sleep? Wouldn't that be ironic! The night would be even longer then, it would be everlasting. Is that what it's like when you're dead? Is that what it's like for you, Granddad? Is it like being asleep forever or is it like having everlasting insomnia? What do you dream? Would you hallucinate? Or is hallucinating a connection to another universe? Maybe that's it. Maybe I could hallucinate Granddad if I tried hard enough.

Do you dream, Granddad? Wherever you are, do you get dreams? Do you dream about me? If I could dream about you and you could dream about me then would that mean that we could meet up? Would we talk like we used to, would you tell me stories and sing to me? And if that looking glass gets broke. I'm sorry I broke the mirror. I know that's what did it because you get seven years' bad luck. When you had your stroke I knew it was because of the mirror and it was my fault. I was only eight and I couldn't bear to think of seven years of bad luck. I couldn't imagine then what it would be like to be fifteen. I still don't know. I am fifteen and I can't imagine what it's like. It's not any different to anything else. It's just me. So is my bad luck over with now? I don't think so. I don't think it can be. I'm in the worst place ever with no friends and no place to go and no sleep.

I don't remember exactly what happened before the mirror broke. I remember seeing the shards of glass and feeling very frightened and your angry face reflected in each one. I knew it was your mirror and in some way special and that it was my fault you were angry. It was the first time you'd been angry with me ever in my whole life. You'd always been so loving and so kind. And then I broke the mirror. It was like I'd broken the spell. Like your kind face was the reflection and really underneath it was your angry face and when the mirror broke that was all that was left. But then your angry face left when Mum swept up the pieces of the mirror. Your angry face went in the bin and all that was left was an empty face. I didn't understand what was happening.

When you fell I thought you'd died. I was only eight. I didn't understand about ischemia and other related cardiovascular stuff. I do now. I know what happened to you in intricate detail because I've studied studied studied. I knew instinctively then that it was me that had done it. My breaking the mirror had caused the bad luck which started with your arm and leg not working and kept on going from there. Now I realise that it was caused by stress and your pipe and perhaps genetics, but if it was stress then that would have been the mirror breaking, wouldn't it, if it was a shock? So it was me after all.

I've tried and tried to remember what happened before the mirror broke and I just can't. I get as far as that I was walking upstairs. I was coming to tell you that dinner was nearly ready. Then there's nothing. There's like this big black gap between walking up the stairs and looking at the broken mirror on the floor of the bathroom.

And if that looking glass gets broke, Granddad's gonna buy you a billy goat. I don't understand the thing about the goat, who wants a goat as a present? Maybe it's just an old fashioned song. Or maybe the person who wrote the song couldn't think of anything to rhyme with 'broke'. Can't have been very clever. I could think of loads of things. Poke, bloke, stroke, okeydoke. Well, okay, maybe they are not the sort of things you could get as a present but even so there must be more things to rhyme, not just goat. I mean what sort of present is it? Goats are smelly and noisy and they butt you and kick you. Almost as bad as cats pricking you with their needle claws.

05:40. That went quick! See, it makes no sense to me at all. I can be thinking of something that seems like totally for ages and only a minute has gone by and then another time I'll blink and it's already ten minutes later. What's going on? Am I having blackouts? Am I in a multiple personality and the other me is getting up and doing crazy things while the me that's here thinks she's lying awake? That would be quite cool actually. I could go around trashing the flat and drive Mum's car and all sorts of things and all the time I'd think that I was lying in bed staring at the LED light on my clock. 05:41. Multiple me, I could totally go for that. That's one way to make a friend, isn't it? Hello me, how are you doing? I'm doing fine, how are you? Not so bad. Wish I could sleep though. Know what you mean, me too. Well you are me. Imagine if you fell out with yourself, though, and you weren't best friends any more. Nightmare!

And if that billy goat runs away. You can't run away from yourself. That's something in one of those self-help books mother dear reads. She really truly believes that if she reads all this twaddle as Granddad used to call it, then it'll somehow make her life better. But it doesn't. Self-help means helping yourself, not sitting around moaning and groaning about poor ickle me my life is so bloody hard. You have to actually do something about your life as well. You have to actually get up and do something. The first thing to do would be to get out of bed yourself in the morning and not expect your daughter to run around after you like a slave. The second thing to do would be to bloody stop snoring.

Men are from Mars, women are from the darkest reaches of hell. Women who run with the bananas. Women off their trolleys. Chicken soup for vegetarians. One minute psychotic breakdown. Twelve steps to achieving putting your socks on. It's unbelievable the sort of crap that gets banded around in these books. And she swallows it all like it's gospel, churns it up and spits it back out. She could probably write her own self-help book full of sicked-up mush that's the same old psychobabble again and again. It's as if nobody actually notices that they whip out the same thing with a different package. If the self-help books worked then they wouldn't be needed, would they? If everyone helped themselves and sorted themselves out then the self-help books would work too well and would put themselves out of business. Has nobody actually thought of that at all, anywhere in the last several generations, or were their brains too fried in the seventies on drugs to have any brain cells left?

Breathe. Calm. I have to stop getting worked up over stuff or I'm never going to sleep. Problem is there's too much stuff. Too much to get angry about. What am I supposed to do? I can't ignore it. I can't wallow in it but I can't put it right. I'm stuck. I tell myself it won't be forever but it bloody feels like it. On nights like this when I lie awake all night, every hour feels like forever.

I've thought about running away, don't think I haven't. But what would I do? I'm intelligent enough to know what happens to fifteen year old girl runaways, however intelligent they are. And I'm not having any of that. I have a plan. I made the plan with Granddad, even though he couldn't talk I knew he agreed. I'm going to study study study and I'm going to get out. And once I'm out I'm never coming back. Mother dear can roll around in bed as much as she likes. She can snore to her heart's content and it won't matter to me because I won't be here. I'll be long gone. Long, long gone. I'll be the billy goat. Little billy goat gruff, me. And if that billy goat runs away, Granddad's gonna buy you a brand new day.

I wish you could give me a new day, Granddad. Just one day with you how it used to be. I'll go to sleep now (I'll get one hour and forty-five minutes till the alarm goes off) and when I wake up I'll be at home and you'll be there just like you used to be, making breakfast and whistling. You'll say, 'Good morning, trouble,' and kiss the top of my head. Except I might be taller than you now. Anyway, you'll give me my breakfast and we'll talk about the birds in the garden and you'll get your pipe out and you'll walk me to school through the park and we'll go to our special places that no one else knows about. You'll let me play on the swings and you'll give me a sweet and say, 'Don't tell Mummy.'

There was one place I really didn't like. It was where the old concrete drainpipe was and it was dingy and smelled of cats' pee. I remember it scared me because it was dark and I ran away from there one time. But you called me a scaredy puss and dared me to go to the other side of the pipe. You said if there were monsters then you'd save me. My guardian angel. But there were no monsters, only you.

It didn't happen. I know it didn't. I'm misinterpreting my memories because of what Debbie said. I was always safe with you. You know I would never believe any of that about you, Granddad. I wish you could just give me a sign that you're here. Make a noise or make something move. Just so I know you're still here being my guardian angel. Has my seven years' bad luck finished yet? Can you come back now? If you did, what would you be like? Back to yourself how you were before the stroke? Strong and standing upright and smelling of soap and tobacco instead of porridge and pee? Smiling and whistling and giving other people the hard stare but never me? Telling me I'm your little girl, your angel, your special precious one? Or will you be stuck in the chair, empty and confused, shouting and mumbling? I think I'd rather you didn't come back if that's what it would be like.

But just one day with you like it used to be. That's not too much of a miracle to ask for, is it? A brand new day. It's already a new day. It's 05:50 and the light is finding its way through my curtains. The light doesn't want to wake up yet but it's inevitable, it has no choice. The particles can't hide here: they have to move ever forward, creeping through my curtains towards the bed. Landing on Uncle Tom's fur and making it shine. The city light is no different to the village light. It's the same sun. And wherever you are, Granddad, it must be the same sun too. Or maybe not. Maybe it's the sun in the other universe where the other Granddad is still alive and the other me is happy and sleeping all night and waking up without the alarm and walking to school.

But a brand new day for me would be exploding myself into particles of light and streaking across the dimension into that other universe so that I could become that happy person again. I would wake up and Granddad would be there with his pipe and his cup of tea, frying his bacon and whistling. I don't care what anyone says about you, you're my Granddad and I want to be with you. If I go to sleep now I'll get one hour and thirty nine minutes sleep and when the alarm goes off I'll be back in my bed in Granddad's house in the village and we'll get up and have breakfast and walk to school. If I fall asleep now I'll transform into the other dimension. If I concentrate hard enough I can do it. Granddad I know you're listening. You can make it happen. You and me together, we can do anything. Remember you said that to me, 'You can do anything you want. Don't let anyone tell you that you can't.' You said that, remember? We can do it if we concentrate together. I'll go to sleep now and I'll dream of you and then when I wake up we'll be together.

I just need to go to sleep to do it. That's all. Just go to sleep and when I wake up everything will be back to normal again. No stinking city, no snoring mother, no stupid rumours about you or about me. The sun will be shining and we'll go to the park and we'll find our special places and it will be just us. Like it always was.

Don't think about anything else, just being together. Me and you. That's all. Just us, together how it used to be. Float. Drift on the light particles. In and out of dimensions. Through the space time continuum. Floating, floating.

Uncle Tom Cobbly is warm against my belly. He's fully asleep now, he's stopped purring. Mum has stopped snoring. I'm floating, I'm floating.

If I fall asleep now then it will all work out. It's 05:55. I'll get one hour and thirty five minutes before the alarm goes off.

One hour and thirty five minutes will be enough time to explode and change dimensions and replode. Or implode. Or whatever it would be. I can do it if I go to sleep now. I need to go to sleep. If I fall asleep now I'll get one hour and thirty four minutes.

Float.

If I fall asleep now I'll get one hour and thirty three minutes.

If I fall asleep now.

If I fall asleep.

If I fall.

If. If. Fffffffffffffff.

10am

The Moon on a Stick

By Hilary Lloyd

Simon's just phoned. He'll be here at eleven, traffic permitting, and it is going to feel like the longest hour of my life because I've done everything that needs to be done. I started too early. Her bag's packed and she's clean and presentable, apart from a scowl, so all I have left to do is try not to watch the clock and hope she nods off in that patch of sunshine.

I couldn't sleep last night, nor could she. She senses something's afoot. She reads my mind and inhales the atmosphere, as she's always done, and my tension is probably manifesting itself in orange banners that will whip her into a fury, or geniality, depending on what she does or doesn't want. It still amazes me that she has such enormous power despite the frailty of her body and mind.

She's tired now, tired of battling, pushing, lashing out, scowling, scratching. My arms hurt. My eyes are sore from lack of sleep. My body wants to lie down and never get up again. My mind is dead while hers may soar into action without warning or reason.

Yet family loyalty persists. Dave wished me good luck as he left for work then promised to talk this evening about getting away somewhere nice. Even after the hell of the last three years, I still bristled at the allusion that she's a problem, a burden, an intrusion into our happy coupledom. Where does my loyalty come from and why do I always spring to her defence even though she's destroying me? But she can't help the state she's in. It isn't her fault her mind is slowly disintegrating and that she can no longer live safely alone.

Safely. If her mind hadn't gone, I know she'd have preferred going out with an electrical bang or in a houseful of flames, or food poisoning, a fall, starvation, anything but dependence on someone else, fierce, fighting, practical, self-sufficient woman that she used to be.

Five past ten. OK, Mum?

Pursed lips. Is she sulking? Again.

Cup of tea and a biscuit? It's too early for elevenses but I need the distraction.

Silence. God, it infuriates me, but I must be nice, especially today when I'm throwing my principles out of the window and shipping her out like a badly-wrapped parcel. *Nice*. How I hate that word. But *nice* is what I am, according to everyone but me. Dave even uses it as an accusation when he can't cope, when he's missing the me he used to know. You're too nice to her, he says, when he wants something. Stop being so *nice*, says my daughter when she visits and sees my pale haggard face.

I am not nice. The devil in me has grown too big for my body. It has spikes and I cannot blunt them anymore. It snarls and kicks at inanimate objects. It screams silently to my brother and sister when they phone to see how Mum is. But what about me? it yells, but they don't hear. They don't see either. When they visit, Mum is pleased to see them, even though she doesn't remember who they are. She puts on her afternoon-tea face along with a pretty blouse and charms them with her benign presence and her sweet exterior. And when they leave, she tears at her blouse and scowls at me, swipes at the teacups and throws cake on the floor and I know she is showing me in the only way she can that I've subjected her to a performance she has neither the energy for nor the inclination. And I decide not to invite anyone again but still they come; it is their filial duty, just as it is mine to care for her in her last confused years.

But why can't they see? Why have they never bothered to

try and read between the lines of my conversations and letters and learn that I am wrecked. Why haven't they offered me a respite before this one? Hey, wait a minute, it wasn't offered this time. I had to ask and they hummed over it for weeks until Dave intervened and told Simon we couldn't even go out for the day, never mind take a holiday, without their help. Then sister dear offered to find a respite home for Mum instead of taking two weeks off work herself or cancelling some precious engagements.

No, I said. There are three of us. Surely we can take turns.

She challenged that all right. Take turns? This is our mother you're referring to, not a game. Look love, I know it's difficult for you, restricting and that, but you did offer to take her in. We could have found a care home for her.

I couldn't. I've seen them. After one particularly awful week, I went to look in hope and came away in horror from those stinking places where televisions clattered through the silence of hopelessness.

Simon was more sympathetic. He knew I was frazzled even if he didn't realise I was flying round the bend along with our mother. I'll try, he said. Give me a week or two to sort things out at work. That week or two turned into months. Christmas, he said at last, and added magnanimously, so you can have a nice family time. With my son in Australia and my daughter totally wrapped up in her career and her friends? I can just see it, Dave and I alone, staring at each other over a glistening turkey and feeling sick at the thought of food. That's what emotional exhaustion does.

But at least Simon offered. He'll be here soon. Fifty minutes more.

She's awake. She's spoken, asked me for a cup of tea and some of that lovely cake I made yesterday. Almost right. I did make a lovely cake but it was a week or two back and it went mouldy.

Now she's smiling. I know what's coming next: you are

good to me, Helen. What would I do without you?

Why does she do that when I've given up on her? Is it coincidence? If not, how dare she play with my emotions; one minute treat me like a jailer then the next flip back into the woman I used to know? She can't help it, I hear the doctor say, or the health visitor, or my brother, my sister, a neighbour; maybe the postman will chip in before long. Her mind is dying. Have some sympathy, they say.

I did have sympathy. Someone's used it all up.

I've escaped to the kitchen. The kettle's on and tears are pouring down my face. They won't stop. I haven't cried for weeks and now there are pools on the worktop that will flood the house and we'll float out of the front door on a tsunami of human anguish. She's uncorked me. Now, after weeks of despairing that she'd ever be able to speak coherently again, out she comes out with pleasantries, lucid enough to convince the shrewdest medic that she's a loving caring mother, a *nice* woman who appreciates what her eldest daughter is doing for her.

You're grieving, Dave says, when my tears come, grieving for the mother you used to know. He doesn't know what other words to use when I'm feeling useless, sodden, pitiful and pathetic. He finds it hard even to touch me and I plead silently for just a glimmer of understanding that I'm also grieving for the woman *I* used to be, that strong, capable, practical woman who loved and cared for her family and friends so fiercely.

But no. The world is now centred round my mother and her needs. She can't help it. I can. I still have my marbles.

I don't want these tears, not when I've made my decision. They undermine my resolve.

I am so very tired. The December sun is reflecting off the units and dancing over the floor. Suddenly I don't want to make tea. I haven't the energy to take it in to her or the courage to brave what her mood will be when I go back in.

I want my real mother back.

I'd even be grateful for the mother of a few years ago, when she was delightfully forgetful and laughed hugely at herself for putting the teapot instead of empty bottles out on the doorstep for the milkman. He'd knocked on the door and made a joke, said he'd prefer it full, if she didn't mind, and she entertained us all for weeks with the telling of it. She'd phone me often, full of girlish giggles about how dotty she'd become. Silly me, she'd say, and I'd laugh with her.

But then, as the months passed, I detected frustration beneath the laughter, then the edges of resentment, then self-pity, anger. And my heart groaned for her and I made the time to drive the three hours to see her, taking more and more days off work to do so, to stock her fridge and fill her freezer with home-made nutritious meals so at least she'd eat to keep up her failing physical strength if not feed her crumbling mind. Eventually my job had to go. Everyone at work wished me well in my 'retirement'. Retirement is not the word for what I took on, the care of a geriatric child.

Dave was good, backing me up, learning to run our household when I was looking after hers. He was my physical prop, an emotional one too when I despaired over what was best for her. Then came the night she fell on her way to the bathroom and the postman was concerned that her curtains stayed closed and alerted her neighbour who phoned me. My drive over that morning was the longest ever, three hours of deepening fear and a nightmare come true when I let myself in.

I cleaned her up, tucked her back into bed, phoned the doctor, noted his frown and knew she'd have to come home with me. I phoned Dave to warn him that he'd have to make hurried plans for the conversion of our dining room into a bedroom. He'd done it by the time we got home.

How long ago was that? Too many years, too much of my life and Dave's, too many dying brain cells, tantrums, sympathy from others and pats on my back from family and friends.

I couldn't do what you're doing, said Ginnie, an old friend from work who turned up one day wanting to whisk me out for lunch and a catch-up on gossip. She was happy to stay in for lunch, happy to talk to Mum, but she stayed too long and Mum couldn't keep up her social face and brusquely stated that Ginnie had outstayed her welcome.

Ginnie promised to come back, but never did. She doesn't even phone me anymore. Nor do Mum's old friends and neighbours. Oh, they were full of concern and sympathy when Mum first moved here, and sent her flowers, letters and cards, but only until the first Christmas. They wished her well, hoped she'd be better soon, but she faded from their minds as quickly as they faded from hers.

I expected it back then. Now I resent it. Am I the only one with staying power, and why don't they see *I* need the contact? I resent the feeling that I've been cast away on a desert island. Maybe no one's aware that I was shipwrecked.

Self-pity is destructive. I soon discovered there is no point in wallowing. No one cares so get up and get on with it, just as Mum used to say before senility was thrust upon her. It wasn't her fault. That's life.

How like her I sound! I inherited her genes, her practicality, her loyalty, her refusal to be daunted by life's injustices. How else did she survive so well after Dad died? And I'm full of admiration for the woman she was then, coping with his last illness like a Trojan, arranging his funeral, sorting out his financial affairs that left her with nothing until she fought and demanded and insisted, then threatened, to see the pension authorities in the courts before she'd give up what was hers by right. And she won. They paid up. But oh, where's that woman now? I want her back. I want to sit and laugh about it with her, watch her lined face become so animated with glee at the recounting of the brolly-waving tactics she used against bureaucracy. They thought I was a useless old biddy, she used to say, but I showed them!

I loved her then but it's hard to love her now. And that fills me with guilt. My love is not as big as I thought it was if it can't stretch even to like her. I am fickle. I've lost the values she instilled in me. I have betrayed her.

Enough. Tea. Only forty-five minutes left to show her, whoever she is now, that I do care.

Here we are, I say, bringing in the tray to find her asleep. A blessing. A respite for her, a few moments escape from this bloody confusing world she inhabits. Her expression is one of peace and I am pleased for her. Sleep on, Mum. Let me watch over you, keep you from harm and pain as you did once for me. Let me kiss you better, cool your fevered forehead, disguise bitter medicines in spoonfuls of homemade strawberry jam, stroke away your aches and sing you lullabies.

Oh, but it's bliss when she's asleep. Maybe she used to think the same when I was a baby when she tiptoed out of my room in the small hours and returned to her own bed sighing in hope that she might, just might, get a few hours of peace before the next cry of distress.

Our roles are reversed. She is the child now and I am the parent. No, not a parent, for sometimes I do not know this woman. Yes, she has the body and face of my mother, and I see her strength of character still, only now she waves her brolly at me instead of at a common enemy. I am the enemy. The mysterious workings of her mind make her see me as the perpetrator of injustice. I am her jailer, her torturer, the shackles confining her. That's why she bites and scratches and scowls and swipes at me. It's why, when she first came here, she used to scream at me to go home and stop *fussing*, to stop treating her like an idiot or an invalid: I am not ill! I am not a baby. *Leave me alone!*

But this *is* my home, Mum, I used to say.

Then why are you keeping me here? Let me go. NOW!

However much I tried, I couldn't always keep back tears of anguish and frustration. And she hated them, told me I should grow up and stop being a baby and then they'd flow faster and I'd run from the room until they'd subsided. I'd return to find she'd forgotten everything and was pleased to see me and would say, how nice to see you again, Helen. You're so good to me. What would I do without you?

Forty minutes left. Forty minutes of hoping and praying that Simon will be here on time. Forty minutes of guilt that I can't cope, that my love has died with my emotional strength, that I have decided to tell him I can't do any more, that she is killing me, that please, please, please find another way of caring for her because I have reached my limit.

But I won't have the courage to tell him when he arrives. And he'll be concerned about getting Mum home, of settling her in. He'll be afraid too, for he knows me well enough to guess I'm nearing the end of my reserves. He'll be brisk and bright, chatty with Mum, wanting to bustle her into the car leaving no time to worry about what she'll do to his family Christmas. He won't dare look at me, for fear of learning something he doesn't want to know.

And I won't spoil his plans or his departure. I'll take the coward's way out and phone him after Boxing Day and tell him in a calm, quiet tone that I cannot have her back. There'll be a stunned silence before he'll find a few kind words, comfort for me when he's oh, so afraid. He's like that. He's a good man and a caring brother. He'll accept my limits, as he's always done.

How can I do that to him? How can I even think of disturbing the equilibrium of his life? I know that I must, if I am not to be destroyed beyond all recognition by a cuckoo nesting in the body of someone I used to know.

The repercussions of my decision will turn my brother and his family inside out, obliterate their routines and their peace, affect their work, disturb their sleep, make them ill. How can

I do that? Easily, it seems, when self-preservation kicks in. After bursts of adrenalin comes a false peace, a state of ticking over, a life as anodyne as a washed-out tea towel. Bleached, worn and frayed. It isn't permanent yet but will be if I don't change something. Something has to be sacrificed to protect me. Love for my mother is all I have left to relinquish.

Will Simon grow to understand why? Maybe, but only after he and his family are destroyed too. The strange thing is that I don't feel compassion for them. It isn't that I don't care, just that I don't have the emotional energy to worry about anyone else but me now. Maybe that's the effect of the tranquillisers, forced gently upon me by my doctor and taken automatically twice a day because I trust that the medics know what's best for me. The pills helped enormously at first; despair ebbed away and physical strength returned. And then I felt good enough, idiotic enough, to suspect I could live without them. Thank God everyone survived that week, when even good calm sensible Dave was almost de-railed by the screaming banshee I became. Even my mother noticed something was different and rose to the occasion. She behaved well and properly when doctors swooped to the rescue and health visitors tutted and shook their heads. By the end of the week, once more doped to the eyeballs, I was back to normal.

Normal? A zombie, more like. But that's what I have to be to cope. I *want* to be a good daughter and a reasonable wife. I never again want to see the devil in me made flesh and emerge to lay everything to waste. That's why I've been careful. This time, I've been clever, taking weeks to wean myself off the bloody pills. I've been me again. I have dug deep and discovered untapped reserves of emotional strength. I learned not to show the slightest whisper of feeling. I learned to recognise the onslaught of tears before they fall and escape from Mum and from Dave. I learned that fleeing the house was the best way to put my fears and resentment into perspective and, because I couldn't ever leave Mum alone for long, wore a path in the garden while doing so. I learned how to smile when I wanted to snarl, how to give a loving pat instead of a slap.

My mother is fooled. Is Dave? I'm not so sure, but surely he must prefer this apparently calm ministering angel to the wild raging sobbing wreck he used to find in his bed night and morning.

Of course, this newfound inner strength hasn't lasted – I was a fool to hope that I could manage without drugs ironing out the deep creases of my despair. But I will not go back on them. Anything is better than that state of nothingness and that's why I've reached this last, desperate stage. Why should I be doped to do a job no one else wants? I'm the only one suitable, after all, and that's why my guilt swamps me. If I can't look after Mum, no one else will offer, not the family, and certainly not the so-called caring services. I don't understand why everyone is fooled by our governing bodies who profess to be pro-family yet do nothing when the family needs help. What help have I had? Bugger all, apart from an occasional visit from a health visitor who cares only about Mum and not me, and a community psychiatric nurse who has a daft smile and coos over Mum then talks about her own problems with me over the kitchen table. How dare she use my carer's ears to unburden herself! Like bloody hell she'll do *that* again.

Oh, this anger is wonderful. It courses through me like a raging river and drowns every pathetic thought daring to cross its path. For the past week or so, as my drug-free strength has been more and more diminished I am refreshed and strengthened by this anger. If I don't think too long about how it must be scouring my insides, I can get up in the morning and survive each day. I don't sleep, of course, but that's a small price to exchange for the control and strength I have gained. How else could I have convinced Dave that all I needed was a respite from Mum, a little holiday, a bit of sunshine, a hotel where staff tend my needs and cook my meals, with a man at my side eager to rekindle displays of affection if not passion? I was clever. He may not have been completely fooled, but certain enough to convince Simon when I couldn't find the words.

I hate this subterfuge but I was driven to it. Being *nice* or pathetic or a wreck doesn't work. No, I had to make a plan and see it right through. And here we are. I've got my way. Mum is going to be someone else's responsibility and I'm not having her back. What will they all think when they find out? I refuse to think too hard about that in case it affects my decision.

Thirty minutes left. Mum's still asleep. Sleep irons her creases in the way the drugs used to iron mine, but in her case I welcome the effect it has. She looks younger. I wonder what her poor brain is up to. Is she dreaming? I hope the dreams are kind to her, stitching pleasant pictures out of the scraps of the girl she was, then young woman, capable mother, wife and indomitable widow.

I am calm again. As always, regret follows the fire of my anger. Fear, too, for Mum, Dave, Simon. Especially Mum. Will this change aggravate her behaviour? I wouldn't wish that on Simon, or his wife. And what about their children, still at home, troubled by the tumult of adolescence? They don't need more aggro that might have them all at each other's throats. It could even split the family. See how far my weakness spreads its tentacles!

Fear for me too. What will I do with myself when she's left? Rest. Sleep. Play. It's so long since there was any fun in my life that maybe I've forgotten how. Will it return? Where will I start? Oh God, let my friends start visiting and phoning again. Yes, a phone call from…who? I suspect no one knows I exist. My identity has been swamped. Yes, I am someone's daughter. A wife too. But where's me?

I will not brood. There is no point, not now when I've made

the decision and Simon's coming to rescue me.

The tea's cold but good. Sip slowly, soothe the waves of doubt and guilt. Let the morning sun shine on, gild her lined face, add a bit of body to her thinning hair. Sit back and count the many blessings. Most are due to her, to the way she brought us up, to her former strength. She still has it, though it's misdirected now. I will take this brief spell of peace to remember, to honour, the woman she once was. Even in her sixties, she came flying to my side when Jake was ill and I was so, so scared for his life. She snatched up the pieces of my shattered household and stuck them back together in her cheerful, capable, organised way, even though she must have been shrinking inside with pain for her grandson and for me. While I spent every second at Jake's side, she filled my house with the smell of baking and made sure all our beds were made with neat corners and fluffed-up duvets. Every afternoon she booked a taxi to fly to the hospital to jack up my spirits, and every evening she phoned Dad to make sure he was primed with the latest news as well as make sure he was eating properly. And when Jake recovered and came home, she sensed we needed family space and quietly slipped away.

Thanks, Mum, I whisper now.

Her eyelids flicker. I hope she's listening.

I'm calm again, and smiling. She was a good mother and that mother is still in there somewhere, the one who decided we all needed a family holiday when Jake was back on his feet, the one who spent what little she had left from her parents' bequest on renting a big house in Cornwall. The whole family managed to spend some of that three weeks there and in the week that our visits coincided, Mum glowed with pleasure at having her happy, healthy brood under her wings again. Yes, she was irritated at times. Yes, she snapped at too many grandchildren under her feet and, yes, she tried too hard to cater for everyone's idea of a good holiday. But her reign over us gave her intense pleasure; I saw it shining in her face and flashing from her limbs as she whisked us round famous sites and gardens or danced with her grandchildren in the cold waves. It was a good holiday, the best really, a time for us all to see just how strong a family can be if it works and plays together. Such a shame we haven't continued that.

Why haven't we?

And why didn't I let the family help with Mum? Because I felt only I could look after her how she would want. Trouble is, she doesn't know what she wants beyond the moment and I can't guess any more. Have I failed her and failed myself in the process? I've been hoisted, as they say, on an explosion of good intentions. My actions and statements from three years back are writ so large they could fill a hoarding that shouts its message to me. No, I told Simon, after he suggested we find someone to care for Mum in her own home. No, I told Sis, when she wanted to find the best care home available. No, I reassured Dave, when he was brave enough to voice fears about losing *us*, just when the children had flown, when the pleasures of retirement and spare time and holidays beckoned. I will not incarcerate my mother, I said, too firmly.

Sis was scathing, but so, so right, when she said I was a fool to put my life on hold for a disintegrating mind. That's not Mum anymore, she told me, and if it is, what about her privacy and dignity? How do you know what she's feeling when you wipe her bum and wash her armpits? Who are you to say she's lost all sense of time and place? You're not God, Helen, any more than I am. Let's work together and find at least a middle way where we can all give our tuppence-worth.

I have no sympathy she repeated, a few months later, when I whinged. I warned you and you took no notice. Just because you're the eldest in this family doesn't mean you know it all.

She has no idea of the sense of responsibility instilled in me by being the eldest child. She and Simon were in my charge from the days of their births. Just mind Simon a bit, Mum would tell me when she needed to see to something on the stove or answer the door. Hold Sis, would you? I must get the washing in before it rains, and, here, hold Simon's hand while we cross the road/find my purse/nip in this shop. On and on, right through my childhood, whether I was busy or not. And later, in my teens, I had to decline invitations to spend Saturday mornings in town or weekends with friends in order to act as an unpaid babysitter. No, Sis has no idea. Simon, yes, to a small degree as he too sometimes had to forfeit fun and games with his mates because his younger sister needed minding. But even Simon got off lightly. Men and boys did in those days. Changing nappies and guarding tots was considered women's work.

I don't blame Mum. She was bound to lean on me. I was six, placid and fairly sensible when Simon was born, and nine when Sis came along. Mum didn't drive and had to do the shopping on foot or by bus. I can see her now, lugging enormous baskets home brimming with food for five, plonking them on the kitchen table and saying, just watch the little ones, would you? I've got to get tea on.

So I do know it all, everything there is to know about responsibility. It was inculcated early, long before Sis was cooing in her cot, and I can no more deny that caring part of me than change the colour of my eyes.

Twenty-five minutes more. Mum still sleeps. She is kind to me in this last hour.

I'm holding her hand and she's stroking it gently with her thumb, easing my path through betrayal. Perhaps Sis is right. My sense of responsibility has grown out of proportion and is too big for my mind. Why else would it explode like this? And I fear the aftermath. Yes, Simon and Sis will forgive me because they love me. Mum gave us that, our family loyalty, that ability to forgive without question. She did it for us. She hacked paths through the jungles of ill health to prop and care and heal. She fed our spirits as well as she fed our bodies. She cared.

Cared. Past tense. What does her mind let her care about now? Little more than whether the sun is in her eyes or her feet are in a draught. What a miserable end to a good life, a life well-lived, its problems stoically endured and its joys celebrated. A cruel and unjust end that most would not wish on a mange-ridden dog. Yet we must endure it. She must endure it, though there have been times when I wanted to end it for her. What do we say about sick pets? Put them out of their misery. Yes, misery, the woeful, confusing mess and contradictions of a life that lacks the ability to love and care and find joy. A life sentence, no, a death sentence drawn out beyond reason, without parole of any kind and without hope for more than the four walls that contain it.

Do I feel guilty about my wish to end her 'death sentence'? Yes, when I receive a rare smile of appreciation if not recognition. No, when she weeps, in frustration, pain or anger. I've gone to her bedside when she's called out in the night and found her moaning in her sleep and tears squeezing through the lines of her face and I've wanted to mop them with the pillow, then press its downy softness onto her face and let her slide into oblivion. But I've talked her through it instead, spoken reams of words in a low monotone until her mysterious fears have subsided and she's slept in peace instead of writhed in fear.

And what about those times when she's hurt me so cruelly, physically or emotionally depending on her mood, when I've left her pills at her bedside in the wild hope that she takes the wrong combination or too many. But I don't. I am no murderer. I can't even tread on snails or swat flies. Life is precious, goes the cliché.

I am so tired. Drained. My bones have lost their rigidity and I am the softest part of this chair, soaking up the December sunshine and the unaccustomed peace like a luxurious cushion. Mum's still sleeping so perhaps she senses my needs. She always used to read our minds and feelings

49

before she was ill so does some sixth sense tell her now, when I'm on the brink of betraying her, that I need this peace more than anything? I'm sorry, Mum. Forgive me.

She will forgive me, because she loves me, or she'll forget what I've done within half a mile of her journey to Simon's. She can't remember what happened two minutes ago. She doesn't know Sis or Simon, or Dave, in fact she shivers when Dave comes into the room. It must be his maleness or bulk that unnerves her for she used to love seeing him. From the day I brought him home, her eyes have shone in both approval and admiration of his character, his looks, his talents and his sense in choosing to be part of her family. The lines of pleasure now grooving her face are part due to him but also to me. Just before my wedding all those decades ago, she patted my cheeks and told me straight that I couldn't have picked a better man. She said much the same when my children were born, that she knew they had inherited the best of me and Dave. They'll go far, she said. Flowery stuff, I know, but Mum could wax sentimental when the mood took her. We children used to wink and nudge and mime playing violins and she'd emerge from her reverie with a belly laugh and a stride to the kitchen to peel yet another ton of potatoes.

No peace allowed for me, it seems. With only twenty minutes left, Mum has woken with a cry for help, the shriek of a wounded animal. Something has switched her on and her limbs shudder and she turns on me with venom.

Mum, it's me, Helen, I say, as she lashes out and catches me across the face. Her wedding ring bruises me, marking me as the enemy, the captor, the one to fight and rail against. I used to be her favourite daughter. Not now.

You are good to me, Helen, she'd said when she first came to live with us. The others don't understand but you do and that's why you're my favourite. What did I do to deserve you? I was embarrassed, of course, but it helped confirm my decision to include her in our life.

I need to escape but can't go into the garden, only to the kitchen. I must stay near the phone in case Simon calls to say he's almost here. Oh God, please don't let him phone to say he's been held up by traffic or he's changed his mind and sorry, Helen, but I know what you're plotting and it won't do. I will not put my family at risk. Would he say that? Probably not. He's a good man. Like Dave, he's strong and honourable. Oh, please come soon, Simon, and rescue me. Please, please, let the traffic be kind and the car behave itself. May the road ahead of you be free from nails and glass, idiot boy racers and macho truck drivers, from road works and police barriers and urgent calls that you must turn round NOW and come home because Helen's plotting to betray you as well as your mother.

I know he suspects something's afoot. Simon can read my mind and mood almost as well as Mum used to. He'll have heard the strain jangling behind my carefully arranged telephone voice. Dave might even have told him on the quiet just enough for concern to burrow into his caring mind. And Simon knows Mum's potential for causing havoc, even if he hasn't witnessed it during his visits of the last three years. He must remember those times before all this when her exuberance verged on manic glee, when she threatened to leave Dad because retirement had turned him from an efficient machine into an idle penny-pinching lump. She asked Simon for help then. It was a son's work to jolly Dad out of lethargy, to ask his advice on a business matter or involve him in male days out. And while they were off inspecting steam engines or whooping it up at air shows, Mum got people in to do the things Dad never got round to, or she went shopping, unchecked by a husband continually asking, 'what do we need that for?' and replaced every scrap of linen in the house with spanking new stuff after dumping the old in the Salvation Army recycling box. 'Just think how many poor people I'm helping', she'd tell me, 'and don't I deserve a bit of pleasure? I may not have gone to work but

I've helped earn every penny of his. It's mine too.'

Simon told me all about their trips and how Dad came out of his shell the minute he left home. Away from Mum and her interminable list of household chores, he regained a sense of importance, of a value lost after the gooey lauding at his retirement party at work. He also told of how Dad's mood plummeted as they neared home again, how Mum would greet them breezily and deliberately wind the poor man up by displaying her latest shopping fripperies. But she needed them. What else could ease the irritation of having Dad around all day? Those two weren't meant to be permanently in each other's company. Their characters clashed and their moods collided either with sparks or swords, after which Dad sulked and steam spiralled from Mum's ears. Sometimes, she threatened to leave him and even got as far as packing her bags. Then she'd phone me or Simon, open her mouth and empty her brain down our ears, threaten to come and live with either or both of us for ever and ever, amen, and never, EVER go back to the man who'd promised her the world but had only given her a kitchen and a badly-designed kitchen at that.

Simon and I had wonderful exchanges after these episodes and we'd chuckle and grin because we knew her exasperation would fade the minute she put the phone down. We imagined her creeping back upstairs to unpack and stuff the suitcase back in the attic, then return to her old-fashioned kitchen to prepare the vegetables for dinner.

And of course, she showed her true colours when Dad fell ill. She worked tirelessly round the clock for him, cooking encouraging little bites, racing to the shops and back for his medicines, or with titbits to tempt him. She turned her precious dining room into a bedroom for him and wheeled him out into the sunshine to watch her tend the garden. And she fought the authorities for extra help, a better wheelchair, a hoist to help her lift him, women to come and clean and, later, nurse him. She honed and burnished her spirit for him and slogged without complaint because he was her husband and she'd promised to love him through hell itself. And after he died, she fought on until her life grew back into one of security and peace.

Maybe that's why her mind has blown. The lifelong fight to protect and care for her family may have kept her firing on all cylinders for all that time, but in the end it exhausted her mind. She has battle-fatigue, or maybe her spirit died because there was no one left to fight for. Apart from herself, that is. But I've sussed the hints of disgust she has for her ageing body. I've heard them in her voice. She used to rail against her failing physical strength, of course, but Mum has always railed against everything. It is part of her character. She's a fighter, a warrior, a champion who has always leapt onto the nearest white charger and ridden bareback into the fray. But age is unconquerable. She is no match for the slow disintegration of mind and body. Maybe that's why I'm the foe. She needs someone to snarl and kick at.

So why can't I forgive her? Some daughter I am.

She's whimpering now. I must go to her. I must override my fears and rush back to her side as she always has to mine. I must tend and care and love her without question for ever and ever.

But I can't. She'll lash out at me with her voice or fist and swamp the last bit of feeling I have left for her. She is an old and miserable woman purporting to be my mother. She is a fraud, a wolf wearing my mother's face and clothes, and she's sharpening her teeth at this moment, ready to sink them into my flesh and my heart. I will stay safe and protected here in the kitchen for the next fifteen minutes and I will hand her over to Simon without a word and only a small smile. I will help her into the car and ignore her bright farewell then return to the house without a single wave or glance back at Simon's car as it takes her away. Then I'll put the kettle on and pick up my life as if the last three years haven't happened. As if they have been no more than a brief interlude, a small cross to shoulder, a passing grey cloud soon to be dispelled by the strength of the sun. And for the rest of the day? I will strip her room, wash the sheets before they are cold, dismantle the bed and take it back upstairs piece by piece. If I open all the windows in there, the sunny, cold December air will remove all trace of her by the time Dave comes home. We will have a dining room again. We'll eat in there tonight. I'll find my posh tablecloth and iron it. I'll use my best china too and prepare a feast, maybe nip to the shops this afternoon for steak or turbot and chocolate. Yes, the best chocolate to make Dave's favourite pudding.

There! My day is pleasantly full. There'll be no time to think or regret or feel guilt. I have done my best and now it's someone else's turn.

But oh, the nagging worms of doubt and guilt. They nibble at my resolve, my plans, my future. How will I be able to live with myself after this betrayal? How will I fill the long empty hours if my friends have forsaken me, and my brother and sister see me in a new harsh and cruel light? And Dave? I have no idea how he will cope with those spikes of self-disgust I am bound to show. When Mum first came, he showed his admiration for me, praised my loyalty and love and even said that he could never have incarcerated either of his parents in some ostensibly suitable but probably stinking care home. Can he guess that I could do that now? If Simon hadn't given me this way out, I could have her booked in next week, this week, today. I know I could pick up the phone and tell the authorities that I've had enough and will someone please come and take my mother away. And then, I suspect, I'd crawl into a corner and fade away into little more than a twitching heap. But Simon is coming to rescue me. I can offload and start to live again.

Who are you kidding, Helen, and where's the fire you inherited from Mum? Come on brain, do your stuff and fill up with happy plans. Dinner tonight. Decided. Tick it off the list. Tonight in bed? I will not weep. I will hit the pillow and sleep solidly for the first time in years and tomorrow – what? Ginny, yes, phone Ginny. We'll have a girl's day out in town, shopping and gassing and giggling. I'll invite her and her husband to dinner soon and show them the last three years have been but a blip, something I've endured and survived and from which I've emerged smiling.

Ten minutes.

I'm back with Mum. I have one arm round her and the other reaches for her hand. We are one, mother and daughter, a mixed bundle of fears and doubt. My guilt trickles away as her head leans into my shoulder and I utter soothing words that it'll be all right and I'm here so you don't need to be afraid and I'll always be here and never leave you to the terrors of your addled mind.

Of course, Mum, I am lying. I am handing you over to Simon for it is his turn to help. You always said we children should take turns and that's what's going to happen now because I can't care for you anymore. You've used up all my reserves and I have nothing left to give. Simon will be the same. You will wreak havoc in his life as you have in mine and someone will rescue him when he can't stop weeping and his wife has been reduced to a shadow and his children, those lovely kids you once adored, have succumbed to a life of unremitting stress without a normal routine to buoy their noses above the spiteful waves. Then Sis will step in and sort it out, find you somewhere to live and see to all the financial side of it and visit you with a cheerful smile and bunch of sweet peas every weekend. Simon and I will come too, not with flowers – for we know how you hate to see the garden in a vase – but with our love restored and regrets duly hidden. We'll probably sing to you, or read – you always liked reading – and we'll ignore the smell and the dismal life we've condemned you to. And as you deteriorate further, you'll grow to not mind the plastic cheer of the carers who talk to you like a six-year-old or treat you like an old mop not realising you were once the strongest woman in the world. And when you die, your funeral will be marked with more flowers – how you'll hate that! – from everyone who ever knew you and we will unite with good memories and forget the horror of your last years and you will turn over in your grave saying what a lot of fuss about something so *natural* as death before giving in to eternal sleep.

So Mum, I'm being honest. About time too, I hear you say. Simon will be here soon but I have just enough time to ring him on his mobile and tell him the truth. He won't answer the phone, being a good and sensible driver, but he will stop at the next lay-by and listen to my message and decide whether or not he wants to continue his journey. Then I'll ring Sis and admit I've been too proud and have taken my responsibilities too seriously. I will make it easy for her to say I-told-you-so and just-because-you're-the eldest-doesn't-mean-you-know-it-all and really-Helen-I-wish-you'd-*listened*-to-me. And I will smile through every second of what she'll blast into my ear and I'll thank her nicely when she's finished and hand you the phone so you two can plot and plan about how bloody wonderful life's going to be from now on.

I'm not bitter, Mum. I know you can't help how you are. I understand every one of your difficult moments. Difficult? They've been hellish recently. The more I've admitted to myself that I can't cope, the worse they've got. You've picked up on my stress and reacted accordingly and I'm sorry I put you through that. Forgive me, Mum. I meant well. I did my best.

Clichés. The road to hell is paved with them. I have become a cliché. I am that dutiful daughter who thought she could make life easier if not good for you. I assumed, being your favourite daughter, that I was the only one capable of easing your stormy passage but I was wrong to force you through my ideal of filial care. I have inadvertently strewn rocks in your path and stirred up storms and whirlpools. I meant well. No excuse. Forgive me.

You're calmer already, I can feel it. Are you sleeping again? Has my voice been a lullaby?

I can't ring Simon. But I will be honest and tell him straight when he arrives and the three of us will sit and talk calmly of what's to be done. We can even phone Sis to include her. We will have a proper family conference just like we used to when we were young, not that you contributed much in the way of calm. I used to like that, the way your emotions sparked and your voice boomed in pleasure or disapproval. Do you remember the time when Sis stayed out all night and, after she sneaked home bedraggled and shamefaced, we gathered round the kitchen table to talk it through? I knew it didn't make one jot of difference. Sis didn't really care what we thought and advice to her always acted like a spur to worse behaviour, but she fooled Dad, if not you. And look where her obstinacy got her: she's what's called a successful woman with an important career and a long wake of discarded men who failed to live up to her standards.

I envy her. I'd like to have conquered the world, gone my own way, made an independent and fulfilling life. Don't misunderstand, I don't regret one minute of marriage to Dave or the lives of my children, but I sometimes wonder what would have happened if marriage hadn't been the only option for women like me who left school with little more than optimism.

Did you know I've always been fascinated by forensic science? Dave does. He teases me about being glued to 'cold case' programmes where intelligent-looking women peer down microscopes at minute dots of evidence then come up with the answer to a crime no one else could solve. With my capacity for attention to detail, I could have been good at that, if I'd had more self-confidence, if I'd defied those teachers who dismissed my efforts and prophesied a career only in child care or secretarial work, for that's all there was available for someone without serious qualifications. I should have listened instead to the teachers who wrote 'could do better' on my reports and got a string of O- and A-levels then surprised you all by winning a place in the best university in the land. Although I don't regret my life one bit, I often wonder what would have happened if I hadn't chosen the easy route.

And what would have happened to you if I hadn't? You'd have been in a care home for three years now. I can't bear the thought of that, Mum. I still can't. I want Simon to succeed with you where I have failed. I want his wife to rise to the challenge, his children to understand that life does not revolve solely round their needs, and I can imagine Simon's goodness stretching as far as giving up his job to care for you. I can see him struggling to set up some sort of work from home so he can be on tap for you, the mother he loves and whose dignity he would never threaten. Of course, he'd never blame me for changing his life and, when I come to visit, he'll do everything possible to prevent me feeling that he's succeeded where I haven't. He's good like that, a sensitive, caring, loyal brother and son who'd rescue any of us without a thought for himself. I wonder if that is because he is the middle child, even though they are usually branded as being the most confused. I suspect they glean the best from life in a family, taking their sense of responsibility from the elder children and their self-worth from the younger.

He's here. He's parked outside but hasn't come in yet. He's sitting out there psyching himself up for what he knows is about to happen.

Don't hurt him, Mum. Are you listening? I know you are, even if you don't reply. Don't destroy him. Soak up his love and his family's respect for you. Try to fit into his routine. Laugh at his jokes and try to smile when the children are noisy or unsuitably dressed. Eat your food without chucking it around and appreciate your new surroundings. I'll come and visit you often and I'll read to you every time for I've only just realised how much my voice soothes you.

I'm asking for the moon, aren't I? The moon on a stick. A cosy ordered life where everyone's content with the status quo and no one, not even you, is kicking at the boundaries. Oh well.

And me? I promise you, Mum, I will learn to live with myself and accept what I have done and what I am about to do as the very best I could do for you.

12 noon

Views from the Beach

By E.C. Seaman

The wind turbines across the bay are new this year and I most certainly do not approve. As long-term and prestigious residents (even if this is now technically not even Caspar's second home, but his third) I really do feel we should have been asked for our opinion. Caspar demurred when I told him so. He said quickly, "I really can't afford to get involved Mother; I can't be seen to oppose renewable energy sources in the current political climate."

Of course I acquiesced graciously to his judgement, as I generally have to these days. And I must admit to a degree of unwillingness to draw too much press attention to this seafront hideaway, Caspar's precious bolthole from the pressures of Westminster. It has been a most challenging year for us, but he is now a mere finger's reach away from the prize; first the party leadership, then in a few more years, God willing... But I hardly dare to articulate that thought, even to myself.

Our family compound isn't the haven it once was. A caravan park crammed with ugly static tin boxes now squats a mile along the coast, and the beach becomes more crowded each summer. I watch the parade of holidaymakers from behind my tinted spectacles. All those dreadful young men with beer-bellies pouring over the top of shorts that are at once too tight in the waist and unflatteringly baggy elsewhere. So unlike my dear Caspar. His belly is held impressively flat by sheer force of will as he speaks into his mobile telephone. He never stops working, even on the beach. The women here are, in my opinion, even worse than the men;

simply look at that family over there. So loud, in every way, the mother's hair dyed that unnatural wine-ish red, so vulgar, and she really shouldn't be wearing that bikini. I absolutely detest the sight of all this puffy flesh, all these bodies stretched out of shape by too-frequent childbearing, by continual overindulgence.

I stiffen my spine; sit upright in my canvas chair. I have always been slim, through rigorous self-discipline as much as excellent genes. But I find that advancing age brings an unfortunate crepiness in the upper arm and thigh areas that even vigorous callisthenics cannot banish. I never wear sleeveless shirts now, rarely indulge in a bathe, though I once loved to swim in the ocean, losing myself for hours in its chilly embrace.

But one has to forgo certain pleasures in this life in order to achieve one's full potential. I know Caspar will prevail – I have always been determined that he would. There has to be some reward for the long hours I have put in, the many personal sacrifices I have made. My late husband, Braydon, was unfortunately never able to stand for leader, owing to a few trifling financial irregularities in his youth, but of course he exerted massive influence behind the scenes. And now Caspar will take the baton forward. And who knows where it will end?

Mind you, look at that great gawky lump over there, my granddaughter, Kathryn. She's hardly dynasty-making material is she? She doesn't even look like a Braydon, so fat and fair, with her face already reddening in the hot sun. She'll go the same way as her mother in a few years, start bleaching her hair, catch some undiscerning fellow with the teenaged blonde plumpness that passes briefly for beauty, then once he's snared, sink back into cushiony fat and un-dyed roots. She's sulking again I suppose. I told the girl not to swim in the sea, making an exhibition of herself, just because she has won a couple of school races. So instead she sits there with her head in that iPod device and a faraway look on her face that makes her look quite retarded.

As this is the first time we have been allowed to see her in years, I keep reminding Kathryn how lucky she is to be spending this holiday with her father's family, though as far as I can see, she is simply too provincial to comprehend the importance of Caspar's work. She will keep trying to distract him by chattering about school or her dreadful mother. I am afraid that she is not top-drawer material at all, and has not got the common sense, or indeed intellectual curiosity, to make the most of a whole week's contact with one of the country's great political minds. I can't in all honesty say the girl is a disappointment, as I never expected anything better from a child of Caspar's first wife, that silly little fool who went running back to Wales at the first breath of marital discord. So limited, so very provincial of her.

By contrast, Caspar's new wife, Jen, lounges elegantly there on the sand, stretched out on a cobalt-blue towel. I have never seen Jen look less than perfect, her hair anything but immaculate ash-blonde. It must be artificially maintained, at great expense to my poor Caspar no doubt, but you would never know. But then Jen's looks are rather her *raison d'être*, aren't they? I suppose that an actress, even if permanently 'resting', has a degree of cachet, but her circle has a certain showbusiness raciness that I don't relish. I hope by now I know better than to try and tell Caspar that, of course. His women are the one area of his life where he has never listened to my advice.

Yesterday, in an attempt to educate my granddaughter, I informed her that the lighthouse in the bay was the inspiration for one of Virginia Woolf's novels.

"Her family also had their summer home near here," I said, though of course the Bells departed long before Braydon times.

But it was Jen who responded, with predictable self-interest,

"Maybe it'd make a script; Virginia Woolf is kinda hot-flavoured right now."

She borrowed my copy of *To the Lighthouse* and devoured it in several sittings then cast it aside disgustedly, dismissing it as totally unfilmable.

"Everything's just too internalised, there's no action."

I reproved her: "It's a classic of English literature, Jen, not *Die Hard*."

Jen simply gave me that truculent stare of hers and said, "Yeah right Mary-Alice, but there are limits, y'know."

Caspar has got a tiger by the tail there, and not for the first time. Jen's bland tanned California-blonde prettiness wouldn't suit arty-type pictures, and Caspar must never allow her to appear in, God forbid, soap operas, or anything that vulgarly displays her figure. If she insists on an acting career, she will have to realise that her glamour days are now behind her; primetime television simply isn't the right image for a future party leader's wife. I do sometimes wonder why my son, whose progress through life is otherwise flawless, has such weak judgement when it comes to women, especially in picking wives. I suppose at least this one, even if she is an American, has managed to produce a son for Caspar. It is so important for a man like him to have a son, to carry on the family name. And Benjy is a dear little chap though Jen mollycoddles him dreadfully, claims he has 'allergies' whatever that is supposed to mean. Sunshine, fresh air and a firm hand, that's all children need.

I do wish the wretched woman would at least try to look a little happier. Her perpetual pout of discontent, her shockingly flamboyant clothes, her wanton extravagance – they do nothing to help Caspar's image. Jen claims not to 'understand' him but in my opinion she makes no effort, instead she continually snipes about him spending days at his constituency or booking into hotels after late night parliamentary sessions. I find my son perfectly straightforward. Men are men and do what they need to do and we must simply accept it as part of the greater good. Life isn't about pleasure, especially as a politician's wife; it's about duty. Where would we all be now if I had put my own desires above the greater good? It is a lesson that Jen would do well to learn.

*

It's only just noon, but I sigh for what must be, like, the millionth time today and I roll over, burying my face in the hot velour softness of my beach towel. Utterly bloody Caspar is still talking to his PPS in London. This call has been going on for nearly an hour now – why does he bother to come down to the beach if that's what he's gonna do? He's hardly even played with Benjy this vacation, just leaves us to our own devices unless someone has a camera pointed his way. Then he's quick enough to play the doting daddy.

He's not even been interested in making out with me, which is a bad sign. A man of large appetites, my husband. When we first met, at that sweet highpoint when it became inevitable that we were going to sleep together, he kinda gave me a hint of how it would be. I didn't listen. He has a name for his schlong y'know. Jeez, how the tabloids would love that little nugget of information.

"Meet QUANGO," he said to me, "in my case, it stands for Quasi-Autonomous Non-Governable Organ." That's a politician's idea of a joke. I laughed of course. Sometimes we laugh at a guy's jokes when we'd be better off punching him on the nose and running as fast as we can in the other direction.

My head's pounding like a road-drill. Those windmills don't help, the razor-edged blades whirling ever faster, making that terrible whump, whump, whump as they cut through the air, slicing off my life in precious seconds. Can I rouse myself enough to walk up to the shop on the cliff-top and buy some painkillers? I know Mary-Alice will have aspirin in her purse but I'm damned if I'll give my mother-in-law the satisfaction of doling them out disapprovingly. Look at her; hunched up in her chair like an old crow, passing judgement, looking down her nose at everything and everybody. Apart from Caspar of course, her mean little eyes light up when she sees her precious son. He's the only person who can really make her smile.

These sunglasses don't do much to shield my hangover from the sun but at least they're hiding me from Mary-Alice's glare. Too many scotch-and-sodas at dinner last night again and I'm not getting any younger, as she keeps reminding me. I hoped to spend this vacation de-toxing after a hectic coupla months, but even here, Mary-Alice can't possibly take it easy; every lavish meal has to be cooked for Caspar by her own fair hand. Her huge lunch hampers and endless flasks of hot plasticky-tasting tea, along with her chair, towels, sunshades and all Benjy's clutter of spades and buckets and fishing lines, mean there's so much to transport down to the beach that it takes two trips to carry it all. People must laugh at us; it's like a freaking royal procession.

Not that I care what the folks here think. They are so utterly, damnably British; Caspar's natural constituency. They all recognise him, but are way too nice, too polite, too consciously well-bred to be seen to be noticing. And so dull, as if they've all been mainlining the Boden catalogue, with their stripy t-shirts, deliberately crumpled linen shorts and neat little frilled cardigans.

I've spent desperate hours browsing the net trying to find a decent spa or salon anywhere west of Exeter or even a few boutiques worth visiting. But Caspar just detonated at me for tying up his laptop for something 'so trivial'. Well, Jeesus, Caspar, this is supposed to be a vacation; time off for Chrissakes. And there has to be some compensation for putting up with a month of Mary-Alice. You'd think after six years I'd be used to the fact that my mother-in-law has a rod up her ass, but the old dear never fails to amaze me. She still carefully refers to me as 'Caspar's new wife'. As our son is now nearly five, I do kinda feel that the novelty has worn off our relationship.

This year, just to finish me off, I've been lumbered with Caspar's *ghaaaastly* teenage daughter for a week. What a *state*. A pasty-skinned little troll who looks as if her hair's been hacked off with nail-scissors. And her clothes! Just *so* awful; baggy black t-shirts with tattered old jeans and her school blue one-piece swimsuit with a racer back that emphasises her over-muscly shoulders. At least she doesn't want to call me 'Mom.' As if! I'm certainly not old enough to be *her* mother.

I decided to take the kid into the nearest town, get her a semi-decent haircut, some layers cut in and maybe a few streaks. Making-over Kathryn could be my holiday project, give me a little entertainment, which gawd alone knows I need in this backwater. I can't possibly do anything about the size of the girl's derrière, not in a week, though I've noticed Mary-Alice has been refusing to give her second helpings of dinner. Mary-Alice keeps reminding the girl how lucky she is to be spending time with her father's family, though as far as I can tell, the kid seems spectacularly unenthralled by it all. She's obviously not even got the sense to make the most of the opportunity; I'd have killed for a rich daddy to give me a leg-up when I was her age.

She's been knocking about with the beach lifeguards, who are obviously *so* embarrassed to have the little mutt puppying around them. Mary-Alice tried to nip that tendency in the bud, get the kid to do something useful, but it backfired 'cos now the kid just sits with her nose in a book or stares at the sea. She confided to me, in a sudden burst of chattiness, that she's, like, under-18 swimming champion for Pantyliner or whichever flaky little backwoods town she's from, which perked me up, like maybe the kid might have something about her after all. But then she said she's doing literature (her 'absolute passion' she says) and drama for her A-levels. Gawd save me from another budding Juliet. If the wretched kid decides to take up acting I guess Caspar will expect me to help. Well, my first advice would be for her to shed at least twenty pounds; there's no point in her bothering otherwise, she'll never ever get cast. Why the hell didn't the kid's mother just send her to fat camp this summer?

But though Kathryn accepted a day at the beauty salon, she made it crystal clear she didn't want my help to change her image. She looked dubiously at the hot-pink tankini I picked out, and wouldn't even try the cutaway surf shorts. She let me buy her a chunky rainbow-striped hoodie, which she's just flung on anyhow over her sawnoff jeans. Kooky kid, I just don't get why she sits on the beach huddled in layers of clothing. You'd think with all that insulating puppy-fat she could deal with the occasional breeze from the sea. I can cope with anything so long as I know I'm catching some rays and topping up my tan.

Oh look, there's my baby Benjy, some seaside treasure clutched in his little hand.

"Come here honey, give Momma a kiss."

He's still pale as a stripped twig, running with that funny splayed-out-feet gait that small kids have. He's shot up this summer, not my plump little baby boy anymore; he seems stretched, almost too tall for his weight. My darling boy. I dream of running away with him, of taking him back to the States. Some days I feel like he's the only good thing in my life. Whatever happens in this marriage, I'll always keep my precious son. That and a hefty chunk of the Braydon estate of course – there has to be some compensation for putting up with his Highness.

But hey, I don't give up that easy, and besides, Caspar's

workaholic tendencies could soon bear fruit, if I'm any judge. Bail-out on my darling husband just as things are gonna get really interesting? No way. I can already see myself in the role of First Lady – dazzling the tabloids with my classy-yet-sexy style. As long as Caspar keeps his dick zipped I know he'll succeed – that golden boy never appears so gilded that he pisses people off, added to which his policies are carefully tailored by focus groups to appeal to the masses. He's the king of the sound-bite, the sultan of spin.

"It's all about building bridges," he'll say earnestly, smiling deep into the camera lens. Is anyone really fooled by that crap? The only bridges Caspar builds are one-way, to advance his career. Even this vacation is designed to demonstrate his green credentials – he'll get big kudos for staying at home whilst legitimately topping up his tan in time for the leadership contest cameras.

Benjy goes scooting off again so I roll over to bronze my boobs and watch the windmills on the hill. Now the wind's dropped, their long white wheeling arms turn elegantly, lazily, like they're doing tai chi, pale and slender against the powder blue sky. That reminds me – I must call my trainer when I get back to London and book extra sessions to make up for this lousy vacation. I can't afford to gain more than a coupla pounds. I have to keep on top of it.

Last year, Caspar and I went through a real bad patch. The usual, but too close to home, so for once I wasn't gonna turn a blind eye. I threatened again to take Benjy away. Mary-Alice got bent out of shape, totally lost her cool, reminded me how Caspar's first wife entered the marriage with nothing, and left with nothing.

"Yeah, well more fool her for not signing a pre-nup," I yelled.

Mary-Alice's mouth puckered up like a dog's ass and she said smugly, "Class will out."

Caspar, when interrogated, always claims his first marriage

was just a boy-girl thing, not meant to last. I guess that means he cheated on her, or more to the point, that she was able to prove it. She took baby Kathryn and ran back to Wales to 'find herself', and a new man as well as it turned out. She never pressed for alimony. Surprising really, considering the second husband is just a firefighter or something utterly *blah* like that.

"Divorce is simply not our way," Mary-Alice said, "it's so dreadfully diminishing."

But she left it at that. Just as well she didn't push me any further, 'cos it's common knowledge in Caspar's circles, though no-one ever says anything to the old dear's face, that Braydon Senior used to have regular bimbo-eruptions. But y'see, the expected way for the Braydon women is to swallow their pride and accept another diamond, another fur, or in Mary-Alice's case yet another expensive redecoration of the house, or extensive re-landscaping of the grounds. That way they maintain the Braydon name and the family fortune. Yeah, right. She's so obsessed that she even calls this beach house 'The Compound', a deliberate copy of the blessed Kennedys. She thinks she's building a British political dynasty in their image, but hey, we all know what happened to them.

It's all about power when you come down to it. It's a dog-eat-dog world, or rather bitch-scratch-bitch. I've always known that if another woman had come along, one who could offer Caspar what he wants politically, then I'd lose him. It's that simple – the sex is irrelevant. But now you know he's *this close* to getting where he wants to be and, when he does, the power becomes mine. Awesome. Yeah Caspar, you'll see; you'll be so scared of scandal that you won't be able to touch me, let alone divorce me. It'll be payback time.

*

This week with my Dad had so much promise. My heart

70

stuttered at my first sight of the navy sea, the flags fluttering above the miles of pale-gold sand, the huge white house perched on the cliffs. My stomach still does flips every time I look out at the lighthouse across the bay; every photo I take looks as perfect as a postcard. It's a major sensory overload. The lush smell of my stepmother Jen's coconut sun-oil fills the whole house, and there are herbs running wild in the garden; straggly thyme, sweet spearmint, and a curry bush, spilling its sharp, spicy scent across the dusty road. Even the clouds are different from back home. They're not grey and lumpy like old duvets, but as soft as whipped sugar, turning candyfloss pink in the sunset while the evening surfers in their slick black wetsuits bob in the white rollers like skinny neoprene seals.

That's how I'd write it all down, capturing pictures for posterity like my English teacher says. But when I started writing notes when everyone was there, they all began to comment and read what I'd written and then Dad asked me if I wrote poetry as well like it was all some big joke. I've been made to share a bedroom with the step-brat Benjy, which is supposed to be bonding, ha ha, but by the time I get to bed the lights are out and all I can do is snatch a bit of reading time under the covers until my torch batteries run down. I've spent most of my allowance this week on spare batteries, so I can get through my A-level reading list and also keep my iPod going. That way I can drown out the sound of Dad and Aunt Jen arguing.

There's nothing much else to do. Aunt Jen took me out for the day, which was sort of okay, except that she made it obvious she was doing it because she pities me. I feel weird calling her Aunt Jen, because she is absolutely no relation to me. I can't bring myself to call her 'Mommy', though to give her credit, she'd probably throw a fit if I tried. She's really scary. When I first saw her I thought she was dead beautiful, like someone out of *Hello* magazine; but she is always so angry. Kind of, I dunno, clenched, like she's going to explode if you touch her. But then the amount she drinks, she must have a pretty much permanent and totally banging hangover.

They are all so obsessed with my appearance. I usually feel quite good about myself, not like I'm a gorgeous model or anything, but you know, okay. I get by. But everyone here is glossier, more golden, more minted than back home, so I feel like a weird pale-skinned fat freak next to all these women with their Pilates-toned bodies and hair that's always three perfect shades of pale caramel.

And my Grandmother is a right cow. I feel dead bad about thinking that, because I always wanted a grandma, someone white-haired and a bit cosy. Mary-Alice is not like that at all. She always has to sit in the exact same place on the beach, right by the cliffs in a kind of little cove and you should hear the fuss she makes if someone else sits there; it's like she owns the place. And when Aunt Jen told her about our day out and showed off the things she'd bought me, Grandmother just sniffed and snapped at me, "You'll have to keep those nice things here at your Father's house; they're not for taking away."

Yes, okay, like I am ever coming back here if I can possibly help it. Aunt Jen rolled her eyes behind Grandmother's back and told me that of course the clothes are mine to keep. Then she ruined it by adding that they probably wouldn't fit me another year. Like I'm a total minger. Thanks a bunch.

I had such high hopes of this holiday, spending time with my Dad. But all week I've been waiting to feel like I've come home. Running along the main corridor of this house there's a table, piled high with what Grandmother calls '*objets trouvées*', which is her posh way of saying 'things we've found.' There are pretty striped pebbles, bits of sea-smoothed glass, huge shells and all types of seashore tat that I know she'd never tolerate in her big London house. They're all piled up anyhow, tumbled memories of past holidays, added to year on year. Each day Benjy adds his little finds to the pile, but there is nothing in it of me. I don't belong here with their talk of past holidays, their shared jokes, their arguments and endless debate about boring political issues. It's not even like it's interesting stuff that people care about, it's just wheeler-dealing about who's in and who's out and who said what about this and that. It's like listening to my mates bitching at school except that Grandmother is trying to calculate who might vote for Dad if there's a leadership contest and then work out who they need to influence.

I keep thinking about home. Steve, my step-dad, is chunky, red-faced, not like my (as I suppose I have to think of him) real Dad. Some illness (I think it was mumps, but I've never asked in case someone gives me the gruesome details) left Steve unable to have kids of his own. It doesn't seem to bother him though. At my big swimming meet this year, he was well miffed when a teacher told him he couldn't video me winning my races. No cameras allowed.

"But she's my daughter," Steve said. He never calls me his step-daughter.

And then there's Mum, as unlike Jen as you can imagine, her hair streaked with grey where she's combed a clay-coated hand through it, her cheeks always flushed pink because the studio Steve built for her is cold so she wears layers of jumpers which she sheds one by one as she warms up. Apart from the days the kiln's firing the studio has to be cool, to keep the clay moving.

"You have to suffer for your art," Mum says and we both laugh, because Mum doesn't seem to suffer anything as she is almost always smiling. And she's not up herself or anything, even though her stuff sells for megabucks these days. She fills up the space in the kiln with keyrings she makes for me and my mates with our names picked out in funky swirly colours. All the girls at school want one. Dad and Grandmother just smiled horrible superior smiles when I told them about

Mum's work, and how she is being exhibited in a big gallery in London now. I could tell they didn't really believe me. But then they don't care about anything artistic. Grandmother was really snotty to Jen about not rating that Virginia Woolf book, but two minutes later she was slagging-off the writer herself, sniffing, "Well what do you expect from a champagne socialist?"

Dad, Caspar I mean, is actually kind of a hunk, though that's too weird a thought, so instead I make myself notice how he sucks in his stomach when he thinks people are looking at him, how he keeps unrolling the top of his wetsuit to make sure his chest tans and how he always turns his face to the left so the camera catches his 'best' side. My mates envied me coming away like this, with my Dad and his family. I mean, he's not like a proper celebrity because he hasn't done anything cool, but he's famous, and rich. And there's something about him that gets everybody jumping.

Just before I came away, I heard Mum having a row with Steve; I listened-in a bit guiltily. I mean, it's unusual for them to argue. Sure they have disputes, but they're usually amiable, with lots of banter, not like this, with a real nasty edge in Mum's voice. I could hear Steve was trying to be reasonable, in that way he has. "Maybe Caspar wants to get to know Kathryn now she's a young lady. He never struck me as someone who could empathise with little kids."

"Not Caspar," Mum hissed, "it's purely a PR exercise. He's using Kathryn, so if anyone asks about his daughter, his first marriage, he can reply that Kathryn went on holiday with him this summer."

"Why don't you give him the benefit of the doubt? Kathryn's a lovely girl; he probably just wants to see more of his daughter."

"No Steve, it's all about saving face and it's bloody typical of him."

"You've never really got him out of your system, have

you?"

He sounded pissed-off. I saw Mum swirl round, pace across the kitchen.

"Not in a nice way Steve," she said. "He's like malaria – something nasty you catch and can never quite shake off."

I'd never heard my mum be that bitchy before. I didn't hear any more 'cos they moved into the lounge, switched the TV on. I didn't want to ask Mum about it. She generally pretends like Dad never happened.

I look at my watch. Just past half-twelve. This time tomorrow, I should be on my way back home. Thank God.

It's been dead boring here. The most excitement I get is watching the wind-farm up on the hill, all the sails twirling happily in the breeze like the little windmills on Benjy's sandcastles. This beach would be way cool if I was allowed to wander, with miles of golden sand broken up by rocky reefs. Pete, one of the lifeguards, says that's why the surf is so good here, and so dangerous. Not that I'd know, because that cow Grandmother threw a hissy fit when I went for a swim. And she wouldn't let me hire a surfboard either in case I gave her precious Benjy ideas.

Not that he'd notice. Benjy and the little kids fish for crabs and play in the tiny rock pools at low tide, but there are also big pools where the water has scooped out deep holes between rocks as big as houses. I like to sit here on one of the high rocks and look down into the glassy depths. The water's so deep that you can't see the bottom and when I've watched older boys jumping in, it seemed to take forever for them to come back up. The pools are still and mysterious until the tide turns and tears back through a gap in the rocks so that the water churns and sucks like a washing machine.

Suddenly, while I'm just sitting here, something finally happens. So quickly, so quietly that it passes unnoticed, except by me. One minute Benjy is sitting on a rock, his toes and his crab-line dangling into the water, the next, with a tiny splash and no time to cry out, he falls. I stand up, waiting for him to surface, but he doesn't appear. I know he can't swim; he only paddles in the shallows, kicking his legs up and screeching if even his ears get wet. But I don't stop to think about it, I just yell, "Benjy!" and jump straight in.

The water tears the air from my lungs. It's icy. I surface, gasping, and then plunge into the depths again, kicking out to force myself down, deeper and deeper, fighting my body's instinct to float. And then I see him through the swirling sand and seaweed, so tiny, so still. I grab for his hand and clasp his wrist which is pathetically thin, so fragile that I'm afraid it'll snap and I'll be left with just his hand clutched in mine. At that totally gross thought, I pull harder, feel a jarring tear, so that for one moment I think I really have done him some damage. Then we're free, swooshing to the surface, and I'm gasping for breath, filling my red roaring lungs with air that feels burning hot after the cold depths.

No time to think, I must get Benjy out of the water. He's all limp and it's scary and I hardly dare look at his pale face, but at least his eyes are open, and his mouth is wide open too, in what would be a scream if his lungs weren't full of water. Oh, thank God! Hands are pulling at Benjy, and one of the lifeguards, his face gone all grey and tight under the tan, lifts him out, placing him tenderly on the sand. The other one has his arms cradling me, pulling me ashore. The first lifeguard is rolling Benjy over, pummelling him, but I know it'll be okay because I can hear the little guy crying, retching up his breakfast.

The other lifeguard stops holding me and I start to shiver.

"Wow, that was so cool. You jumped straight in, you knew exactly what to do," he says.

He wraps a crackly foil blanket round me, steps back, but the look in his eyes is good, kind of hot. I want to tuck that look away somewhere, so I can pull it out and remember it later, when I have time.

And then they are all there: Dad, Jen, Grandmother. Jen's wailing like a fire-siren, mascara smeared over her face and Grandmother's interrogating the lifeguards about what happened. Benjy's now sitting up, clinging desperately to Dad's legs, his little face wet with tears and snot.

Dad looks embarrassed. He furiously turns on Jen. "Can't you bloody well stop him from making such a fuss? He's drawing attention, Jen; if anyone recognises me…"

And then Jen hits him, just the once, but good and hard.

I don't believe it; they're going to have another row, right here, right now. Instead of comforting that poor little kid, Dad's going to bawl Jen out. But then just when I think he's finally going to lose it, Dad's face changes, goes blank. I guess he's far too experienced to be pushed into a fight in public, because he picks Benjy up, turns away and stalks off, tight-lipped.

Grandmother watches him for a minute, her eyes narrowed, then turns to me. "You've got blood on your legs," she says.

"It's just a few scratches from the rocks," I reply. She nods at me, almost approvingly.

"You'd better help my granddaughter carry our things up from the beach, young man," she says to the stunned lifeguard, and she clamps an arm around Jen, who is still sobbing, and almost drags her away.

I don't exactly rush back. Helping Pete the lifeguard pack up the beachbags is the most fun I've had all holiday. My legs feel a bit wobbly, and he notices this and helps me up the steep cliff path with a hand at the small of my back. When I finally go into the house, Benjy's sat at the kitchen table with a big plate of pudding. Grandmother says it's because he was brave, but really it's like a plaster, something to cover up a bad patch. Jen can't take her eyes off Benjy. He has soft, deliciously clean-smelling bandages on his arm, fastened by a smiley-face sticker. It was his wetsuit that snagged on the rock, so he only has a little graze.

"Am I going to have a scar? Wow," he says, now the anaesthetic cream and all the attention has taken effect. He can't stop chattering about the fall, but he seems a little bit better every time he tells the story.

"Bless him, by the time he's finished building it up, we'll be hearing how he saved *you*," Aunt Jen says to me, but not as nastily as she sometimes says stuff. Benjy has turned away, doesn't hear, his full attention now on the lavish amounts of strawberries and meringue she's squashing up for him.

I want something to eat too, it's nearly one o'clock, but Grandmother pretends not to hear me when I ask when lunch will be. Dad's just got off the phone to London and wanders in with a sheaf of papers and his laptop under his arm. He and Grandmother now get their heads together, plotting the next stage of policy on some obscure Countryside Bill that's up for discussion. Can you credit them? I mean, it's like Benjy's accident never happened. Then Dad actually turns to me, assuming I've been hanging on his every word, and says with his big fake shiny-toothpaste smile, "Of course – you live in the countryside, don't you Kathryn? What do you think about it?"

I can't be arsed with this anymore.

"Since you and Mary-Alice have already decided it between you," I say, "what does it matter what anyone else thinks, Caspar?"

Grandmother's head snaps round, her face horrified.

"You may think it very modern, calling your father by his Christian name, but that's not what we do in this family," she says sharply.

I hardly know how I dare, but I look straight at her and say, "A father is the person who raises you. I don't think Caspar deserves that title."

There's a sudden intake of breath; I see Caspar's face darken and Grandmother's mouth purse up in that nasty tight way that means she's brewing an almighty put-down.

But Aunt Jen's been at her secret booze stash again and she cackles happily, "You've got a real chip off the old Braydon block here; a disputer, a born politician."

Then – "Can I call Dad 'Caspar' too?" says Benjy, all innocence.

We can all see that Caspar is totally busted. He can only take it like a man and laugh or he'll look bad. He doesn't try to ask my opinion again. I lean forward and nick the last unsquashed strawberry off Benjy's plate, giving him a grin.

Tomorrow is home day. I'll be back by teatime and then I still have two weeks of the summer holiday left and they stretch out before me like blissful eternity. I mean, my mates don't need to know quite how crappy this holiday was, do they? And at least I've got a bit of a tan – and Pete's email address. Before I leave, I'll put the keyring Mum made for me into Grandmother's pile of holiday-treasures, slipping my name right into the heart, deep among the driftwood and shells and pieces of soft-green glass. I'll get Mum to make another, she'll understand. Maybe sometime she could make one for Benjy as well.

2pm

End of Innocence

By C L Raven

If you had your time again, would you do anything different?

"Not guilty."

I gasp, the shock and disbelief feels like a red hot dagger, ripping through my soul with the force of a speeding train. I grip the hard wooden seat in front of me, gouging my nails into its solid flesh until the pain nearly cripples my fingers. I close my eyes and hope that when I open them, time will have reversed and they will read the verdict as guilty. It can't be real. I've been brought up to believe that justice always rules in the end. This isn't justice. This isn't right. It has to be a mistake. I am dreaming, living the worst nightmare possible. But I'm not. I open my eyes and nothing has changed. The harsh reality is like a cruel slap to the face and I know I will feel its poisonous sting for the rest of my life.

"Dean Bradshaw, Luke Johnson, Thomas Brown and Stacey Jenkins, you have been found not guilty of the murder of Liam Scully. You are free to leave."

"No!" I shout, before I can stop myself. "They did it! You can't let them go! They killed him!"

The judge's solemn voice shatters the remaining piece of hope that, for so long, I have clung to desperately. Now I have nothing and his words echo around my tumultuous mind, slowly destroying me from the inside. He glares at me for disrupting his court while the four defendants hug each other and squeal with delight. It is the best day of their lives and the worst of mine since Liam died.

I sink back on to the bench, my body weak and shaking. I

fight back the torrent of tears – tears of anger, tears of disbelief – and feel the pain of losing Liam all over again, reliving that horrific night he died. I watch my brother's teenage killers walk free from court through the eyes of a stranger. Dressed in their suits and adopting remorseful expressions they had fooled the jury, but I know the truth. And I am going to do something about it. I just don't know what. All I know is that I cannot live with the knowledge that my brother's killers escaped retribution for stealing his life.

Mind and body numb, I stalk them from the oppressive courtroom out into the harsh sunlight. The city looks different to me now, malevolent, unforgiving. I hardly recognise the place I have lived all my life. It's a darker, colder place without Liam and it is even more sinister and gloomy now his killers will go unpunished.

I shield my face from the sun's mocking rays and observe the swarm of reporters who pounce on the teenagers, hungry for the first taste of blood from the supposed 'innocents.' I hope they will tear them apart and leave them with empty shells like the one I have been burdened with. I listen to the noise as the reporters jostle for space, each making sure their face is in line with the lens, hoping for the exclusive. To the four teenage murderers, this is just another chance to get in front of the camera. To the journalists, this is a chance to prove how useless the police are. They don't care about Liam, they only care that their name is under a headline that boasts of his chilling death and the day his killers walked free.

"Liam Scully was brutally attacked last year, beaten to the ground where his head was kicked and stamped on until he died," a reporter bares her teeth at the viewing public as, all around her, cameras flash, blinding me. "Today the four teenagers who, all aged fifteen and sixteen, were accused of killing the happy, friendly twenty year old Liam Scully, walked free from court despite eye-witness testimony placing them at the scene of the vicious assault. It is not known why

Liam was attacked. Police believe it could have been another case of the 'happy slapping' craze that's sweeping the nation, as teenagers indulge in increasingly violent activity then post their crimes on a popular internet video site. No video footage of the attack was found, but all four suspects had recently bought new mobile phones. Lack of concrete evidence was instrumental in the court's failure to secure a conviction."

There was nothing happy about his murder and they certainly weren't slapping him. Their voices blur into a fog of noise as I stand, stunned, on the court steps in the shadows, watching Liam's killers parade themselves before the cameras, enjoying their notoriety, their five minutes of fame. Some people will do anything to get on TV, even take another man's life. They are smiling, laughing, gloating, posing with the 'V' sign, as though they have escaped the worst possible miscarriage of justice in history. They have got away with murder, but they won't get away from me. For months, the court case has kept me going with the belief that justice would prevail, that my brother's murderers would be punished. Now, I have nothing left to live for. When Liam died, part of me died too. Now all of me has perished. I have no life. And a man without life is dangerous. Liam's death has left a darkness that consumes me. I can feel its cold arms embracing me, dragging me into a world where rules no longer apply. The hope of bringing his killers to justice had kept that darkness at bay, but now I have no reason to fight it and I surrender myself to it. Nate Scully ceases to exist. With the judge's utterance of those two, seemingly small, words, 'not guilty', my life has changed forever.

The teenagers reluctantly move away from the baying reporters, slipping back into normality after their brief stints as celebrities. They are skipping down the steps to freedom, back to their lives as though Liam never existed, as though these past eighteen months had never happened. I have been sentenced to a lifetime of emptiness and pain. But I am determined I will not serve my sentence alone. If I am going to the world of eternal darkness, I am taking them down with me.

I wait until they reach the pavement then I follow them, pushing through the crowd that lurks on the steps. Nobody seems to notice me as I walk in their wake. A ghost among the living. Everyone perhaps assumes I am a suspect walking free from court – because I am not wearing a suit, I am a criminal.

Nobody knows I am Liam's brother and nobody cares. The rowdy teenagers are laughing, high-fiving each other, singing. I hang back, listening to them as they gleefully recount the trial, comparing whose performance was best, and boasting about how smart they were for dumping their phones before they were arrested. But worst of all they are laughing at how my brother's life had ended. To them it was a bit of fun, like a video game. To Liam, it was a terrifying, horrific and painful way to die: defenceless, outnumbered, hideously butchered by malicious strangers for no reason. His life extinguished for a cruel and sick bit of fun. No matter how much anger I feel, the crushing agony of my guilt is stronger – I wasn't with him, I wasn't there to protect him, and that guilt will haunt me forever. It will chase me to my grave.

Their gloating words chill my soul. I feel intense, pure hatred burn through my veins as if turning my blood to electricity until I become alive with malevolence. They are so engrossed in their victory that they fail to notice the dark figure stalking them. They catch a bus from town and I board with them, making sure not to sit too close. They are noisy on the short journey and I see other people looking uncomfortable. I drum my fingers on my knees, silent in my plotting. They eventually rise and move to the front of the bus. I remain seated, waiting until they have all disembarked, then I slide to the front and step off, pretending to head in the opposite direction until the bus glides away. I turn abruptly and shadow them along the road until they enter an off-licence. They emerge minutes later with a bag full of booze. They are not old enough to drink alcohol but no doubt they think the law doesn't apply to them. They are murderers who have got away with it. They think they can do what they like and never be punished for it. They drink as they walk, toasting their success.

Thomas Brown is the first to reach his house and he disappears inside, the door slamming shut behind him. I make a note of the address. I might need it later. A few streets on and Luke Johnson leaves the group. I memorise his address as well. They are making it too easy for me. Being drunk and high on victory has made them easy targets. Now there are just two of them, Stacey Jenkins and Dean Bradshaw. Now I know what I am going to do. My heart begins to pound, my legs feel weak. I don't know if it is fear or adrenaline coursing through my trembling body, but I know I cannot back out now. If I don't do this, I will have failed Liam and I will never be able to live with myself.

I spy Stacey's phone poking out of her pocket so I seize my chance and barge between her and Dean, knocking them roughly aside. Both of them stumble and nearly fall. I reach into Stacey's pocket and grab her phone whilst she is distracted.

"Hey! Watch it arsehole!" Stacey yells, clinging onto a lamppost as I run off at full pelt.

She is not so charming and demure now she is out of court and away from the judging eyes of the jury. She fails to notice I've got her phone. Neither of them have any idea what I have planned for them. Maybe that is better, because if they knew, they would run and I don't want them to see this coming.

They don't recognise me. I conceal myself round a corner and wait for them to pass. I try to steady my ragged breathing and control my shaking hands. I hope they don't turn down this way, or they will see me. Luckily they continue straight ahead and don't even glance in my direction. I am not important enough to notice. I wait until they are some distance ahead of me then I resume tracking them. They lead me to a nearby park. I'm glad it's empty. They sit on a climbing frame, drinking and laughing. As I watch, rage festers inside me, growing like a malignant tumour, one I will never recover from.

I become impatient as I lurk in the prickly bushes. Cramp inches its way up my legs, eating into my muscles and I shift position to ease it. I pray they can't see me or hear the bushes rustling. I feel like a soldier keeping watch on the enemy before invading their camp. Eventually, the girl staggers off, laughing and shrieking, leaving Dean Bradshaw alone. I spy a strong branch lying half buried in the leaves so I pull it free and grip it tightly. I feel safer with a weapon. I survey the area again and, finding it deserted, approach from the shadows. It seems to take an eternity to reach him though the distance between us is less than one hundred feet. Time, distance and everything around me is distorted. I hesitate at the gate, suddenly uncertain. My sweaty hand grips it, but I am frozen to the spot and cannot move. I summon the courage from somewhere and push the gate. It swings open, squeaking and protesting, creaking like the rusted hinge of an ancient coffin. I step across the threshold onto the darkened earth of the playground and allow the gate to bang shut behind me. I want him to see me. I want him to feel afraid. He doesn't once look in my direction as he finishes off the drink and tosses the bottle to one side. It rolls and stops at my feet. I stand staring at him until he notices me. The heavy branch hangs by my side. I let him see it. Fear is the cruellest punishment of all.

"What you looking at?" he spits. "Freak." The venom in his voice surprises me. He doesn't know who I am and yet he hates me.

I say nothing as I move closer. He jumps down from the climbing frame and barges past me. I grab him by the collar and for the first time, he looks afraid. I can almost taste his fear and I savour it.

"Get off me you perv!" He shoves me. He is angry, drunk, scared and vulnerable. An easy target.

I swing him around and strike him in the face. He stumbles backwards, shocked. His face distorts into a grotesque, hate filled mask. This repulsive face was one of the last my brother saw. It carried him to his death.

"I'm gonna get you for that!" he snarls. His seeming bravado doesn't fool me. I know he is scared and I am enjoying his terror.

He runs at me, so I move aside and ram my knee into his soft stomach. He falls to the floor, gasping for breath but still managing to shout out horrific agonies that he threatens to retaliate with. I pause to free Stacey Jenkins' phone from my pocket then just have time to select the camera option and press record as Dean struggles to his feet. I prop the phone on the climbing frame, where it can record every vengeful moment. He swings his fist and it catches me in the nose. I can feel blood streaming down my face, seeping into my mouth. I spit it out, hating the foul taste it leaves behind. I raise the branch and use it to club him on the side of the head. While he is disorientated, I kick him to the ground. This is too easy. I had expected him to put up more of a fight but he is letting me overpower him. He doesn't say a word to me as I hit him, unleashing my pent up rage and grief on his murderous body, beating him with the branch. Without his gang, he is weak and vulnerable. He attempts to throw dirt into my eyes to blind me, but it falls uselessly back to the ground, not even hitting my boots. The camera-phone silently watches as my weapon punishes him in a way the courts wouldn't. I can see his blood seeping from his wounds and I don't stop, I can't stop. A strange feeling of serenity washes over me and it feels as though as I am viewing him through a stranger's eyes again. I was expecting him to beg for mercy, apologise for killing my brother. But he doesn't. He doesn't know who I am or why I am doing this and he doesn't care. It fuels my anger. They had taken my brother's life for no reason except entertainment. Why should a life mean so little? I see his blood seep into the dirt and force myself to cease hitting him. When he lies still, I grab the phone and press stop, breathing hard. The branch now feels unbearably heavy, as though attached to a lead weight. My rage and hatred has subsided to a dull thud. I then hit the nine button three times, leaving a bloody fingerprint.

"Ambulance please. A young lad's just been beaten up by a gang of youths. There were three of them. Two boys and a girl. They were dressed in suits."

I give the location then hang up. If the courts won't punish them for killing Liam, maybe they will punish them for beating Bradshaw up. I am surprised how cool and calm my voice is. Moments before, I was a quivering wreck. Now I am in complete control. I scroll through the phone and find numbers for Thomas Brown and Luke Johnson. With a few simple clicks, the video is sent and my mission of revenge has begun. If they enjoy the entertainment of filmed beatings they will love my gift.

I walk away, amazed at the lack of guilt I feel. I never break the law. I always own up even if I knock a wing mirror off someone's car and I still feel guilty about it for days afterwards. I've never been nasty to anyone. But these murderers have awoken part of me I never knew existed and I feel nothing. Perhaps it is because I know that what I am doing is right. This is Karma.

I run from the playground and retrace my steps, leaving Dean Bradshaw lying in abject misery and a pool of his own blood. I don't look back to see if he is okay. I don't want to know. It's true when they tell you ignorance is bliss. Ignorance is what helps us sleep at night. I toss the branch far into the thorny undergrowth and sprint from the park. I don't want to be anywhere near Bradshaw when the ambulance arrives. I do not deserve praise for calling 999 when I want him to die.

The skies overhead darken and the clouds weep shamelessly. But they are not crying for Dean Bradshaw. They are sobbing for me, weeping for who I once was and the person I have now become. I pull my dark hood over my head and keep my eyes to the ground. I know I can stop at any time, but I am driven on by a consuming hatred that destroys my rational thought and drives me to a place I never thought I'd stray. Now I am its prisoner.

I walk the streets alone, not encountering a living soul. I wipe the blood from my nose, conscious that blood arouses suspicion, then I conceal my stained hand in my pocket. I know that I can turn back, I don't have to continue along this path, but I have crossed a line and nothing I do now will erase the damage I have caused. The walk seems to take forever but it is over much too soon. I am not ready for the next stage…but it is ready for me.

I loiter in the shadows outside Luke Johnson's house, the passing car drivers pay no attention as their black tyres splash me. They don't care who I am or why I am here. If asked about this moment, they would not remember me at all. I watch and I wait, picturing Johnson inside, celebrating, mocking my brother and plotting how to execute his next innocent victim. Maybe the next one's gruesome death will be featured on one of those video websites the journalist referred to. Maybe their next victim will be the internet's newest star, thousands logging on to witness a savage killing purely to entertain their sick desire to watch someone suffer. A modern twist on medieval executions. A new low that society has sunk to.

An ambulance speeds past me, its lights flashing, the siren screaming news of an emergency. There is no emergency. If Dean Bradshaw dies, the world will have purged itself of an evil person. Society won't shed a tear if his life is erased.

The longer I stare at Luke Johnson's house, the more it seems to change before me. At first it looked like an ordinary house, but not now. The windows seem to glint and narrow, light reflects from them, flashing as though the house is possessed. The white paint appears to darken slightly, looking dirtier than before. The house looks bigger, looming above the other houses in the street, swallowing them whole. It is daring me to defy it and enter. I consider ignoring its call but I know I won't.

I had assumed that once Johnson received the video he would leave his house, rush out to find Bradshaw, but I was wrong. He obviously doesn't care that his friend has been beaten up, possibly killed. I cross the road, dodging the speeding traffic and stop at Johnson's gate. Once I cross this threshold there is no going back. Time seems to stand still for the briefest of moments before I shatter the spell. I go through the gate. It is like entering a different world; I know that there is no return from this madness and I march down the path, allowing the rage to swell inside me again. I need it. I want it. I crave the courage it gives me. I scan the garden and see a rusting scaffolding pole abandoned under the hedge. I swiftly cross the garden to retrieve it then bang on the door, pounding the cold wood with my fist, listening to the sound echoing around the house. I don't even stop to consider what I will do if it is not Luke who answers the door. Finally the door is flung open and he is standing there. He is sixteen, the oldest of the gang. He has changed out of his suit, no longer looking like the respectable, innocent teenager he had claimed to be. He looks every inch the vicious thug I know he is and I feel better about what I am about to do.

"What?" he demands. He doesn't recognise me. I mean nothing to him. But he and his friends mean everything to me.

"Are your parents in?"

"No. Piss off, I'm busy."

"You're on your own then?"

"Yeah, what's it to you?"

I say nothing as I push him out of the way and kick the door shut behind me. It bangs loudly, trapping us inside. Silence joins us in the hall as we stare at each other. I haven't planned this out. I don't know what I am going to do. For a split-second I have forgotten why I am here. Then he head-butts me, dislodging my hood. I slam Stacey Jenkins' phone on the hall table and allow my subconscious to take control. I surrender to my darkest desires as I grab him and shove him up against the wall; all the while the phone films the action. He knees me in the stomach and shoves me away from him. His eyes don't seem to register what is happening to him as I hit him. It's like he's in a trance, this blank expression in his eyes. Or is that my reflection I'm seeing? I no longer know.

All I know is that I don't stop myself as the pole connects with his body knocking him to the floor. His taunting voice goads me into hitting him harder, harder, until I can no longer feel what I am doing, until I'm pounding and kicking with a mania I never knew I possessed. His hands are up, trying to grab at the pole but I beat them down and stand on them to keep them still. I can barely feel my own hands and feet and the pole I am using to batter him, but I know he can. I know he can feel every punishing blow that rains down on him and that thought keeps me going. I hope he feels every single physical wound to match one of my agonising mental ones. I pray he hurts as much as I do. I want him crippled by the same fear and pain that tortures me. Like Dean Bradshaw he doesn't speak to me. He doesn't apologise for his crime. He doesn't know why I am doing this and I can't bear to say Liam's name to explain why. To hear his name would force a cruel dagger through my heart, bringing back the pain of losing him and the icy knowledge that I will never see his face, never hear his voice again, no matter what I do.

Then I stop and pick up the phone. It tells me it is 2:25 p.m. Only twenty five minutes have passed since the verdict was read out. I send the gruesome images to Thomas Brown's number then call for an ambulance before I pocket the phone. I stare down at him, but I no longer recognise him. He's not Luke Johnson anymore. Then I catch sight of my reflection in the hall mirror and don't know the stranger staring back at me. I am alien to myself. My nose is still bleeding, my lip is split open. My cheek bone is bruised and swollen from Johnson's head-butt. I feel shaken, disturbed, but not sorry.

I walk out, leaving the front door wide open and pause at the gate before stepping over the threshold and moving undetected alongside the traffic. I pull my hood up again, to shroud my colourful face, and I hide my right hand in my pocket so no one can see my bruised and bloodied knuckles. They ache and throb, the pain forcing me to cradle them. My left hand holds the pole by my side, shielding it from the traffic. Lightning rips open the sky, silent in its attack. I hope the pole doesn't attract its electrical rage. A sharp pain in my stomach has me doubled over, coughing and spluttering. I don't want to vomit and draw attention to myself but the cramps are unbearable. I avoid looking at the faces of people who pass me. I'm not sure who they'll see when they look at me. I don't know if they see the pole, but if they do, they say nothing. Saying nothing means it doesn't exist. The pain in my stomach nearly forces me to cry, but I fight back the tears. I don't deserve even my own sympathy.

Once the pain has subsided, I head down the rainy street, searching for Thomas Brown's house, trying to remember where he lives. I know I'm close. I hope I don't get lost. I need to finish this. Up ahead, I spy Stacey Jenkins and change my mind about hunting for Brown. For now. Stacey is still wearing her suit, she's still drunk and she's alone. I watch her as she staggers around, shouting abuse at people she thinks are looking at her judgementally. Her suit is dishevelled and she can barely walk in her high heels. She looks older than her fifteen years. Make up and violence has aged her. Any innocence she may have had was lost long ago. I hurry to catch up with her, pleased when she moves down a side street, Thomas Brown's street. I recognise it now. It's a quiet street, no cars, no people, nothing but me and Stacey Jenkins and this blackness that lurks between us. I'm glad I won't be seen.

I creep up behind her, putting the camera-phone on a low wall and raise the pole, poising it for damage. I grab her pony tail and yank her head backwards, forcing the jagged edge of the pole against her throat. She stumbles as I drag her further from the junction and any hope of salvation. She starts squealing and struggling but I'm not going to let her go. I cross the street with her and haul her into a narrow lane that joins this street to the next, where no one will witness what I am about to do. She had filmed Liam's death and I want her to suffer for revelling in his misery.

She starts crying and pleading with me not to hurt her. I hesitate for the briefest of moments. An unbidden notion hits me, pricks my conscience like a poisoned thorn. *She's a girl.* I'm an eighteen year old full-back for my local rugby team. This is wrong. I feel sick. I hate what I have become. I release my grip on her and allow her to escape. She grabs the opportunity to gouge my face with her sharpened talons. My cheek and neck sting as blood rushes to seal the wounds. As I'm standing there, horrified at the depths I have sunk to, she turns around and looks me straight in the eye. Her bravado has returned now she is no longer fighting for her life, and with it comes vileness.

"Hey! I know you! You was in court. For the dead guy. You his boyfriend or somethink?" I hold my tongue, unable to speak. This isn't me. I am not like them. "Wait 'til I tell the guys we pounded a poof." She starts laughing then examines her nails. "Bugger it! You made me break one."

All her tears have gone. I begin to wonder whether they were ever there. She doesn't know what pain is. She has never suffered before. But I will teach her what suffering is. I want to make her sorry for what she has done. I want her guilt and misery to destroy her. I don't see a girl anymore. I see a hideous monster. Something inside me snaps and I rush towards her. I seize her and hurl her into the wall with ferocity I never saw coming. She crumples to the ground and the false tears flow again. I feel no compassion for her now as the impartial, unfeeling camera screen shows me what my foot is doing to her body. But it's not my foot. The small screen removes reality from my actions.

"They made me do it! Said they'd get me!"

Still no apology. She had a choice. Everyone has a choice, no matter what. Even if they had threatened her with the same treatment if she didn't comply, she still had a choice. She could have chosen to try to stop them, or she could have walked away. She chose to join in. She chose to stand by and film while her friends killed an innocent man. I have a choice. I choose to punish her. I choose to inflict on her the same cruelty she inflicted on Liam. I choose to live with this decision forever. She seizes my ankle and sinks her fangs deep into my flesh. I swear and hit her with the pole until she releases me. She reaches for my foot again so I stamp on her hand to save myself and then raise the pole high above my head, bringing it crashing down on top of her.

I drag her to her feet and allow my eyes to rove over her bloodied face. Her eyes roll back in her head and I'm not sure whether she is conscious. I still feel empty. I look in her eyes, searching for something inside, guilt, remorse, the crushing shame of what she's done, what they've all done, but there's nothing there. I toss her to the sodden ground among the cigarette butts and discarded alcohol bottles. It seems that throwing away a life is as easy as throwing out the rubbish. I pick the phone from the floor and send the video to Thomas Brown. I then delete it, before phoning for an ambulance. I leave her there, the rain soaking through her torn and bloodied clothes, as if washing away her sins. She looks pathetic, like a drunken tart who has collapsed and fallen asleep among the rubbish. But she and I know the truth. We know of the monster that lurks beneath her human façade.

I stand and look at her for a moment, desperately trying to feel remorse, guilt or shame for what I have inflicted on her, but I can't. With each attack, I lose another piece of my soul, a piece of the young man I used to know. I can't go back, I can't change it. The girl is lying unnaturally still, a physical statement of the person I have become. Turning, I stagger away, kicking an empty lager bottle as I go. It clatters into a wall and I pray no one hears it. I move along the side street, deliberately slowly so as not to attract attention but there is nobody about as I walk the deserted street, hunting for my final target – for Thomas Brown.

The rain is drenching my clothes and they stick to me, making me cold inside and out. The icy droplets streak my bruised and bloodied face like tears. The rain runs down the pole, merging with the blood and dripping off the end as it scrapes the ground. I leave behind the destruction I have caused. The rain seeps into my open black boots and the laces trail in the puddles. I can feel my energy slipping away as pain takes its toll on my body. I can feel each scratch burning, as though carved with a red hot dagger and not a young girl's nails. My face aches and my knuckles throb. I drag my body towards Brown's house, the route dictated to me subconsciously. I arrive, ready to storm through his door, but there is a car in the drive that hadn't been there earlier. I want him alone. I conceal myself once more in the shadows, watching the house, but see no sign of him. I know I can walk away but I also know that I won't. If just one of Liam's killers goes unpunished I will have failed him. So I wait, my anger and hatred growing stronger with each fleeting second until I can barely keep still. I know Stacey Jenkins is lying in the lane at the entrance of this street and that makes me edgy. If someone finds her now, I am still in the area. Someone may remember me. I pray nobody finds her until I have long gone.

After minutes of futile, frustrating waiting, Brown opens the door and steps out, sealing his fate. I wait for him to walk past me then I trail him. My scratched watch tells me that thirteen minutes have passed since I left Luke's house. To me it feels like an hour.

We walk along the cracked pavement, him swaggering, me trying to remain inconspicuous and keep my pole out of sight. He takes me in the opposite direction to where Stacey is lying and I'm relieved. I do not want to look at her broken battered body and be reminded that I did that to her. I'm hoping he is leading me somewhere quiet but then I realise he is heading for a busy high street. Panic begins to seize me. If he reaches it, I will lose him and I know I will never get a second chance. My brain is working overtime, frantically trying to change the situation to my advantage. I spy an alleyway ahead. Everyone is warned to avoid alleyways when walking on their own. Brown is about to learn why. He has nearly reached it. I run up alongside him and sling my arm around his shoulder, startling him.

"Alright mate?" I ask.

"Yeah." He thinks I'm a friend. Then he looks at me through narrowed, confused eyes. "What you doing man? Get off me." He tries to struggle free but I'm holding him tightly, pulling him closer to me.

I steer him towards the alley. "Got some stuff for me?" I adopt a role I know he will trust. He has to trust me or he might flee to safety. I don't want him safe. I want him harmed. I want him trembling on his knees, begging for my forgiveness.

"Dunno what you're talking 'bout."

"Ain't what Dave says."

"You know Dave?"

I nod. Not his Dave, but everyone knows a Dave. He is willing to accompany me now. He feels safe, believing I am a customer. Trust is such a fragile thing. Trust the wrong person and the result could be catastrophic. Thomas Brown is about to find this out. I cross the entrance to the alleyway, hearing faint rumblings in the bowels of the sarcophagus grey clouds. We venture further into the alley. It reeks of urine, stale smoke and used condoms. A horrible place to be alive but an even worse place to die. I think about the place where Liam died, out in the street in the dark with no one around to rescue him, with those four evil faces leering at him, laughing at him, kicking him, stamping on him, striking him with their fists as he lay helpless on the ground. Even if there were people around, they wouldn't have stepped in and stopped it. People don't. They see someone being beaten up and they walk away – or stop to watch. It's not their problem. It's society's fault these kids are killing people, it's their parents' fault, it's not theirs for standing by and letting them do it.

As he fumbles in his pockets for the drugs, I raise the phone and hold it steady as I punch him in the face. My hands no longer shake. He stares at me, stunned, a look of disbelief on his face. He was not expecting that.

"Hey man, calm down. I got your stuff." It hasn't yet sunk in that I'm not here for a bit of light relief. And it annoys me. I want him lucid, cornered and afraid.

I decline to answer as I grip his shoulders and ram my knee into his stomach. A packet of white powder falls out of his hand and lands on the floor. As he doubles over, I thrust my knee into his face, hearing his nose break as we connect. His blood stains the leg of my black combat trousers. I know that no matter how much I wash my clothes that stain will never leave. I can see that the alcohol he consumed earlier is rapidly wearing off and he is becoming very sober. He mumbles something incoherent but I ignore him. I thrust my elbow into his broken nose then punch him in the mouth. Blood spills down over his chin, dripping onto the floor and leaving a crimson trail down the front of his white t-shirt. He groans and swears.

"You *killed* my brother!" The venom spewing from my mouth shocks both of us.

"I dunno your brother." There is no denial of killing somebody. I wonder if he's done it before.

"Liam Scully."

"Ain't what the courts say." He gives a nasty, half laugh through his broken teeth.

He snorts and wipes the blood from his face, but only succeeds in spreading it further. It's all over his hands and all over mine. He wrestles me for the pole, but when he fails to prise it from my fist, he knees me hard in the ribs. I gasp for breath as a sharp pain pierces my body, spreading across my chest and I know a rib is broken. He tries to deprive me of my pole, but I hang on. I know if I lose it, I will lose this fight. Thomas Brown is the biggest of the gang. He's bigger than me. I kick him in the knee cap and he releases his grip on my pole.

My fingers grip his hair and drive his head backwards into the wall, silencing him. I hear a dull thud and when I release him, I swing the pole at his head. He crumples to the dirty ground and lies still. I stand over him, breathing hard and waiting for him to get back up but he doesn't. He doesn't make a sound, doesn't move. In the distance I can hear sirens. They gradually grow louder and I freeze. I press against the wall and hold the rusty, blood-stained pole against my forehead. Did someone see me? Have they phoned the police? An ambulance races past the alleyway and I slowly release my breath. I glance back at Brown. He still hasn't moved. Blood has seeped from the wound on the back of his head. His eyes are closed and I can't tell if he's breathing. I hear a noise up ahead and swiftly wipe my prints from the pole then toss it over a wall and flee.

I don't know where I am heading but I walk quickly, my strides devouring the ground as I hurry away from the alleyway. Each step sends blazes of pain across my chest and I resist the urge to hold my ribs. I wipe my fingerprints from the phone after dialling 999 then drop it on the ground. I no longer care about framing them. I keep walking, faces blurring as I avoid eye contact. I'm worried that if they look into my eyes they will see what I have done. I keep my hood up to protect my battered face from the judging world. I lurch along the pavement, lightening tearing through the sky then thunder crashing in the clouds overhead. To the people around me, I am just another hoodie. Someone to be feared and avoided. This time, for once, they are right. I shove my cut hands into my pockets so no-one can see they are stained with other people's blood.

I stop to cross the road and my heart freezes. I can see Dean Bradshaw talking on his phone. He's laughing, completely oblivious to anyone else around him. He's changed out of his suit and is now wearing jeans and a t-shirt. I tear my eyes away and when I look again, I see it isn't him. Shaken, I stumble away from the kerb and keep going. A police car races past me and I turn my face away, praying they can't see the blood stain on my knee or the bruises on my face. The rain falls harder now, soaking me, its cold cruel tongue licking at my injured flesh. I sidestep a teenage boy and look into the scowling face of Luke Johnson. I choke. He notices my strange behaviour and looks at me accusingly, like he knows what I've done; then my vision clears. It isn't Johnson. He doesn't even look like him. He has the same hair style and that's it. I move on, feeling sick. How does that boy know? The way he looked at me. How does he know what I've done? I vow not to look at anyone else in case they also guess. What if he goes to the police? My face must be imprinted on his mind. The guilty face of a brutal criminal. I catch sight of my reflection in a parked car window. I pause for a moment to study it. I look no different, except for the bruises. I have the same face I had this morning. It's the same face I've always had. It should look different. It should look like those twisted faces you see in the *Crimewatch* line ups, but it doesn't. I still have the same dark hair, the same dark blue eyes. It frightens me. I am still Nate Scully, but I no longer know who that is. I feel that the enormous change in my mind should be reflected in my physical appearance. Everyone has an idea of what evil looks like and it should look like me. I never thought I would be a person the nation could read about in the papers, the one that everyone fears. And yet I look the same as I always have done; does that mean I have always had evil lurking somewhere in me, waiting for the chance to come out?

I don't know where I'm heading but I keep going. It feels like I've been walking for hours but I know I haven't. I check my watch. 2:47 p.m. Not even an hour has passed since I left the court, yet my life has changed forever. I don't know where I am. I think I'm lost. A car passes me and stops at the traffic lights as I glance up. Stacey Jenkins is in the passenger seat. She stares at me, her face free from bruises and blood, but it's her. I know it is. But it isn't. The girl is blonde like Jenkins. But her eyes are different, so is her nose, her mouth. She's younger. Prettier. Not yet warped by the world she lives in.

Panicked, I keep my head down as I slink along the pavement. The world should be looking different, the scenery should have changed, but everything is exactly the same. Everything except me. I will never again be the person I was before Liam was murdered. I dread seeing Thomas Brown's face in my nightmares, on the streets, those glassy eyes staring at me before he dropped to the ground, the back of his head smashed open. I can still hear the dull, sickening thud as his head met the wall. I could sense that life was leaving his body as he collapsed in the dirty stinking alleyway and I still felt nothing.

There is no-one else on the street. I am completely alone. Even the traffic seems to have vanished. But then another police car cruises by and the driver looks at me, like he knows what I am thinking. It is as though he has x-ray vision and can see into my soul and scrutinise the darkness residing there. Alarmed, I avert my eyes. They are looking for me. My face is plastered on posters, they each have a copy. It will be on the news tomorrow. They drive on and I notice my hands are shaking. My whole body is trembling. I spy a group of teenagers up ahead. They're laughing and shoving, pretending to push each other into the road. I silently pray that they do. They could be another group who enjoy murdering people for kicks. I long for a car to plough into one of them, but it doesn't happen. Someone needs to stop them before another person loses their life for the momentary enjoyment of these vicious yobs. They may not have done it yet, but they will, I know they will. Thomas Brown is with them. I think he's their leader. They don't look at me as our paths cross. Thomas Brown does though. He catches my eye and stares hard at me, acting tough. But it isn't Brown, this kid is about seventeen. Once again my anguished mind is playing tricks on me. It is definitely not Brown; this boy is good looking and has a friendly face. Brown looks the brutal thug he is. This kid is only about a year younger than me but I feel much older. I glance back. The back of his head is unharmed.

Then they all turn around. Bradshaw, Johnson, Jenkins, and Brown. They face me square on, challenging me, begging me to take them on and teach them a lesson. I turn away. I wait for a few seconds then glance back over my shoulder. It's not them. They've gone. The leader is still staring at me, I try and avoid his gaze but when he catches my eye he smiles a warm, friendly and slightly concerned smile, before his friends pull him out of the way of an oncoming car shouting at him for not paying attention to the road. Yesterday I would have smiled back. Today I am incapable of that warmth.

I duck down an alley, breathing hard and push my hood off my head. If that kid had known what I had just done he would not have smiled at me like that. My heart pounds a rhythm of doom. I double over, gasping for breath. Nausea wells up inside me like a tsunami, surging through my body and flooding it. I am helpless to do anything but vomit. Once my body has purged itself, I sink to the floor, my knees raised. I stare at my knees, not seeing them, seeing only four faces. I can no longer hear the traffic, only the sounds of my feet, fists and the pole crashing into their bodies. I can no longer feel my rage, just their lives slipping away.

I grip my spiked hair in my fists as my body shudders violently then I realise I am crying. But somehow I know it is not because I took something I can never give back, but because I know that I have lost a part of me forever. I read somewhere that a person experiences two deaths. The one that everyone knows about and another one. I never understood it, but now I know that I have just died the other death. The death of the soul.

I wipe my eyes then rise unsteadily to my feet and edge towards the opening of the alley, pulling my hood back up. I wait for a break in the crowd then I join it, just another face among a throng. I can hardly bear to have people around me, knowing that I possess a deadly secret. I can feel the weight of the knowledge pressing down on my shoulders, seeping into my flesh and crawling around my body. It festers in my gut, replacing the fury that had resided there.

I surreptitiously scan the faces of the people I pass, my mind feverishly wondering whether they also harbour a secret. I see a woman with a black eye. Does her husband beat her? Does he unleash cruel punishments if his dinner is cold or she buys the wrong newspaper? As she's walking the wet streets, is she vowing that the next time he hits her will be the last? I spy pretty Goth twins. Are their clothes a filtering system so that only someone special will be able to see beyond? Do they use this filter because they have been hurt in the past? Do people shout abuse at them because of the way they choose to dress? Is it their armour for keeping people away?

Everywhere I look I see agony, hate, loneliness scarring peoples' faces, clouding their eyes as the person they once were slowly dies, crushed by the burdens they are forced to carry. I don't know how they can live with their burdens and I don't know how I will live with mine.

A bus pulls in up ahead and I run to catch it. I sink down in my seat and watch the grey rainy world speed by. Some people on the bus are talking to each other. I say nothing. At the next bus stop I get off. I walk up the street and find myself standing outside a police station. Should I tell them I have witnessed the teenagers being beaten up? They will question why, having seen four attacks, I did nothing. Should I tell them only about one of them? Say I found an unconscious person? Or should I go in and tell them what I've done? If I confess, I will go to prison. Why should I rot in jail while Liam's killers are allowed to walk the streets, free to do it again? But I don't know if I can live with this for the rest of my life. The police officer behind the desk glances up and looks at me. I think he is going to arrest me. I hurry out without looking back.

"Nate, it's time. The jury are coming back in."

I look at the barrister then scan the corridor I am sitting in. I haven't been asleep. Yet I have experienced something so real, I cannot believe it hasn't happened. It wasn't a dream. You have to be asleep to dream and I am wide awake. Was it a premonition? Have I just seen the future?

Suddenly I feel very nervous. My stomach clenches and nausea swirls in my gut. My hands are shaking, my legs are weak. My whole body is numb and soaked in a chilling sweat. I don't want to go into the courtroom. I don't want to have to face Liam's killers again. I don't want to see them walk free for the second time today. If it was a premonition, I know what the result is going to be. They are going to get away with murder.

"Come on or you'll miss the verdict. Relax. You have nothing to worry about. There's no way the jury will return a verdict of not guilty. I saw the looks on their faces when I described their brutal attack on your brother. I told them to imagine that it was *their* child on the floor being kicked and beaten and filmed. They know about society's problem with these feral yob gangs." The barrister is smiling, looking completely confident. To him it is just another court case. To me it is a life-changing moment.

His words fail to comfort me as I slowly rise to my feet. The corridor is spinning around me. I cannot breathe, my throat is closing and I'm choking on my own fear. I trail inside and sit at the front of the viewing gallery. I want to witness the very moment they are told they will spend the next ten years locked away for killing my brother. Though ten years compared to taking his life is nothing. And they're too young for prison. They will be sent to a youth offenders' institution, taken on day trips, allowed to play snooker, watch Sky TV. That isn't punishment.

"Would the foreman of the jury please stand?" the judge asks. The foreman rises, looking nervous. "Have you reached a verdict upon which you are all agreed?"

"Yes."

"On the count of murder, do you find the defendants guilty or not guilty?"

I hold my breath, praying, begging for him to say 'Guilty'. Time seems to stand still and a stifling atmosphere seeps into the ancient courtroom. I want him to don his black cap and sentence them to death. They don't deserve to live for what they have done. No prison sentence is sufficient. It won't bring Liam back. He is gone forever and they are responsible for that. They have robbed me of my big brother and stolen part of me. The only way to redress the balance is to steal something from them.

"Not guilty."

I feel my world explode and lie in pieces at my feet, its burning ashes are all that remain. I can feel my heart being squeezed and my head feels like it is spinning. The reality is unpleasantly familiar and I feel violently sick. My nails gouge the wood and I half expect to find the grooves my nails made before, but they are not there. My fingers ache, but I can't let go.

"Dean Bradshaw, Luke Johnson, Thomas Brown and Stacey Jenkins, you have been found not guilty of the murder of Liam Scully. You are free to leave."

The judge's firm voice rings out through the courtroom. I know exactly what I am about to do and yet I can't stop myself.

"No!" I shout. "They did it! You can't let them go! They killed him!"

The judge glares at me as Liam's murderers celebrate in the dock squealing and hugging each other, just like I had seen them do before. I want the jury to change their minds, but they don't. The teenagers rush from the courtroom, smiling and loudly proclaiming their victory. To them it is the best day of their lives. For me it is the worst. I know I will follow them out and I do, a numb, silent shadow stalking them to the court steps. I stand on the steps, shielding my eyes against the harsh sunlight as I watch them parade in front of the adoring cameras. The scene plays out like a video on repeat. I play the smiling journalist's speech through my head and she recites it word for word, as though she can hear my thoughts. The accuracy frightens me. I can feel severe nausea and stomach cramps. I feel more scared than I ever have been before.

I watch Liam's killers reluctantly tear themselves away from the cameras and their chance of fame. They skip down the steps, laughing and celebrating their win. I can feel rage rushing through my body and I savour its familiarity. I know where it will lead me if I let it. My eyes are fixed to the murderers' backs and as I start to move down the steps in their wake, I'm faced with a choice. The most important decision I will ever have to make. Do I allow them to walk away, leaving them free to kill another person just for teenage kicks? Can I live with *that* guilt for the rest of my life? Or do I take their lives and at the same time ruin mine? How can I live with *that* guilt?

I feel as though a hideous future has been ripped from its grave and its bloodied corpse shown to me as a warning.

I step onto the pavement and watch them as they begin to walk away.

3.00pm.

What would you do?

4pm

Fifty-Minute Hour

By Kevin Chandler

We pull up across the road a full ten minutes early. I suggest we wait in the car.

"We don't want to be late!" she says, in that all-encompassing way of hers I find impossible to challenge without it being taken as, not merely a difference of opinion, but a personal attack. Actually, I wouldn't mind being late. In fact, I wouldn't mind not turning up at all, but last night she was adamant that if there was going to be any chance for us then I'd better get my arse along too. I say nothing; just stare out of the window at the shabby entrance across the street. She gathers up her handbag, gets out, and then stoops to peer back in at me.

"Well…are you coming?"

The room is large and square, very much the cheap side of chic. IKEA chairs, that look more comfortable than they feel, line three walls. A large square coffee table sits like an island in the centre of the carpet, bearing a neatly fanned assortment of what I take to be women's magazines, a box of tissues, and a weary looking pot plant that, like me, might have preferred to take its chances outside. A tidy six-shelf bookcase adorns the remaining wall, the spines on the left-hand side half-veiled with ivy tendrils snaking down from the top shelf. The tendrils have one more shelf to go before they reach the floor, where, if they've any sense, they'll veer left and make straight for the door. I try to ignore my urge to make a bolt for it myself, and focus instead on the books. From here I can barely make out the titles although I notice the word 'sex' features prominently. If we were alone I might wander across and take a closer look but we're not and it would only draw attention; right now I'd rather be invisible.

The room mimics a still life, something with a title like 'A Study Of Disengagement'. Directly opposite us sits a woman of uncertain age, so still she could be almost a waxwork. She looks sad and weary. Above her head is a poster, blu-tacked to the wall. I can tell it's blu-tacked as the emulsioned wall is daubed with little greasy marks, the remains of earlier attachments. The wall's latest tenant pronounces: 'Relate: The Relationship People' below a photograph of two smiling faces lost in each other's features; white 30-somethings, actors I guess as no actual person looks that happy. There's no background or context to the picture, just endless white space through which bright eyes smile and brilliant teeth shine, a vision of disembodied health, laughter and happiness that, with different words, would make a good Colgate advert. Just as well the sad-looking woman can't see the poster above her head, it would only make her cry, either that, or she'd tear it from the wall and rip it to shreds. I wonder if we ever looked like that, so engrossed in each other that the world around us disappeared? For us the world was only too real from the very start, her kids an ever present part of our equation, even though it was a full month before she'd let me meet them. Until then I had to park around the corner, as if we were having an extra-marital affair.

Away to the right sit another couple. I observe them out the corner of my eye, older than us, mid- to late-forties perhaps. I was wrong about total disengagement, they're holding hands, and I am suddenly conscious of the gap between our two chairs, a gap I feel embarrassed about but unable to bridge. I'm tempted to reach out for her hand, to show the other couple we're as good as them, but fear she'll only snatch hers away or, worse still, flinch and tolerate.

No one else seems to be taking surreptitious looks around.

I envy the other couple's stillness, so content within themselves. Even the sad lady, with the shopping bag of sadness cradled in her lap, appears to wait more patiently than I. If there were more of us I could fill the time playing 'doctor's surgery', trying to guess who's contagious, who's terminal, and who's just here for a top-up jab. I expect the other couple will survive, that handhold looks well set. The lone sad woman's had it, I'm afraid. I wonder what we look like? I suppose by keeping still, we all hope to become part of the furniture, with nothing to answer for.

I amuse myself with these idle thoughts because it's easier than thinking about why we're here, and the unknown 'Farrell' we are waiting to see. Mr Farrell? Mrs? They didn't say when they gave her the appointment. I'm not sure which I'd prefer. If Farrell turns out to be a woman, I'll be outnumbered, but I'll feel more threatened if it's a man and he sides with her. I let out another silent sigh.

Not a fidget, or a cough, or a whisper. The creeping ivy seems more alive than any of us; it's enough to make me want to run amok with a 4-iron. I'd start with the wall clock above the door, one of those cheap round plastic things, its red second hand jogging along, one click at a time. It says, three fifty-nine and twenty seconds. Smooth backswing, head still, I could send it to smithereens before it has a chance to reach the hour. Instead, I count down silently in ten-second intervals, like the talking clock. I promise myself that when it gets to one minute past four, I shall declare Farrell officially late and head off to find the loo. At ten seconds past the hour, the door swings open and we all look up. An old-ish woman with a kindly face loiters in the doorway and smiles at the sad lady, who gives a brief grimace of recognition before rising slowly and following her out; not a word passes between them. A second face appears, again female, although considerably younger; her torso, legs and feet are resolutely hidden behind the door, as if she had forgotten to put on any clothes, which incidentally, is akin to how I've felt since we arrived.

"Bob, Mary, do come through," she whispers.

So much for confidentiality, but Bob and Mary seem more relieved than exposed, and beam back at her before they also rise and depart, leaving... just us. I take advantage of the new found freedom to let out an audible and extravagant sigh, at which point a third figure appears in the doorway, this time male and full-bodied, about forty I guess, close-cropped receding hair, tan chinos, boat shoes, denim shirt, no tie. He establishes our names without revealing his, and beckons us to follow. Stella rises first, as seems fitting, whilst I remain seated, just long enough for it to register with them both.

The room is small and the three of us squeeze in, hovering uncomfortably on the limited floor space. The unnamed one invites us to sit down. I allow Stella first choice of the two chairs positioned to one side, a little away from the one with an A5 diary upon the seat, which I assume marks it out as his. Against the adjacent wall, a narrow coffee table has on it a pot plant and box of tissues at the ready, clearly a signature of every room in this place, although there are no magazines this time. At the end nearest his chair rests a pen and what looks like a receipt book. The tissues are placed at our end and in one of those cubed cardboard boxes with flowers printed around the sides, hardly man-sized. The plant is an orchid in full bloom. I want to touch it to see if it's real but Stella has taken the seat closest the table and I would have to reach across her, so instead I take the chair next to hers and merely stare across at the rich, purple, and quite possibly fake, petals. Staring at the plant is preferable to meeting Farrell's gaze, for I take it that our un-named host is he. I hear him clear his throat, he welcomes us, establishes that he is indeed Farrell, and concedes that, yes, it is rather an odd first name, but they operate a first name policy here, and he hopes we might all work together on that basis. Stella readily gives her consent;

I acquiesce via the mere hint of a nod.

"Good. Stella and Jack it is then," Farrell says, and sounds pleased with the progress thus far. I still haven't looked at him.

He goes on to outline Relate's confidentiality and payment policies, and the aim of this fifty-minute hour, which appears to be to establish and explore the main issues we are bringing, then negotiate a contract for a number of weekly sessions in order to address those very issues in more depth within the boundaries of our therapeutic alliance; at least I think that's what he said, he rattled it all off like he's learned it by heart and has to say it rather a lot. I'm not sure which aspect of therapy-speak I find more amusing, the notion of a fifty-minute hour, or the fact that the problems that brought us here have been instantly expunged and replaced with...issues. Issues, such a softer notion, almost desirable, the sort of thing no aspiring couple should be without, and of course, rhymes neatly with tissues. I notice that between our two chairs sits a wicker basket containing several crumpled ones, presumably bearing the remnants of Farrell's previous clients' problems, or issues. I only hope he can get rid of ours as easily.

The preliminaries over, Farrell tells us to go back to our respective corners and when the bell sounds, come out fighting; at least that's what I take him to mean. Stella is first to advance, which suits a back-pedalling counter puncher like myself. I jest. I'm endeavouring to lull you, and myself, into believing that listening to the woman I love relate my worst and most intimate excesses to a complete stranger, who sits in stark and solemn judgement, is not one of the most embarrassing and humiliating experiences of my entire life.

The gist of what she tells him is that she can't trust me anymore. I note her use of the word *can't*. She does not say that she *won't* trust me, or that she *chooses* not to trust me anymore, but that she *can't* trust me because of what I've done; the responsibility for her lack of trust thus placed squarely upon my shoulders. Stella's victim status duly established, I am designated the guilty party. Saving the more vivid details of my crimes for some later point in the proceedings, she simply informs our judge and jury that I have behaved appallingly to her two children, so much so that she fears for our future together.

"Objection your honour! I have no trouble with Clare, Clare and I get on fine; the problem lies entirely with Sam!" Humour, you see, is my defence; it's an old habit, one I know I overuse, but at times like this I feel the need of it. In the actual event, I voice no objection; I don't leap from my seat, or even raise my voice. I try to explain to Stella quietly, but pointedly, (and I cannot bring myself, *choose* not to bring myself, to look at Farrell) that Clare and I get on all right, most of the time. Not wonderfully, we're not soul mates, she's not my little princess nor I her adoring father, but we get on. Clare (who is twelve, by the way) does what I ask of her, most of the time. We greet each other on arrival, acknowledge each other on departure, even the odd half-smile has been known to pass between us on occasions.

"The fact is, Stella," I conclude, "Clare and I get on all right."

Stella says nothing; just stares back with that look of cold contempt I have become so accustomed to of late. Farrell clears his throat again. I realise this is no unsavoury grunt on his part, no grand clearout of phlegm, just a subtle, barely audible readying of the apparatus, like an opening batsman raising his bat from the crease in the moment just before the ball leaves the bowler's hand. It serves as a speech mark, to indicate that the next contribution we hear will be his, so we'd better listen up. Farrell uses my name. He speaks it with a rising intonation and then waits. I feel my name stretch far beyond its four component letters and wrap itself around my neck; my shoulders tense and stiffen and I plant my feet ever more firmly on the carpet. I should hold my ground, perhaps recite Farrell's name back to him, with the same rising intonation he used, so that, like two gunfighters at High Noon, we can size each other up whilst around us the street and sidewalks clear. But I am not confident of being quick enough on the draw and already feel a knot squeezing my throat. Lassoed by a word, I feel my head being slowly, irresistibly, pulled around to meet the eyes of the man who dared to call my name.

Now he has me tethered, he says it again, more softly this time.

"Jack… you seemed at pains to point out to Stella that your relationship with her daughter, Clare, is not as big an issue as your relationship with Sam, her son? Is that right?"

I reply that my relationship with Clare is not an issue at all; the issue, if that's what he wishes to call it, although I would call it a problem, lies entirely with Sam and his behaviour towards his mother, how she lets him get away with murder, and how, when I try to intervene to back her up and point out to Sam when he's out of order, she takes his side against me.

This is red rag to the bull, and I feel my head being jerked again, this time from the other direction, by a lioness leaping to the defence of one of her cubs.

"Of course I take his side! He's my son, a mere child, and you're a grown man, or supposed to be! I take his side because he has no one else to stick up for him when he's being bullied by you!"

I sidestep the accusation of being a bully and seize the opportunity to fire off a couple of rounds of my own,

"Sam? A mere child? Who are you trying to kid? He's fifteen, going on sixteen, he's taller than me, he smokes cigarettes, and worse, up in his room despite you repeatedly asking him not to. He comes and goes as he pleases, never lifts a finger to help around the house, and if I tell him to do something, he gives that sneering look. Then, when I challenge him, you always take his side. He laughs at you behind your back, he's got you wound around his little finger and you can't bloody see it."

"Jack, he's a teenager! That's what they're like. Sam is not a *bad* boy. You've not had kids of your own and that makes a big difference. There are a lot of pressures on kids these days. It's hard for a young boy when his father leaves home, and it's hard for a teenage son to adjust to his mother's boyfriend moving in with them."

More throat clearing from Farrell. He needn't have bothered. I wasn't about to say anything more, I couldn't see the point.

"I'm getting a sense," he says, "of what it must be like for the two of you at home. There's a heap of tension here, and anger, mostly from you Jack towards Sam, but also from you Stella, towards Jack, for being so…"

And in that pause, for the first time since entering the room, I look my judge in the eye. Conscious of my stare, he looks hesitant; his mouth opens and for a second it looks like he might close it again. He doesn't.

"I was going to say…unreasonable. Is that how you see Jack's attitude towards your son, Stella?"

"Yes, I think Jack is unreasonable, at least where the children are concerned; he's far too ready to tell rather than ask." (I find that rich, but hold my tongue.) "But it isn't only Jack's attitude that's the issue here, it's his actions. Things have got to such a stage that Jack beat up my son, and I find such behaviour totally unacceptable."

Stella pauses for a moment to let the charge sink in, and then repeats it, with an extra helping of moral outrage. "He beat up my son!"

I register the change from 'Jack' to 'he,' and feel another, 'objection your honour' rising within, but clamp it down.

Farrell half turns his head and gives me a penetrating look. I hold my ground; I'm damned if I'm going to let him shame me into looking away.

"Do you want to tell me what happened?" is all he says, looking straight at me, and I note that this time, he too jettisons the use of my name. I am fast becoming an object, a 'you' or a 'he.'

Farrell takes a fleeting glance back at Stella, and then turns again to face me, at which I shrug, and gesture with a vague wave of my arm in the direction of Stella.

"Stella's already laid the charge at my door, 'I beat up her son'. Why don't you ask her to fill in the crime sheet, she seems to know all about it."

"You're so bloody sarcastic, Jack. You know I wasn't there!"

Ah, at last, a concession to fact. That's an improvement, and I seize the opportunity to underline the point.

"That's right, Stella, you weren't there! You came home from work just as it was all over and thought you knew everything. Well, I'll tell you what happened if you'd care to listen for a moment to anything other than the edited version of events your precious son told you. For your information, I did not beat up Sam. I got home from work and, as usual, he was lounging in front of the telly, curtains drawn against the sun. I could smell cigarette smoke on him, and the dog was scratching and whining at the back door. I asked Sam why he hadn't let the dog out. He ignored me. I said something, he sneered, and there was an altercation that developed into a scuffle. It was not a full-on fight, no one was punched or kicked, and the whole thing lasted no more than thirty seconds, including the initial argument. There was some yelling on both sides, a bit of pushing and shoving, and yes, a little blood was drawn; my hand caught his lip as I reached to grab his collar. I backed off, he ran upstairs. Next thing I know is you walk in and tell right away something's gone on. You didn't bother asking me. All you said was, 'Where's Sam?' and rushed upstairs. By the time you came down your mind was closed, you'd already decided who was innocent and who was guilty and, as usual, you took his side."

"I abhor violence," Stella solemnly announces from on high, "and I am simply not prepared to have it in my home." Her final plea to judge and jury, delivered straight as a die.

"I'll leave now and go and pack my things, shall I?" I ask, only partly sarcastically. But Stella is no longer looking at me, her eyes are trained on Farrell. Which is where my eyes now also turn looking for… I don't know… help, I suppose. This time, Farrell doesn't clear his throat. He speaks, softly, slowly, with what sounds something approaching tenderness. Either that, or it's a good act.

"This must be very distressing for *both* of you, in fact, for all concerned. It must have been distressing for you, Jack, in what amounts to a newly acquired step-father role, trying to instil what you view as much needed discipline into a teenage boy who you see sneering back at you and, in your opinion, winding his mum around his little finger. Distressing, too, Jack, for you to lose control, to the extent that you're reduced to scuffling and fighting with a boy, albeit a tall fifteen-year-old, but still a boy. And, Stella, it must have been distressing for you, as a woman and mother, to realise that the man you love, the man you had trusted enough to bring into your home for the last year, had been fighting with, and harming, your son, your own flesh and blood. And whatever exactly went on that afternoon, it must have been distressing for Sam, and also for Clare, if she happened to witness it."

"Clare was upstairs in her room doing her homework," I explain. "She must have heard the row and came down right at the end, just as we were scrapping."

"Huh, scrapping!" sneers Stella, "you make it sound like it was playful. You were fighting! Sam was bleeding! It was lucky for you he didn't need stitches. I'd like to know how you would have explained that away at the hospital, a grown man resorting to violence with a young boy, you a police officer and all? Get it through your thick head. You damaged my son! You bruised his lip. You drew blood! Not once have I ever done that to him, not once in fifteen years, and neither did his own father. Rob may not have been faithful as a husband, but he would never have beaten up his own son. My children have never had to be frightened in their own home."

It was the riot act and she read it brilliantly, and despite her persistent inaccurate use of the term, 'beaten up,' I wince.

I feel awful, truly awful. So bad I could throw up. I want to leave this room now, leave this place, this woman and her children and the half-built platform of a new life I have been constructing these past eleven months; I want to run away somewhere safe, crouch down in a corner, out of sight. I could get up and walk out right now, I don't need their permission, but my legs feel too weak to propel me from the chair.

"I'm hearing you wanting to play all this down, Jack, as if you feel Stella's getting the whole thing out of proportion?" and Farrell cocks his head a little to one side, like a spaniel wondering if a choc-drop might be coming his way.

I take a moment before replying; I feel I must answer, but not in the blood and heat of emotion. I must choose my words carefully.

"I'm not saying I think what happened that afternoon was right, or that I'm proud of my part in it; I'm not. Things shouldn't have been allowed to reach that stage. Sam should have behaved differently when I asked him to do something, and so should I when he sneered at me. Things escalated, they got out of hand."

"Well," says Farrell, "I'm not here to measure this up and pronounce whose version of events I deem the more accurate. I'm just saying to you both that this whole episode, which sounds to me like a sudden eruption of a brooding volcano in your household, must have been extremely distressing for both of you."

"Not half as distressing as for Sam!" Stella can't resist

tossing this in on the back of Farrell's summary, like an extra piece of fudge being sneaked into the paper bag after it's been weighed and priced up. I wonder how Farrell will react. I'd like to see him take her on, ask her how the hell she knows who's been most upset by this? But Farrell is different to me, he turns his body more towards her, again puts his head a little on one side, before addressing her directly.

"It seems important for you, Stella," he says, "that both Jack and I are aware just how upsetting this incident has been for Sam. Perhaps far more than you think either of us appreciate; is that right?"

"Yes," she replies, solemnly, "no child should have to live with fear in his or her own home." And with that she looks down at the carpet.

Farrell looks across at me, his eyes pose the question that I know I can no longer evade.

"All right, I accept that," I say. "No child should have to be frightened in his own home. But if we're talking about 'shoulds' then there are a few I'd like to add to the list."

"Whoa, hold on a moment, Jack," says Farrell sharply, leaning towards me, hand raised, palm showing. "Something happened here just then and I don't want it to get lost, which is what would happen if you launch straight into a round of tit-for-tat point scoring. You both walked in here today brimful of conflict, each of you nursing a heap of hurt and anger and unable to see eye-to-eye about anything. Then, just now, almost out of the blue, you agreed on something. I heard you say, Jack, in as many words, that you regretted what happened in that bust-up with Sam, and felt bad about your part in it. I also heard you say you agreed with Stella's fundamental belief that no child should have to live with fear in his, or her, own home. And I'd like to make sure you both really heard that moment of agreement between you, because I think that agreement is really important, it's like a first building block, and neither of you should let it roll away down the hill by retreating back into the conflict."

I'm not sure I know how he did it, but something happened as Farrell spoke; I felt, in some strange way, that me and Stella, were, well…being held is the only way I can describe it. I'm not sure if that makes any sense, even to me, let alone anyone else, but that's how it felt.

However, I don't think Stella was as impressed by Farrell's intervention. She muttered something about actions being more important than words, and reiterated how I had destroyed the trust she'd placed in me. But Farrell picked up on the quiver in her voice, and for the next few minutes the focus shifted away from our momentary note of agreement to Stella and her bitter feelings about being let down by all the men in her life. He got her talking about her ex-, in some detail, more than she'd ever said to me. Rob was a real charmer, by all accounts, with a roving eye and wandering hands. I already knew from Stella that he'd had an affair and that's what ended the marriage. What I didn't know until now was that his lover was her best friend; 'a double betrayal' she called it, and that was all she'd say on the matter. Farrell then asked about her childhood and she skirted around her father until Farrell asked her outright about him. She didn't seem to say very much, I could tell she wasn't keen on the subject, and after a while it dawned on me that I was no longer listening; I'd turned off down a lane, stumbled onto a side track, and was lost in the tangle of my own undergrowth.

I see the living room of my boyhood, my father standing in the doorway, completely filling it, a great swathe of a man, shirtsleeves rolled up, tattoos down each arm, trademarks of his years of service in the Royal Navy, mermaid on the left, pair of crossed cutlasses on the right, his stern warning…'Don't you ever get any done!' still ringing in my ears. How I loved his arms, so richly inked and pleasured, the gypsy in him, the would-be pirate in my soul. Arms that reached and dipped, sawed and hammered, and wrenched tough roots from the ground; arms that swung me up onto his shoulders, galloping all the way back down the lane from the pub, a mustang ridden by a tiny jockey. Dad, how I came to fear your arms, when fists closed and muscles swelled like Popeye's, and I learned to run and hide. Sooner or later, you'd come to find me, late at night in my bed, or at breakfast the following day, you'd seek me out, summon me to you, and give me that look, you know the one, the look of a man who can't bring himself to say the word 'sorry.' Instead, you'd stroke my hair, your palm now soft as butter, and tell me "you're all right", and "you must know that I don't mean it, it's when the drink gets hold of me, and when the devil's in you"; then you ruffle my hair and tell me, "be a good boy for your Mammy." Fourteen, I was, when I stood up to you. Got between you and her, took you on. I expected a thrashing, but you surprised us both, threw your head back, looked down your nose at the pair of us; "What's this?" you sneered, "Huh, you can have her! You deserve each other." Then you turned your back and walked out the door, and that was the last we ever saw of you.

I shake my legs free of the tangled stems, retreat through the long grass and trudge back up the lane, to where it seems my absence has been noted.

"Jack… Jack, anything you want to say?" Farrell's voice is soft, but fails to conceal the hint of irritation.

"I'm sorry?"

"About what Stella was saying, about feeling let down by the men in her life, and especially about her father."

"I'm sorry."

Stella gives a loud sigh and Farrell's eyes dart back and forth between us. I realise that, once again, I've said the wrong thing, or not said the right thing well enough. Either way, I got it wrong.

"Stella, you seem frustrated with Jack's response, as if you were looking for something more, and perhaps are left feeling, a little…disappointed? Or even let down, yet again?"

I'm tempted to raise an objection: 'That's right, tell her what she feels, put words in her mouth, why don't you?' Instead I settle for just a withering stare, which Farrell misses. I knew coming here was not a good idea.

"Jack, you've got to learn to open up with your feelings!" Her voice is full of passion and the self-confidence that stems from conviction. "Not just your angry ones," she implores, "your *soft* ones, your *vulnerable* feelings. Don't you understand what this is all about?"

Silence.

I understand something. That she speaks words differently to me, in a way I cannot emulate. The way she said the word 'soft' as if it were the longest word in the dictionary. I realise something is being asked of me here, and there's two of them doing the asking, but that just makes it harder to know what it is I should say. I expect I look dumb, sitting there, an empty sheet of paper before me, just like the first time I took the Sergeants' Exam.

"What do you want me to say?" I plead.

She closes her eyes and wearily shakes her head. Wrong again.

More throat clearing. Farrell to the rescue, or coming to kick me when I'm down?

"Jack…this is hard for you. I can see that. But what Stella's asking is important. She seems to be wishing you could express some of your more vulnerable feelings, whether it's about the abuse she suffered as a child, or the stress you feel when Sam winds you up. Maybe bottling up your vulnerable feelings is what leads to the sort of angry, violent emotions that spilled out with Sam the other day? Have you ever thought about that?"

Deep pockets. Even as a kid I always had deep pockets. Places for coins, rubber bands, shiny marbles, matches, unfinished ciggies, and what Farrell now calls my vulnerable feelings. 'A right little hoarder' Mum called me, like when she washed my school trousers and found the aforementioned items along with the dry crusts off the morning toast I'd secreted and forgotten all about, the crusts *he* wouldn't allow me to leave on my plate. "Kids in Africa would fight over those crusts, you don't know you're born, son!" Boys learn early not to show vulnerability. Two worlds, outside and inside, best if you keep them apart and never, ever, get them mixed up – that's what gets you into trouble. It was he who taught me to lie; fear is always a good teacher. "I'm going to ask you one more time. Was it you that broke the bathroom window?" – "No Dad, honest," and he cracked me across the face. "Don't ever, ever, lie to me again!" It took a day for the swelling to go down. I was kept off school until it did. Made some excuse about running a temperature, at least that's what the note I took to school said. I swore I'd never let him catch me out again. 'Poker Jack' they called me at Hendon Police College, and my poker face won me more than a few quid. The other lads could never tell if I held nuts or nix. Deep pockets, that's me, and I keep them well zipped.

"I don't know what you want me to say. I've already said I'm sorry about the fight, I shouldn't have let it get to that stage. And for what it's worth, I'm sorry about what Stella's father might have done to her twenty-odd years ago, but I wasn't around then and I don't know what more I can say." My cheeks feel hot, and I realise I must be blushing.

Farrell is biting his lip, clearly distracted. He is looking at Stella, my eyes follow his and I see that she is crying. I wait for Farrell to speak but he says nothing, just sits, his body facing hers, his face angled towards the floor. I notice my right heel is jigging up and down on the carpet but I don't remember it starting. At home when she cries I ask her what's wrong. 'Nothing' she replies, more often than not. 'Of course there's something wrong, no one cries for nothing, what the fuck is it?' I say, and then we have a row and I get it in the neck. That's how I learned to leave her alone, take the dog for a walk, come back later, make her a cup of tea and see whether she's ready to come round. Sometimes she is, but sometimes her silence will last all day, and then at night in bed she'll turn over and go to sleep without her usual 'ni-night,' and I lie there, wondering whether to reach out or say something, but I trust neither my tongue, nor my hand, to come up with the right thing.

I sense Farrell preparing to speak.

"For what it's worth…that's what you said, Jack, 'for what it's worth,' just before you expressed sadness about what happened to Stella when she was a girl, as if you're unsure what value your feelings have to Stella, or perhaps to anyone?"

He's staring at me, good and straight, waiting for a response. I can tell an answer is required but I'm not sure I even understand the question. And so I look away, down at my boots.

Feelings? I'd rather speak of emotions, more active, more concrete: frustration, anger, jealousy, confidence, pride; I know what these are. Feelings are vague, things sensed rather than experienced, and hard to trust. Two kisses at the bottom of a birthday card, I can do that, but not the self-composed lines above; 'all my love', 'you are the sun that lights my life', 'with deepest sympathy' and, worse still, 'I f-e-e-l your p-a-i-n.' What are they worth these expressions, these declarations of…solidarity, desire, need, or compassion? Are they really gifts, or just arrogant demands? 'See how much I love/adore/need/understand you, now love me in return!'

"Words are cheap," I say aloud, for no good reason other than it is what comes to mind the moment I look up to find Farrell still staring hard at me.

"So they say, Jack," he replies. "Yet I've noticed you use words sparingly, as if they're actually very costly and you're scared of running up a huge bill."

"Look," I snap back at him, "I don't know what's happening here. We came to talk about Sam and the fight, and whether Stella wants me to stay or leave, and now we're discussing the price of words. I don't like it and I object to being the only one in the dock!" And having surprised myself by standing up to Farrell, I immediately wonder what price I'll have to pay.

"Jack…"

It's Stella, looming up on my right; again I'm outflanked.

"Don't you see, this is *precisely* what we need to talk about. Feelings and how you bottle them up, and how they burst out in anger whenever the kids, whenever Sam, does anything remotely challenging to you and your values. It's like living with a tyrant. I'm always watching out for some little thing out of place, or that the kids do wrong, that'll give you reason to pounce. Because that's what you do Jack, you pounce on Sam. It's as if you're watching him all the time, just willing him to step out of line, so you can feel justified in having a go at him. I know he's not perfect; I know he can be difficult, but it's you Jack, you've changed in the year we've been living together, you've changed into someone I don't understand and, at times, I don't even like very much. Sam is not a bad boy, he really isn't, but I see you trying hard to make him into one and I can't just sit by and watch that happen."

For a moment or two, I consider taking issue with her argument, but there's no point, she'll just turn it back at me. I could get up and walk out, but it would mean just another closed door and I've had enough of those already.

"I don't know what to say," I say, weakly, but honestly.

Stella lets out a weary and exasperated sigh. "I give up," she whispers, and I hear the cushion groan as she slumps back in the chair.

Farrell's throat clears.

"Well, I don't," he says softly. "Jack, you said more or less the same thing earlier on, 'I don't know what you want me to say,' but it sounded different then. Then it was as if you were saying it resentfully; as if you felt Stella was getting at you, demanding more than was reasonable, and you felt under pressure to come up with the goods. But just now, although your words were much the same, you said them differently, as if you really wanted to say something to Stella, like you really wanted to give something back to her, but felt helpless to know what it was, or how to offer it. Is that right? Is it hard, Jack, to offer your helplessness or your vulnerable feelings to another person?"

I swallow hard. I want to say again, 'I don't know what to say,' but this time my tongue won't let the words take shape, it's too busy pressed to the roof of my mouth, keeping back the…

And I swallow, great gulps of air, in an effort to suck in the oxygen that might restore my composure. I fail, miserably.

Can't remember the last time I cried, really cried, and I feel so stupid, out of control; it's like throwing up, but without the excuse of food poisoning, or a night on the piss. Sure, I well up every once in a while, usually at a film, or when I watched my team get relegated at the last game of the season, or before passing out parade at Hendon, when I realised I was the only one of my mates whose parents weren't there. But that was not like this, those tears I could manage; I allowed them to coat my eyes, wiped one or two away, then swallowed the rest down. But now they keep coming, wave after wave of the little bastards; it's like being on riot duty, but I haven't been issued with a shield. I keep spluttering, 'I'm sorry, I'm sorry,' but can't say it without choking.

Farrell leans forward, forearms on his knees, staring up into my face. Stella's angled her body to face mine, but it's arching away, as if I might be contagious. I'm the centre of something, but I'm not sure what. I hate this.

It is the middle of the night and a child is crying, somewhere far off. I lie in bed, half-awake, listening. It's more of a whimper, like a puppy locked out in the rain. It's stopped. I think I must have been dreaming. And then it starts again and I realise it is coming from Mum's room. Mum is crying, Mum's heart is bleeding. I get out of bed and stand by my door, listening out for her, willing her to swallow hard, stay the tears and drift back to sleep; things always seem better in the morning. But the tears keep coming, and she's whimpering like a puppy. I open my door, pad across the landing, and listen through her door. 'Mum…' I whisper. 'Mum…' and give a tentative knock. The whimpers halt for a few seconds then start up once more. I squeeze the doorknob slowly, and enter. I stand still, adjusting to the gloom. Her bed is over against the left hand wall. She's lying on the far side, back turned away from the door. 'Mum?' Her throat gives a stutter and whimpers turn to sobs that she tries to stifle, and a low groan comes from somewhere deep inside her. I go across, slip in beside her, edge towards her, and reach out my arm to draw her to me, away from the pain and the cold. Her body gives a shudder, and the tears cascade. I clutch her tight to me, her back pressing against my chest, tight and strong, against the storm. I don't know what is happening. I am here, my mum is bleeding, I am at the centre of something, but not sure what. I make my right arm stronger still, pressing her back into my pyjama'd chest, to give her my boy-strength, my would-be man strength. I want to pour it into her, and make her whole again. It is working. The sobs turn again to whimpers, gentle whimpers, with deeper breaths between them, and I feel her resistance melt as the tension in her eases and she snuggles back into me, and we lie there, together, still, and warm, and safe. And I hear Farrell's voice, calling softly through the door.

"Jack…"

What's he doing here?

"Jack"

I look up. I'm back in the room. Both of them are staring at me. Farrell is still leaning forward. Stella, as rigid as a dummy in a store window, looks aghast.

"Jack," he says again. "What are your tears about?"

I give a sniff, and wipe my fist across my nose. Stella thrusts the box of tissues towards me. I grab one; it rips as it comes out and I screw it up, drop it straight in the basket and give a sigh.

"I don't know," is all I say, and I'm speaking the truth.

Again, it is the wrong thing, my words propel Stella from her chair, she rushes from the room, and the door bangs shut then swings open on its hinges. I watch her striding away down the corridor.

I look across to Farrell. He is still leaning forward but his eyes are trained on the open doorway. It seems an eternity before he looks back at me.

"What do you want to do, Jack?" he asks, as if he doesn't know either.

"I don't know." I close my eyes and slump against the chair-back. "I don't know."

I hear Farrell get up and move to the door. I hear it close and for a moment I think he must have gone after her. Then I hear his voice, clear, strong, and as welcome as an ice cube clinking in a tumbler of whiskey.

"It's up to you, Jack." he says.

I open my eyes and meet his gaze.

"Do you want to leave too…or shall we continue?"

I don't talk to men, never have. Men are for doing things with, fishing, fighting, ogling the barmaid's arse as she bends down for that cold bottle from the bottom shelf of the fridge which you and your mate ordered for that very reason. Men are opponents, comrades in arms, fellow sufferers; that's men, they're not for confiding in. But when Farrell said '…shall *we* continue?' something makes me say, 'Yes.' And as I do so I start to weep uncontrollably again.

The shoulder of Farrell's shirt is wet with my tears. Can't remember the last time I was held by a man. On riot duty, I badly sprained an ankle and the guys took it in turns to support me as I hobbled back to the hooli-van, bricks and rubble raining down around us. My dad was always lifting me up when I was little, 'Let's show the cat's arse to the sun,' he'd say, as he swung me onto his shoulders. We wrestled and rolled in those early days, before the drink curled his hands to fists and turned his spirit to vinegar. But he never hugged me, not like this. And when I cried, he'd scuff my hair with his great hand, make a fist, gently prod my chin, and say, 'C'mon, pecker up, son, don't be a ninny.'

And I tell all this to Farrell as we sit back in the space created by the absence of women, and the atmosphere in the little room is different. I half-expect Farrell to reach down under his chair and pull out a big box of man-size tissues, plonk them down on the table and chuck the girlie ones in the bin. He doesn't say much, just listens, nods, and offers up the occasional observation, such as, 'It's hard, trying our best to be men, when inside we still feel like little boys.' And again, I notice his use of the word, 'we,' and my eyes well up once more but this time the tears don't flow, and I give a nod and a weak smile. I tell him about the day I stood up to my dad, when, as a result, he walked out of our lives for good. Farrell listens, says something about the price we pay for becoming men. He tells me a story, about a river with two banks, one male, and one female. He says we all start out on the female bank with our mothers. He says that girls, in order to become women in their own right, have to separate from their mothers and find their own stretch of bank. But we boys have to do something extra, not only must we separate out from our mothers, we have to make it across the river to the male bank, where our identity lies buried. Some of us, he says, face only a narrow brook, and are lucky enough to have a generous dad, willing to reach out a hand and help us wade across. But too many boys, Farrell says, face a wide stretch of water with either no dad at all to help him across, or a mean-spirited, tyrannical father, who defends his bank against all invaders, including his own son. Such young men either fail to cross the river and never really find their maleness, or they focus so hard on being the big strong man who has to swim against the raging torrent to claim his manhood, that they leave the little boy in themselves behind. And once they've established themselves on the far bank, he says, they're too scared to ever go back and look for him. And as Farrell tells this story, I hang on his every word, and think of my own father, and myself, and Sam, and I wonder whether Farrell's got sons of his own. Farrell says the story is a kind of fairy tale, and that fairy tales are powerful, and have much to teach us. He says I can take the story away with me and imagine that it's tucked inside my wallet, to be taken out every once in while and given a little thought.

And now we're talking about sneers, and why they have such a powerful effect on me, Sam's being a vile echo of my dad's. Farrell says he hasn't seen me sneer, but sometimes, when I'm talking to Stella, when I'm reacting to one of her criticisms, he says he hears what sounds like a sneer in my voice, and asks whether I recognise it, and if I do, maybe it would be useful to think about where it comes from. I say nothing but stow this too, away in my wallet, for later.

Farrell asks about women, what they mean to me, and what

it was that made Stella special? I try to explain, but it's not easy. I like their roundness, their soft edges, I like the way they move, not just their bodies, but the way they speak with their faces, hands, and eyes, in a way we don't. Farrell smiles, as if he agrees, but he doesn't say so.

"And Stella?" he prompts.

Stella. There was something different about Stella from the word go. She was strong as well as feminine. Nice shape, full lips. I've always liked her lips, until they began to curl up in disgust. I tell Farrell this, and he says that a look of disgust is not so different from a look of fear. I tell him I respected the way she protected her kids from a new man in her life, even though at first it kept me at arms length. I tell him I like the way she says 'Ni-Night.' First time she said it was the first night she let me stay over in her bed. It felt like she was talking to a child, and I fell asleep thinking about it.

"She seemed like a good mum," I say at last. "She let me in." And with these last four words a leaden lump of tears catches in my throat.

My palm rests on the flat of her chest; I feel the ribs beneath her skin. She is so small. Last time we snuggled like this she was bigger than me. My arm and hand and the strength in my chest seems to have soothed her, and the whimpers are gentler now, nothing more than little groans really, kinder, more content. And I feel her snuggle against me, nestling into me, safe and warm; so very warm. Her spine arcs away momentarily, and then melts back into me, melts right into me, the soft roundness of her bottom melting into me and I feel my heart race, breath quicken, as something is happening, something moving, hard, growing, down there, snuggling against, up against, pressing, nightdress, lifting, burrowing into, slips into, warm, soft, wet…and she stops. I stop. Two bodies. Frozen together in the dark, a train halted at red, going nowhere. 'Jack….' she whispers, 'you must go back to your own bed, right now. I'm sorry.' And I peel away from her, slip from the covers and leave her bed, and as I reach the door, I hear her speak softly, 'Jack, everything will be better in the morning.' I turn the doorknob, step outside and as I half turn to pull the door after me, I hear my name called out sharply from the darkness, 'Jack! This never happened.'

I have finished. I am crying again, not loudly, not sobbing, just slow, aching tears of release running down my cheeks.

Farrell lets out a huge sigh.

"That's quite a secret you've been holding onto, Jack, quite a secret. Have you told anyone at all, before today?"

I shake my head.

Farrell nods and lets out a grunt of what I take for understanding.

"Did you or your mother ever mention it again?"

"No."

"What about next morning at breakfast? Guess there must have been quite an atmosphere?"

"Sort of. Nothing was said. Me and my kid sister got on with our breakfast while Mum was scrubbing out the inside of the oven. I remember she had these pink rubber gloves on and the cleaning stuff stank to high heaven. She said she had to get it done before she left for work. I remember wishing she would look at me, but she never once did. She was down on her knees, scrubbing away. She just kept saying she had to get it done before she left for work."

"Hmm, like I said, Jack, that's a big secret for any boy to have had to hold," repeats Farrell, and I'm glad to let him speak for me.

There is a tentative knock at the door.

"Yes?" says Farrell.

"It's me, Stella."

The door half-opens, she's looking across at me. She has

been crying.

"Can I come back in, or is it too late?" she asks, of us both.

"Is it too late?" replies Farrell, looking directly at me.

"No. It's not too late," I say.

Stella sits down and Farrell closes the door after her.

He sits back down and looks at us each in turn. Stella and I, waiting on words, words from the man who holds our relationship in his hands. The silence is unbearable and I long to hear him clear his throat. When at last he speaks, it is slow and measured.

"I think you both have a lot to learn from each other, if you can bear to really listen. But I'm afraid our fifty minutes is up, for today."

Farrell reaches for his diary.

"Shall we make another appointment?"

8pm

Needs

By Nick Tyler

On the surface, her placid brown eyes express their love for me; beneath that easily destructible layer they convey their helplessness.

Being the responsible one is somewhat new to me. I feel like an imprisoned man, yet it's a prison I never want to leave. My love is this child's only hope, and in a time when a single father is as rare as chivalry, I sense her life is already damned.

The average lifespan of a black man in this neighborhood isn't long enough to offer sustained guidance, dedicated support and constant love. Even if I'm to be one of the lucky ones, how tainted will her world be? Will those eyes grow into steel, untrusting and deceptive by necessity?

These are the concerns I ponder on a daily basis…when things are good. Right now, that isn't the case. I only have one priority: money. Without any family or affordable child care, I've needed to stay home to care for Leshaundra. The problem is that funds have run out, my baby's mother has fallen in love with a pipe, nobody will hire me, and I haven't received my welfare cheque. It's been quite a fall for someone who only needed two more semesters for an English degree; someone who traded in his potential career for passion.

I peer down at Leshaundra in her crib. She shuts her eyes and drifts off to some other place. Maybe it's a world filled with princesses and unicorns, or beautiful sunsets and white-capped mountains, or where a kiss is gently planted on her cheek by a mother who abandoned her not so long ago.

Her naps always last an hour, give or take a minute or two. I'm fully aware that the time must be maximized.

A double knock like guttural thunder sounds from the door, causing my shoulders and heels to jump in tandem.

"I'll be back soon, baby," I say, stroking her hair.

Not many people would knock on my door at 8.00pm on a Tuesday. Most people I know in the building go out for a drink, a fix, or they stay home to watch whatever is on prime time television – if they own a television.

"Donnovan!" an angry woman's crackly voice barges through the wooden frame that separates us.

I open the door, curious to know who this strange voice belongs to. The increasing angle of light reveals a destitute face riddled with pock marks, scars and blisters. The skin under her eyes sags like a bloodhound's. Wrinkles are fast approaching despite her youth. Her frail body rocks back and forth like a ship on unsteady waters. But this ship doesn't know it's rocking.

This woman's appearance and soul don't belong to my wife. I search for a hint of her, but find none. I don't even recognise her voice. I must admit to myself that she disappeared months ago and had no intention of ever returning.

"Dee." I say her name, but it's not like it used to be. When I used to roll that syllable off my tongue, it was always accompanied with compassion. Now it's filled with a hopelessness, like a word trapped in a pitch black, padlocked box.

"What do you want?" I hurry my words. I have too much to worry about right now to be dealing with a half-dead, withdrawn crackhead.

"Gimme some money." Her dark brown eyes cleverly shift to the top of their sockets, giving her the appearance of a starving dog begging for a leftover crumb.

"I told you not to come here." I close the door behind me and make sure it's locked. Only the two of us stand in the dimly-lit, nicotine-stained hallway. It's a place where drug abuse, prostitution and countless domestic violence disturbances have occurred, and Dee represents every possibility. "I'm off to the store."

She grabs my arm in a weak attempt to coerce me, but can't muster the force. "What about our baby?" There's something sincere in her tone, but it leaves her as quickly as it arrived, as if the crack stepped to the forefront of her mind and shouted, "Hey! What about me?"

"She's not your daughter anymore." I pull my arm free and glare down at her, hoping this non-verbalized form of communication will get her attention; nothing else has so far. "When you stop using, we'll talk. Until then, I consider you an enemy."

"That's my baby!" she shrieks and throws her fists into my back as I walk away. The impact of her strikes is nothing more than a temporary nuisance, which resembles what the former love of my life has become.

I contemplate the irony of her words as I continue toward the staircase. Her strikes weaken with each step. Her energy has faded; I can hear it through the gasps in her breath and the awkward shuffling of her tired and abused feet.

Though the big blue door slams behind me, separating me from my contaminated wife, a new danger lies ahead, one I've learned to deal with on a daily basis.

It's hard not to remember the shakes, sweats, blisters and tears but still it's something that tempts even the strongest-willed, law-abiding citizen when living in the ghetto. The rent is due, there's no money, violence in the backyard is an everyday occurrence, and some form of escape is desperately needed. Luckily, I hit bottom. Those who don't, crash right through the bottom floor and straight into hell.

A constant challenge of living under these circumstances, with an addiction my body will always crave, is being forced to walk down the drug-user-infested staircase because of a broken, never repaired elevator.

I approach the third floor, knowing that's where the users and pushers usually hang out. I only have fifty minutes to complete my mission and return. If they impede my progress, I'll be tempted to use any tactic necessary to displace them.

"Donnovan." A scrawny, long-bearded man known as 'Cookie' stands up from the steps. I pass him as if he doesn't exist, wondering how the man is still alive. There's a reason for his nickname, one which relates to cooking up methamphetamine – a lot of it.

"Hey, man!" he shouts as I make my way to the second floor. His voice echoes off the walls with vigor, giving it more power than it deserves. "You can't treat a legend like that. I own this building!"

That last statement is one that many in these parts often use. It doesn't refer to real estate ownership, but how long a resident has been around. Someone's ability to survive for so long often leads to respect from neighbours and hang-arounds.

"The only thing you own is desperation, old man," I say as I exit the stairwell, not giving him time to respond, at least not for me to hear it. Part of me feels like I disrespected an elder, but the better half of me knows that as a pusher he's a destroyer of lives and thief of good souls. He's not the same man who got Dee, but that doesn't matter, the only difference is his physical form.

I continue my short trek to the local strip mall, which only entails a half-mile hike through a small, littered wooded area behind my apartment building. I could take the road, but based on what I have in mind, that would be an unwise decision.

I exit the woods and traverse a small hill. Once at its base, I study the stores and their neon signs, all shining bright with pride. My target is a small jewellery store squeezed between a supermarket and a martial arts studio.

More cars are leaving the parking lot than entering. Aside from the supermarket, the other nine stores will most likely close at 9.00 pm, leaving me forty minutes to get in, out, and back home before Leshaundra wakes up crying and in need of attention.

It's not something I want to do, but with no current or savings accounts, and only scattered nickels and dimes around the apartment, it's something I need to do. Any other father in my situation would do the same. They might not think they would, but when it came to it they would probably act even more desperately than me, simply because they'd never weathered such a storm. They would be lost in their emotions like a stray city dog abandoned in a national forest. It doesn't matter though. I'm not them and they're not me. My only concern is the task at hand.

I take my first steps toward the jewellery store, knowing they're the first steps toward a different life.

The bell above the door rings, sending what feels like a shot of adrenaline through my body from head to toe. Is it real adrenaline pumping through my system or just a bundle of nerves masked as such? I'm not sure.

"Can I help you, sir?" A man with a neatly-trimmed white moustache leans forward from behind the glass display to the left. His grey suit is a few sizes too small, looking as though it's choking his blood circulation. I see it as a representation of who this man is, as well as the way he lives. I imagine him stepping into a Jaguar after work and arriving at a gated mansion, where a butler awaits to serve his supper, and a wife is there to offer him the love he deserves. I then force myself to realise it's a stereotype, one bordering on hypocrisy. If what I imagined were true, why would he work to such a late hour, if at all?

I approach the counter and smile at the man, knowing my straight, glinting white teeth and honest eyes are my greatest assets. The man seems calm on the surface, but shakes beneath; I can tell by his trembling hands.

"I'm looking for an engagement ring for my wife," I say,

peering down through the glass top, at the diamond options below.

"Your wife, sir?"

I sense the man's head tilting to its side as I realise my slip-up, but I don't move. I continue focusing on the rings, wanting to present a state of calm, not fluster.

"My mistake." I offer a brief laugh, one nonchalant enough to make it sound like an error anyone could have made…even a white man. "Can I see that one right there?" I point to a ring with a square setting.

"The Princess Cut?"

"Yeah." I nod, even though I have no idea what he's talking about. I don't care about the make or appearance of the ring, only its value.

The man behind the counter doesn't respond with, "of course," or "sure, let's see if you like it," which leads me to believe he's suspicious. I can't sweat that, though. I need to play my role: cool, calm, and potential buyer.

He removes the ring from the display case and presents it over the counter with both hands. A sparkling ring that so many women would covet is set on a cushioned platform inside a small case. The case is opened like an oyster shell, but offers more value than anything most people would ever find at sea.

I lift my head and casually glance around the store, acting as though I'm looking for other ring options before I study this one, but really I'm searching for other employees. There are none. The man behind the counter, who I now assume to be a jeweller and not just a salesman, might think he's doing the wise thing by presenting the ring with both hands. Maybe he thinks he'll have an advantage if I try to swipe it. But what he doesn't realise is that he's increased the distance between his hands and the alarm behind the counter.

"That's nice," I say, maneuvering my hands toward the boxed ring.

"No touch." The jeweller releases his right hand from the tiny box and moves his index finger in a tick-tock motion.

This is my chance. The window of opportunity has opened and will slam shut within seconds, blocking the storm's path – my path. The importance of acting as a good citizen crosses my mind, but is immediately overruled by thoughts of Leshaundra and my need to provide for her.

I outstretch my arm in a whip-like motion, snag the ring, and stare deep into the jeweller's eyes. I instruct my brain to send the message of disaster, hoping he'll understand, and that we can avoid any complications.

"I'm sorry." The words slip out. I had no intention of displaying weakness, but I guess the better part of me took charge. I fear it's a peak for the good man I've become, and that each move I make from here will send me back to the doldrums of despair.

"You're sorry?" the jeweller asks as he slowly lowers his hands to his side.

Acting out of desperation, I place my hand in my right coat pocket and form the shape of a pistol, then stretch the jacket toward him.

"Put your hands up!" I scream. It's a tone of voice I haven't used in years, one filled with untrusting rage.

"Fine." He puts his hands in the air, but not fast enough to show he's overly concerned. If anything, the fear he showed earlier has turned into confidence. I'm unsure if this is because fear is often worse than consequences, or if I'm overlooking an important detail.

"I know you don't have a gun," he says with a smile, one that indicates he thinks he has the upper hand.

"Oh yeah? How do you know?" I know this question blows my cover. It's an obvious attempt to buy time. If I had a gun, I'd have shown it.

"Don't worry. You can take the ring. I'm going to end up getting it back, anyway." His eyes flick toward the corner at the front of the store. I suddenly realise I've forgotten about the video cameras.

"Sound the alarm and I'll come back and tear this place apart," I threaten, before lowering my head and moving toward the back door. It's a weak threat, but I don't care. It's getting too hot in here, and I need to get out fast.

My gait quickens with each horrible thought that crosses my mind: police beating, being shot, prison.

Once within arm's reach of the door, an alarm sounds. The sirens, whistles and lights send my thoughts into unfamiliar confusion, like they've been placed in a piñata and repeatedly whacked and spun.

A solid wall lowers behind me, blocking my view of the jeweller and store. A thick bolt locks the door ahead, leaving me trapped in a five foot cage, stolen goods in hand.

There's air in here, but my breathing pattern has faltered. Hiccups follow gasps and gasps follow quick exhales. Panic is confirmed by the beads of sweat forming on my skin like boiled warts. My grip on the engagement ring weakens, and I ask myself if I've fallen victim to a classic mirage.

The sirens screech, the lights flash and turn. My eardrums thump inside my head like the drums of a tribal battle call. This jeweller is the system, I am just the little man. I have no chance. But if I want to get back to Leshaundra, I can't be caught. Though the door ahead is bolted, it's still glass. Not the kind of glass that can be broken with a swift kick, but perhaps the kind of glass that can be broken by a father imagining his baby daughter in her crib, stretching her arms out, wanting his love, needing his care.

With her image at the forefront of my mind, I back up as far as I can. Once my back is pressed against the thick wall behind me, I lower my shoulder, point it toward the bottom half of the door and charge ahead.

In that brief second, I conjure up all the love I have for that baby girl. My blood pumps faster and harder, rushing my most prized emotion to the core of my heart. Based on the sudden, superhuman strength I possess, this time I'm certain it's adrenalin. I now understand how a mother can lift a car to save a trapped child. What most people fail to realise is that this amazing power can stem from love, not just fear.

I crash through the bottom half of the door, screaming like a black-belt smashing a dozen bricks. A black-belt screams in order to diffuse temporary pain, but my pain is constant; it doesn't disappear after a single strike at one overwhelming challenge. If only I had the ability to become a black-belt of my emotions. Then, maybe I'd use a different technique.

The thick glass shatters. Most pieces follow me as if wanting to punish me for my crime. A few pieces shoot to the sides as if understanding my plight. I wonder if these pieces of glass represent how many people would call for my beheading versus how many would be willing to listen to my desperate situation.

I reach my hand to my eyebrow and remove a shard of glass stuck into my skin. I see it as a piece that intended to alter my vision, but even if it had, it couldn't alter my vision of a healthy, functional family. And it is this vision that spurs me on. I have less than forty minutes to get home before Leshaundra wakes up, before she has any clue that I abandoned her, that I didn't wait by her side like a trusted guardian who would take her hand and lead her through a world littered with hate, sin and greed.

A sound like a steady metallic waterfall comes from the jewellery store. I look up and watch the thick wall rise. The jeweller's shined shoes and ironed pants come into view. His attire represents my most feared enemy. Even if he doesn't capture me now, he still possesses invaluable weapons, ones I can't compete with. Desperate men like me use guns and knives and end up in prison. Men like him use pens, keyboards and lawyers and end up in newspapers as heroes.

The wall rises high enough to reveal the jeweller's

midsection, as well as a tightly-gripped revolver in his right hand.

I hurry to my feet and race around the corner. I realise I've turned toward the populated parking lot, which isn't where I want to be. But facing a potentially loaded gun wasn't an option.

My steps are awkward. I'm forced to drag my left leg. I'm certain it was the first leg to crash through the door and it's numb. I wipe my hand across my face, wanting to look as alert as possible in case I come across anyone. But my hand is wet, and when I hold it in front of my face, I watch blood drip from my fingers with each step I take.

My physical state is deteriorating, a dangerous sign. As long as it is a sacrifice for Leshaundra, it's okay. If it ends up serving no purpose, then I've only added to the long list of no-good criminals who hit the streets on a nightly basis seeking to harm, rob and kill.

I turn the corner, toward the front of the jewellery store, and slam into a thick, blubbery object. My medium-sized frame falls backward and onto the sidewalk. I'm unable to keep hold of the ring, which bounces and dances tauntingly on the cement.

"Donnovan?" a deep male voice asks. I recognise it as one of my neighbours. "It's me, Antoine. Whatchu doin', bro?"

He's one of the good ones, one of the reformed few who fight the scum that invades our neighbourhood. He's also one who fights the system and feels oppressed by it. I remember a conversation we had one night over a few beers. I agreed that the 'system' caused us to be where we were, but then asked how much worse off we might have been without that same system. It's always been a habit of mine to play devil's advocate, to see the other side, but that time it finished our conversation and ended up being the last time I spoke with him. If I had just passed him on the sidewalk, I wouldn't have received, or offered, much more than a nod. But in this moment, our lives cross paths, providing opportunities for questioning, assistance, and/or judgment. With blood smothered all over my face, having just run from the back of a jewellery store with a heavy limp, and having dropped a diamond ring, I know judgment will precede all other possibilities.

"What's with the blood? And whatchu got an engagement ring fo', bro?" He points to the ring on the ground.

I haul myself up and shake my head, attempting to gather my thoughts, wanting to piece together a logical response.

"I thought you were already married?" he presses, this time with a more derogatory tone.

I look over my shoulder and down the alleyway. No sign of the jeweller yet, but it won't be long. I might have thrown him off by heading in this direction.

"Donnovan!" Antoine shouts, recapturing my attention. "You okay, bro?" He snaps his fingers in my ear, taking me back to that trapped sensation: irritating sirens, flashing, buzzing, eardrums pounding, caged, enemy in control. My body reacts before my mind has a chance to act as a buffer.

I grab his fingers and bend them backward, forcing his 230lb frame to its knees. I see the agony in his face. He doesn't even realise the pain is temporary, something that will heal within the next few days. He probably thinks his suffering is the worst thing imaginable, and that he'd trade places with anyone in the world for that moment just to relieve the pain. But I would trade my pained heart for his broken fingers any day.

"Digressing," I whisper.

"What!" Antoine screams. "Ow, man! Stop! STOP!"

I release his fingers and realise that all I'm going through for my daughter is bringing pain to others. Is that what causes all the hurt in the world: defending and fighting for your own at all costs, no matter what the expense to others? Our own country operates this way, why not its citizens?

"What the fuck is wrong with you, bro?" Antoine grimaces as he holds his now-deformed fingers.

"I'm sorry," I reply with sincerity. "Society forces me to behave this way." I grab the ring and place it in my pocket.

"Hey!" the jeweller shouts from the alleyway.

I know he's holding a gun. I don't need to look back to confirm it. Renewed adrenalin forces my numb leg into action and I run into the parking lot, weaving between parked vehicles, trying to confuse my pursuer by ducking behind large SUVs and pick-up trucks.

"Hey!" he shouts again. I'm eased by this. It lets me know that the word is the only weapon he's willing to use in a public setting.

I manoeuvre my way to the opposite end of the lot, where a puttering, white Oldsmobile approaches. It's moving slowly. As it comes in line with my body, I pounce on the driver-side door and yank it open. I find myself jogging along with the car, staring down at a little old white woman wearing a red wig and white nightgown. I immediately know what she's thinking: these damn niggers. Our generation knew to keep them in their places. Look where our country is headed!

But what if she knew me? What if she could watch me hold Leshaundra and see the love for her in my eyes? What if she knew why I wanted her car? Would she let me have it? Would she then feel ashamed for prejudging me? Or should I be ashamed for prejudging her on how she would think of me?

"I need your car, lady!" I scream as I struggle to keep pace. "Move over!"

She glances in my direction and makes a face that screams: "I'm not ready to die!"

She slams on the gas. I lose my grip on the door and flop to the ground, rolling over four times, my limbs contorting in random directions as if they don't contain any bones.

The sound of the jeweller's shoes slapping against the concrete comes from behind, intensifying with each step. I struggle to my feet and lift my arms, which feel like they've been banged against a steel wall by a steroid-induced weightlifter, and then shot up with large doses of Novocain.

"Hey!" The jeweller's voice is frighteningly close. "Give me my damn ring back, you stupid n…asshole."

I look to the left and spot a teenage black girl witnessing the event. I didn't need to see her, though. As soon as he stopped himself from saying that publicly condemned word, I knew one of my kind was in the vicinity.

He's within ten yards, closing in with increased speed. His gun is still at his side, visible to the public. I laugh at how he fears using the 'N' word more than displaying a gun. To find a laugh at this moment is refreshing. His foot connects with my chin, altering the shape of my smile, forcing blood to spit into the air like a primed geyser. My chest collapses to the ground, momentarily stealing my breath.

"Give me the fucking ring, you piece of shit!"

His words are filled with anger and hatred. What I at first assumed to be a good, respectable man, has turned out to be no better than a violent criminal. This time his foot connects with my gut, sending my body a few inches upward. An 'ugh' sound escapes my mouth. I don't want him to hear it, but I can't help releasing the word. It had nowhere to go.

"I said, give me the fucking ring!"

I grip the ring tighter. He doesn't realise that his words and tone only motivate me further. If he had approached with, "We need to talk about this. If you're having trouble, I understand, but that doesn't give you the right to steal from me. If you hand it over, I promise not to press charges, and I'll see if I can help you out," it might be different.

But who acts like that these days? What would I offer him in return? A smile? A hug? A high-five? He's not looking for any intrinsic rewards, only monetary ones. And that's something I can't offer, which makes me a nuisance; someone who doesn't belong.

"You best stop beatin' that black man, mista'!" the teenage girl shouts, leaning her upper body toward the jeweller as an intimidating gesture.

"Stay out of this," he rebuts.

She reaches into her pocketbook and removes a digital camera. The jeweller has now found himself in a situation that would put him in the newspaper for all the wrong reasons. No matter what the circumstances, the public loves to be sympathetic as much as the media craves controversy.

"Put that away if you know what's best for you, little girl." The jeweller's crazed eyes shift in her direction. He cocks the hammer on the gun.

The jeweller has gone over the edge. Maybe he can't pay his bills; maybe his wife has left him; maybe he's withdrawn from his own addiction. No matter the case, I'm the one who put this chain of events into action. Now I must be the one to stop it, which is a much tougher task.

"She's got nothing to do with this." I glare up at the jeweller, even though he's not looking back. Suddenly, the ring seems irrelevant. The issue of life and death has come into play and I have gone from crook to potential hero. But 'potential' shouldn't enter my mind in this situation. If I fail to save this girl, I will have failed to save someone else's Leshaundra. And after watching years of development and forming forever-lasting memories, would the parents' pain be even worse?

"Put the gun down, sir." I have no interest in calling him 'sir' but I have to treat him with respect if I want to save this girl's life. I choose to stay on the ground between them, remaining in a more unthreatening position.

The girl lifts her camera and points it at the jeweller. "You can shoot me if you want to, but I'm gettin' it on record."

The jeweller's face turns bright red. I watch the blood rush from his chin to his forehead. It's the most horrifying movie I've ever seen. "If you snap that shot, I fire this gun."

It's about hatred for him, not evidence. The ugly zeal in his eyes gives it away.

"Sorry, mista, but you're not gonna be goin' round tellin' me what to do." She steadies the camera, looks through the small window and clicks the button.

"No!" I scream as the click resonates in my mind, knocking around like a metallic ball in a pinball machine.

The jeweller doesn't hesitate to fire back. The bullet leaves the barrel like a miniaturized rocket ship, only this ship has death written all over it. Once it's in the air, it can't be called back down due to complications. The sound of the gunshot is deafening, yet still not as loud as the fateful click of the camera had been.

I jump in the air as fast as possible, wanting to intercept the small, manmade object that will end this girl's life. But the bullet has already passed and collided with this girl's heart and future.

Her dark brown, innocent eyes first reveal shock and horror. I can sense them asking if she could go back a few seconds, admitting she didn't believe he would shoot. Then, for a second, they convey anger and desired vengeance. But something else quickly takes over, something peaceful that rides along with death.

Her body quivers and drops to the ground like a deflated balloon, her arms and legs squiggling on the way down.

My eyes begin to shed quiet tears. The jeweller looks at me with a fear I've never witnessed before. He releases the gun and I listen to its steel surface bounce on the ground. He shakes his head, indicating he didn't mean to do it, that it was an accident, that I should help him. Just a smile, hug, or high-five would do. But I can't help him, because just as he now seeks something of intrinsic value, I must avoid criminal penalties. There's also no doubt in my mind that once he comes to his senses, he will pin me for the murder. And what kind of chance will I have? I'm a poor, black man living in the ghetto who just stole a diamond ring from a jewellery store. I even made the motion that I had a gun in my jacket pocket while in the store, which has all been caught on tape. The jeweller will claim he chased after me and I fired at him. The teenage girl was a civilian who happened to be in the line of fire. Who will believe my side of the story? No one. Especially if I run. But I must run. Leshaundra will be awake in less than thirty minutes and her life and future are more important than my own.

*

Today's events race through my mind faster than my legs can churn. A robbery. A beating. A murder. All because of my love for Leshaundra. And was it all worth it? Yes.

What would I do if forced to make a decision between a nuclear warhead being sent to a populated city on foreign soil or the death of my one Leshaundra? I'd order the missile strike without hesitation. Does that make me a bad person, or a good father?

As it stands, she has a questionable future. The recent events have confirmed this prophesy. And what if she somehow beats the odds of growing up in such a perilous environment? It would be great on the surface, but most things great on the surface come with some form of cost. Today's events would weigh on me like a hundred-pound dumbbell hanging by a thick cord, wanting to yank my mind from my head, away from reality.

I step onto the soft dirt of the trail that twists through the small patch of woods behind my apartment building, thinking of nothing but getting back home. But those once focused thoughts come to a halt as I watch Cookie walk toward me. His sway is controlled, like he's become a professional drug abuser, experienced at how to present himself while in altered states of mind.

I stop, but for no other reason than being in need of a friend.

"Hey, man," he says, brushing his left hand through the knotted, grey beard hanging from his chin. "Looks like you got a date with fate." He laughs.

He's not laughing at me. It's something more sinister, like he knows something I'm not yet aware of.

"Hey." I nod, unsure how to respond, unsure if his company will make me feel better or suck me into a downward spiral that might spin forever if I make the mistake of stepping inside.

"Remember what you said, man?" He points at me with a long, accusatory finger.

"No." I shake my head, not remembering. How could I? I have too much on my mind.

"Just over half an hour ago, man, you went and said the only thing I owned was desperation." He tilts his head as if he still couldn't believe I'd say something like that to someone who was supposed to be a respected elder.

I remember now. "Yeah? So?" I need to play it off as if it was just a form of trash-talking.

He studies my condition. "Looks like that would mean I own you."

I ignore his comment, not having the time to argue with a junkie. But as I stand near him, I see a lack of care for all potential worries in his demeanor. I smell the aroma on his filthy jacket; it's the aroma of a substance that has the potential to take me to another place. It's a place that I know can destroy my body, but it can also send my mind to a land with less strife and no cares or worries, a land where I'd only have one need: another escape. And is that really such a bad life after all? It might be a shorter life, but I won't be judged, I'll accumulate close friends with similar interests, and I'll experience the greatest sensations ever created by man. Maybe that should be the hint to stay away: 'created by man' but I don't recognise it as such.

"I'm not desperate," I blurt, as if I'm the defendant being asked how I plead.

"Not yet, my man, but you're hungry." Cookie steps closer. His admired stench intensifies. "Your eyes are bigger; you're grinding your teeth. You want something. You *need* something. I know." He points to himself. "I seen it befo'."

"That's a bunch of bullshit." *Leshaundra. Leshaundra. Leshaundra.* I need to get out of here. He's sucking me in like a needle sucks blood from a patient. Only this needle is open-ended, never stopping until the patient is drained of all life. I'm aware that bad times lead to relapses by disguising themselves as relief, but temptation is the most seductive creature I know, and she's knocking.

"You want this shit or what?" Cookie displays a half-burnt crack pipe. It's like seeing a former lover who disrobes and wants to rekindle an old flame. "I remember your favorite flavor, my man. I always keep myself prepared for a potential customer." He smiles, this time revealing his crooked, yellow teeth. "You get one blast for free, but after that, admission will cost ya."

One blast. That's one hit. One chance to temporarily relieve the pain. But will one hit lead to two, and two to three, and three to seven?

"No thanks," I reply with a tremble in my voice. I'm certain my tone reveals my lack of conviction. "I only have twenty minutes to get home before my baby girl wakes up. I need to go take care of her."

"You need to take care of yourself first. Your baby girl ain't at home, anyways. She right here." He stretches the crack pipe toward my hand.

Sirens sound in the background. It won't be long before a crowd forms in the parking lot, yellow tape secures the crime scene, and the jeweller begins spitting lies. Police are probably already on the hunt for a black man carrying an $8,000 ring.

With that thought in mind, something hits me. Up until this point, Cookie has seen me as the target, easy prey, a potential cash machine. But he's actually provided me with an excellent opportunity. At least that's how it seems.

"Forget the blast," I say, thinking only of my potentially ingenious plan, and not the temptation that will come with it. "Give me ten boulders if you got it."

"Ten boulders? I know you don't got a hundred bucks on you."

"Nope. I've got much better. Check this out." I open my hand and present the ring, hoping my persuasion will at least equal what his had been when he dangled the crack pipe in front of me.

"It hot?"

I nod. There's no sense in lying. He knows it's stolen. I suspect it's only a test to see if I'd tell the truth. Not that it matters, though. I'm certain he'll take it. He has to take it. He's a drug dealer who's addicted to his own merchandise. People like that become less than human; the all-mighty dollar owns their souls. They'll do anything to get their hands on something that can pay for their alternate, artificial worlds.

"Deal," he states. "I'll find a pawn shop." He reaches inside his jacket, takes out a bag filled with crack cocaine, and places it in my hand along with the pipe and a lighter. Part of me hopes the pipe will burn, not allowing me to get a hold of it, but it fits into my hand perfectly, like a baby and her bottle, and this baby can't wait to drink the milk inside.

"This bitch always there when you need her. Ain't no denyin' that." Cookie slaps me on the back as he passes, leaving me and my desired nemesis alone in the woods, allowing me an opportunity to make any move I please with no possibility for rejection.

I smell the fumes from the pipe. They ease their way into my nostrils with a tantalizing scent, sending messages to my brain that relief is only a hit away. I place the pipe to my lips,

153

not to smoke it, just to see how it feels. Is it something I'll want to experience again, or will that bitter stench turn me off? Of course I already know the answer, but I can't admit it to myself. Circumstances have designed a puzzle without a realistic solution, which leads me to the need of an altered perspective.

I study the lighter. Its rebellious scarlet color motivates me. I try to force in the thought of blood and death, but it's more of a sexy hue, one that lifts its skirt so I can take a peek, letting me know what's around the corner if I make the right moves.

Fewer than two minutes ago, I held a diamond ring. Now I hold a lighter and a plastic bag filled with crack and a pipe. Was I subconsciously heading to this the entire time? Was that why I really left Leshaundra alone in the apartment? The mind of an addict works in manipulative ways, always planning and plotting new attempts to drag you back in. Sometimes it takes minutes, other times years, but once you become a user it's always there, waiting for its chance to strike. It will allow you small victories to increase your confidence, but it's really only a setup for a bigger letdown when something goes wrong.

I rub my finger on the wheel of the lighter, sparking a flame. I can see my legacy's future burning inside the fire if I'm to continue. Flickers of white light, resembling hope, try to fight through the flame, but they're overpowered. I place the fire to the crack-rock in the pipe. Closing my eyes, I inhale.

A stampeding bundle of euphoria races to my brain, sending oxygen to every corner, allowing my mind to breathe and forget all worries. Though I'm not touching them, my ears feel clean, as though I just washed them with a damp Q-tip. I see the definition of the leaves on the trees. Like people, they look similar to one another and live in the same vicinity, although keep to their own branches.

I shake my head in an effort to rid myself of such absurd thoughts at such a critical moment in my life. But remembering there's a critical moment is what leads to a second hit.

I see that the path winds through the woods like a snake. It's harmless now, because I'm standing on the middle of it, but I'm concerned about what it might do when I try to exit. Will it strike or let me find my fate without interfering? Which would be better? Which would be worse?

I see Leshaundra on a tree branch, giggling and waving as she plays with her plastic, blue dog.

"Hey, baby." I wave. Her sweet, heartwarming smile widens. To my horror, Cookie's head suddenly appears behind hers. He's standing behind her, his legs stretching ten feet high so he can reach her level. I feel like I'm watching a clown in a tilted mirror. He lifts his beard to cover his face and then splits it apart as if he's peeking from behind a curtain. In a way, he's letting me know he'll always be there – a part of her life. And even if it's not Cookie himself, I know he's right.

"He's got his whole world in his hands." Cookie sings, his eyes focused on the crack pipe in my hand. "And I've got her whole future in my hand." From behind, his fingers crawl like spiders onto Leshaundra's face. They stop and squeeze her chubby cheeks like a loveable grandfather. And that's what scares me the most. She's too good-hearted not to accept his love. She won't recognise that he's just setting up another customer, probably planning on offering her a first hit at the age of three.

"Fuck you!" I throw the pipe at what turns out to be an unoccupied branch.

I stand still for a moment, waiting for Lesaundra and Cookie to return, but acknowledge that it was a hallucination.

"You abandoned our baby," Dee's voice calls from behind. "How could you, Donnovon? You have to find her."

She's right. I hurry across the path, sit on my knees, and begin to run my hands through the scattered leaves, frantically searching for the crack pipe. "I know you're in here. Come back. I promise I'll never hurt you again. Please."

Footsteps from behind. I jerk my head as if I had no neck. All I see is an empty path. No feet, no footsteps. There can't be footsteps without feet, can there? Unless they're testing me. I know what they're doing. They want to see if I'm high. They want to know if I'm the man who shot the girl, if I'm the one who robbed the jeweller. This has all been a trap set up by the system. They want to take my baby. They want to prove my incompetence.

"Fucking bastards!" I scream as my hands continue to sift through the foliage.

My hand makes contact with a hard surface. I know it's the pipe. My fingers have made love to it so many times before. No debating or justifying this time, I light up and take three more hits.

To the right, I notice three trees with vertical vine-like branches. They resemble metal bars to a jail cell. I can already feel the cold surfaces around me, the lack of love and abundance of hatred of those within these walls. Beyond the bars, on the side of freedom, stands the jeweller.

"You're a crackhead who needed a fix, so you went to my store and stole a diamond ring. I followed you to keep track of my ring. A teenage girl tried to help me by telling you to stop, that you were doing the wrong thing. What a perfect story for the media: 'Local Girl Dies a Tragic Death by Acting as a Hero'. Because of your rage, which was brought on by your craving, you shot the bitch! Ha Ha! You shot the bitch." He laughs, bending over to hold his stomach. He then straightens faster than a cadet spotting a sergeant. A morbid expression replaces his smile. "You're a deadbeat. No matter how you look at it, there's no denying that. You're worthless."

He disappears before I have a chance to respond, as do the

vertical, vine-like branches. But his words remain, confirming my worthlessness. I consider taking my own life, but I don't know how. Plus, who would watch Leshaundra? Who's watching her now? Minutes ago, being caught by the police, beaten, or shot, frightened me more than anything. Now what frightens me most is the call of the crack being more powerful than my baby's cries.

I have to find the goodness that remains in my heart. My demon might have taken control again, but I know good can outlast evil if I focus. I've only got ten minutes to get back to the apartment before Leshaundra wakes. Despite all the wrong I've done, I find strength in taking that first step toward the apartment, toward a helpless baby who loves, needs and relies on me.

The hallucinations come and go, but I fight them off. I've seen them in the past and I know how the demons try to disguise themselves. My breath shortens, my heart rate increases, and I see lights around dark objects, which I know aren't there. I begin to feel nauseous and desperately want to throw up. Not so I'll feel better, but to get rid of the poison I've put in my body. All I want is to be a good father, but I don't know if I have the ability. This saddens me most.

A small, bright circle of light flashes on a tree to the left. Voices come from behind. Real ones. They sound anxious and determined. The circle of light moves off the tree and in my direction. I drop to the ground as if preparing for a push-up and watch the light move to the trunk of a tree on the opposite side of the path.

Another light shines on another tree. More voices follow. They're nearing at a steady pace. I hear a constant sniffing. An army of dogs has followed my scent.

I place all the drug paraphernalia in my pocket and crawl as fast as I can, feeling like I'm a soldier on the sands of Iwo Jima. Perhaps that's not a fair comparison, considering it's not a matter of life or death. But it is a matter of freedom. Is there that much of a difference?

Staying low, I avoid the flashlights, but this hungry posse is gaining on me. I reach the end of the path, stand, and race for my apartment building.

I'm only a few feet from the front door when I hear a man scream: "Right there!" I look behind me to find dozens of circles of light on my back. I continue my frantic pace.

Dee is sitting on the ledge, picking the scabs on her arms. Once she spots me, she stands and blocks my path.

"Move!" I scream as I approach the door.

She seems unconcerned with my warning.

"Dee, move! The fucking police are after me," I yell as I reach her. She studies me carefully.

"You're high!" she says with excitement.

"Dee. If you don't move, I'm going to move you. I don't want to have to do that. Our baby is upstairs and she's about to wake up. I need to get upstairs."

"Give me some shit first. Whatever you got."

"You're sick."

"You're not? I said, give me what you got!" She grabs my arm, this time with more ferocity and determination than earlier. Knowing I possess her medicine clearly gives her more strength. It's what she lives for. When she can smell and taste it she's a machine, not stopping at any obstacle, until she gets it.

I hear the cocking of a hammer on a gun from behind. Then another. And another. "Don't move, sir," one of the voices call.

I hand Dee my only potential escape: the pipe, crack, and lighter. She doesn't seem to care that an army of police officers are watching the transaction.

"Thank you, honey," she says as she steps aside.

I'm happy she moved, but now I have a decision to make. Now that they have a clear shot, will they shoot if I try to enter the building? But like with most things in life, if I stand still, I'll lose.

In the quickest motion I can muster, I reach my hand forward, swing the door open, and enter the building, hoping the circles of lights won't turn into bullets.

I make it inside safely. All I heard were screams, warning me not to go inside. I run for the stairwell. They don't know what floor I live on. I might have a few minutes before they find me. Hopefully, it will be enough time to make sure Leshaundra is okay.

No addicts or dealers in the stairwell this time, only graffiti-covered walls, a stale acidic stench and tar-stained steps.

I reach the 8th floor without incident. I peer down the hallway, in the direction of my apartment, and find an unexpected sight. Three little girls in Girl Scout uniforms stand in front of my door. I recognise one of them as a girl who lives two floors below. They're all staring at my condition in disbelief. I see the fright inside them, but they're each putting on a strong front, acting as if they didn't notice the blood smeared on my face, my bloodshot eyes, my limp.

"Hi, girls." I wave as if it's just another jolly day in the neighbourhood. "How can I help you today?"

The girl in the middle, the one who lives downstairs, twirls her braided hair with her fingers as she begins to speak. "Well… um… we heard you were having a tough time feeding and taking care of your baby." She waits to see if I'll respond, which I don't. "We raised money for you by selling 'Say No to Drugs' and 'Say No to Crime' stickers."

She extends a cheque. The amount reads: $500.00.

"I can't accept this."

"Why not? You deserve it. Good things happen to good people. My mommy told me so."

My heart feels as though it sinks below my waist, waiting to be excreted. "Okay." I take the cheque. Not because I want to, but because it's nearly 9.00pm and Leshaundra will wake any minute now. "Thank you." I nod.

"Anytime," she says with a smile, looking past my condition as if she figured I was just out playing a silly game with other adults. "Have a good day, mister."

"Thanks."

I open the door to my apartment and hurry to Leshaundra's crib. To my relief, she's still sleeping. I pick her up and hold her against my chest, feeling her heartbeat pound against my own. But then I remember that I'm dirty, bleeding, and high. I immediately extend my arms, holding her away from my body.

"You're a good person," I tell her. "I need to be one, too." I place her back in the crib and walk over to the phone.

I dial a number that I've memorised for weeks. It's a number I've feared, but now it seems right. I hold the receiver to my ear as I begin to weep. I tell myself to be strong, to do the right thing.

Once the phone rings there's no turning back. I know it's a ring that leads to a better life for Leshaundra.

"Better Home Adoption Agency, may I help you?" a woman with a sweet and caring tone asks. Does she sound caring just because I want her to? Maybe. But I know whatever she can offer is better than the alternative.

"Can you take my baby today? She needs a new home right away."

"I'm sorry, sir. You have to make an appointment."

"She doesn't have time for an appointment. She's at 131 Broadline Street. 8th floor. Apartment 16. If you don't arrive within a half-hour, she'll most likely die." I hang up the phone right away, not giving her a chance to respond. It was a necessary lie, one that will ensure someone will be here to pick up Leshaundra and place her in better hands.

I walk over to the crib. She wakes from her nap with a cry, but once her eyes are fully open and she sees me, she smiles and giggles. That's a sight I'll keep in my mind, playing it over and over again until my final breath.

"I love you." I bend down and kiss her forehead. "I have to go now. I hope you understand."

I move away without looking back. I continue into the hallway, down the stairwell, and straight into the hands of the police.

I might have become a criminal, but I've also proven to myself that I'm a good father – one who does what's best for his child. I've given Leshaundra what she needs: a chance.

10pm

Maria's Mother

By Jackie Blissett

10 o' clock. Dickory dock. Hickory dickory dock. Where's my Mouse? She's not in the house. If I make it rhyme she'll come home on time. But I said half-past eight, she's already late. If I count to ten 1,2,3,4,5,6,7,8,9,10, then I do it again 1,2,3,4,5,6,7,8,9,10, she'll walk through the door just like before...Mouse...Mouse... ... ... she's still not in the house! She's an hour and a half late. I think that gives me cause to worry. It's an hour and a half! Ninety minutes of lateness! She's never late, maybe ten minutes, and only now and then. But ten minutes late was eighty minutes ago. What can I do? What should I do? Really I can't just sit and wait, can I? Do I have a choice? Wait and listen. Listen and wait is all I can do. Wait and listen...listen and wait...

If I strain my ears hard enough I'll hear her footfall on the gravel path. Listen...listen...silence. I need to hear that familiar crunch that tells me she's here, that tells me she's safe, and I know she's at home and I'm no longer alone. If I make it rhyme she'll come on time. Dickory dock. Come on Mouse crunch, crunch make a gravely scrunch. Your quick, light steps crunch, scrunch, crunch on the gravel. Come on Mouse ...crunch... ... ...silence. So strange, usually I love silence. Rare and precious in a life...stillness...silence: no noise to create the pounding pressures I dread, those pressures which clang and spin around in my head. Silence brings me peace – when there's silence I can stop thinking and float on my ocean, the one without motion. But this silence makes me feel sick. I want to vomit. I want to scream. It brings me darkness...uncertainty...fear. No window or door, no chink of light to bring respite. I need my Mouse. Where are you? Silence. I want the light. I need my Mouse.

Tap, tap tippety tap. Tap, tap tippety tap.

Tap, tap, tippity tap… tap tap tippity tap. My nails, beautiful, long, strong … … …

"The usual?" Pedicure, manicure – French of course. This morning, was it only this morning? No prelude or warning. Thinking only of my nails I sip a cappuccino whilst Tina files away and tells me that Terry wants to take her to Ibiza for their honeymoon. Tina's worried; she's not sure that Ibiza is really her scene. I try to assure her that the island isn't entirely about clubbing. Ask at the travel agents or look on the internet. I hope she takes my advice, but I'm not really that bothered one way or another. She over-files one of my nails and it really annoys me. I know that nobody will notice, but to me it's markedly shorter than the rest. It worries me. I rub it self-consciously and look at it all day…well, all day until an hour and a half ago. It doesn't worry me any more. Tap…tap…tippety tap. If I do four sets of four I'll hear her key in the door.

Tap…tap…tippety tap. Tap…tap…tippety tap.
Tap…tap…tippety tap. Tap…tap…tippety tap.

Tap…tap…tippety tap. Tap…tap…tippety tap.
Tap…tap…tippety tap. Tap…tap…tippety tap.

Tap…tap…tippety tap. Tap…tap…tippety tap.
Tap…tap…tippety tap. Tap…tap…tippety tap.

Tap…tap…tippety tap. Tap…tap…tippety tap.
Tap…tap…tippety tap. Tap…tap…tippety tap.

Beautiful nails…long, strong, strong and long. Mouse has the same shape nails as me. The same hands…almost identical! Except that hers are paler and smaller; and of course younger. My Mouse. So small. Where are you? Why don't you come home? Where are you?

Such small hands…small, so small. I gently rest a finger in the palm of her hand. I expect the tiny fingers to curl instinctively around it, but they do not. We are a tragedy. I sense that young nurse watching me. I know this scene is breaking her heart and that she's trying to be professional, but if I look up I'm sure I'll see tears in her eyes. I resent her sympathy, I resent her presence. Tonight, when her shift has finished and she returns to the normal world, the one in which we no longer live, she'll either forget us, or tell people, strangers who should not know our business, about her bad day and how upset she was at work. They'll sympathise with her and wonder whether she is strong enough to work in the Special Care Baby Unit. I prefer the hard-faced ones. It plays down the tragedy – makes it somehow nearly acceptable. Count the tubes…watch the lights…bleep bleep bleep bleep…I can't remember why they've taped her eyelids closed.

Bleep, bleep, bleep…

…ring…ring…ring.

Ring her phone again. Yes try again and then again. Four sets of four. If I do this thing her phone will ring:

07741017811 07741017811 07741017811 07741017811

07741017811 07741017811 07741017811 07741017811

07741017811 07741017811 07741017811 07741017811

07741017811 07741017811 07741017811 07741017811

Connect… "Hi. You've got through to Maria. Sorry I can't

take your call at the moment, but I'm obviously having too much fun to answer. If you'd like to leave a message after the tone, I'll get back to you when the fun's finished. Bye!" *Bleep*.

Disconnect..
....
....

I've left four messages. She must have got them. Scrunch, crunch, scrunch. Come on Mouse make that gravely crunch. If I make it rhyme she'll come home on time...

What must I do, I don't have a clue.
My God how I hate to sit here and wait.
Gripping on tight
trying to fight
my imagination
source of dark creation...No.
I don't want to go to that terrible foe
but in a scary cold place – it squats – it waits.
Maria. I love you. Maria. Where are you?
The dark place cracks
it grins at me,
"I'd like to invite you in to tea.
There's a very special delicacy
something we'll share just you and me...
Perhaps a bit broken.
Perhaps a bit bloody.
She's been dragged through the dirt
now her hair is all muddy.
Perhaps a bit twisted.
Perhaps a bit torn,
She's been used and abused
by a drunk with the horn.
She tried hard to scream.

She tried hard to fight.
But he was ever so big
and she ever so slight.
His calloused crude hands stank of fags and beer
as he wrung out the life of the one you hold dear.
Oh dear! Oh dear! Who's in the house?
I don't think it's poor little Maria Mouse".

No. Don't do this to yourself. No. Mustn't do it…mustn't do it. Stop. Now. 10:03. Where can she be? Make it rhyme and she'll come home on time…I'll count to ten 1,2,3,4,5,6,7,8,9,10, then I'll do it again 1,2,3,4,5,6,7,8,9,10. What's wrong with her phone? Phone…phone…Tara. She's with Tara…always with Tara. Where's the number, number, number, number. There got you. Here we go…433959… … No. Disconnect, quick disconnect. Doesn't feel good, doesn't feel right. Four sets of four and she'll be at Tara's house or Tara's mum will know something…Dial…

433959 433959 433959 433959
433959 433959 433959 433959
433959 433959 433959 433959
433959 433959 433959 433959…*Now ring…*

Come on pick up…
"Hello."
"Good evening. Can I speak to, umm, Linda please?"
"Speaking."
"Oh, this is Maria's mum. I'm sorry to bother you, but I don't suppose Maria's there is she?" Please let her be there. Mouse, please be there…
"Sorry? Who?"
"Maria's mother; I need to find her, is she there?" Come on…come on…
"Mrs. Taylor?" Ah! Finally the penny drops.

"Yes, is Maria there please?"

"No, no I'm sorry…Maria isn't here." This is wrong. Not the answer I want at all. "Is everything alright Mrs. Taylor?"

"Yes, no, I mean no. She was meant to be home by now and I'm getting a bit worried. Is Tara there?"

"No. She's out with some friends." Speak up woman, I can hardly hear you.

"Perhaps Maria is with them." She must be, mustn't she? Oh Mouse. Why aren't you there?

"Yes, perhaps she is." She doesn't sound too sure.

"What time are you expecting Tara home?"

"Oh, I don't know. She usually comes home around eleven or twelve on a Saturday night." What! Is this woman insane? She's asking for trouble. I can't believe how irresponsible some parents are; makes you wonder how much these people really love their children! Oh God. So late. What do I say?

"It's just that I was expecting Maria home at eight-thirty and I rather worry about her. She's small, fragile." She thinks I'm an idiot, but I don't care, I just want my Mouse.

"Oh." Is this all she can say? What's wrong with this woman? She sounds confused, drunk even.

"She's only fifteen and a half." But I haven't got time to give her a lesson on good parenting. I've got to find my Mouse. Silence… … "Well, would you mind calling me if you hear anything?" The least she can do.

"Yes of course…Mrs Taylor?"

"Yes?"

"…Nothing…goodnight."

"Thank you, yes, goodnight." Disconnect. Goodnight? Yes, a very good night.

Maria, and in fact Tara, could be lying dead in a ditch for all that awful woman cares. Okay. Calm down. I need a drink to help me think. Yes, just one glass. One glass of wine and I'll feel just fine. 10:05 and a glass of wine, and then my

Mouse will come home on time. Go in the kitchen, open the bottle, slow, slow, don't rush. Find a glass and pour…not too generous.

Kitchen, glass, wine – red or white?

Red: passion, sex, danger, depression…blood.

White: Light, pure, summer, happy.

Red…a Merlot, fruity but not happy. First sip…Oh so good! But doesn't feel quite right. Four sips…just small sips. Four sets of four. Empty glass. Damn. Just one more. Two glasses are okay. Sip slowly…slow, slow, quick, quick, slow. Here in the kitchen I can't hear the scrunch – perhaps it's best. Less torture.

Red: passion, sex, danger, depression, blood…blood. Blood. Dark and thick. Like a freshly opened vein. Pungent. Iron. Enlivens every sense whilst you are dying. Taste, touch, smell. Smell. Iron and sweat. And fear. I don't need the scars to remind me.

Two little incubators sitting in a tree
K – I – S – S – I – N – G.

Two little incubators in the S.C.U.
No one knows just what to do.

Two little incubators make a sorry sight.
The parents pray from dawn till night.

Two plastic oysters. Two little pearls.
Just tiny, fragile, preemie girls.

Two little skeletons – wearing over-sized, but tiny nappies and stockinet hats. Two little skeletons – loosely clothed in fragile folds of muscle and skin. Pink tissue paper hanging from chicken bones. Masks and tubes and monitors. Screens and lights and blips and buttons. Hot, sterile, bright.

Yet another day in the S.C.U.
But now one incubator where there were two.

Drink the wine and you'll feel fine. Rich – heavy. The blood of Christ. In heaven with baby Jesus. Baby Bethany…such a large name for a tiny, tiny frame. Bethany and baby Jesus…like Bethlehem and baby Jesus.

She was always inside a vessel. Swirl the wine, whirl the wine. Always inside a vessel from start to finish. First inside me – flesh – warm – thriving; then inside a plastic incubator – warm – but dying; then inside a wooden box – cold. Full stop. Her only destination, a white box – so small. So sad. The smallest, saddest thing. White – not so happy. That frilly doll's dress…nothing else to fit her. Frilly, starched, Victorian – dead. Dead cold. No blanket to keep her warm. Drink the wine and you'll feel fine.

"Another my dear?"

"Well, I shouldn't really, but seeing as you're offering."

Such a beautiful sunny day to wear black, blue skies and sun, dreadfully at odds with the tears and genuine condolences for the parents of the dead baby. I don't understand this day – but I understand the night. So cold, so full of shadows and dark corners – so long and so bitterly cold. I beat myself. She's all alone in the graveyard – no mummy or daddy near to calm and ease her fear.

How can I leave my baby alone in such a dreadful place? So far away and in a flimsy little dress. No jacket, little ski-suit or blanket to keep her warm.

White – white and red. Large heavy drops – red on red they fall almost silently. Ssh! You'll wake the baby! Pat, pat, pat – I watch the drops as they join the rivulets which flow down the sink and into the plug hole. I watch the black–blue blood run onto white – dark, thick, heavy from a dark blue vein. Blue on blue, red on white. I watch – until I can't watch anymore.

We are a tragedy. I sense that the young nurse is watching me. I know that this scene is breaking her heart and that she's trying to be professional, but if I look up I know I'll see tears in her eyes.

Too much wine. Three glasses too much. Down the drain…drain away like life blood…red on red, red on white, red on silver. Tonight I won't float on my ocean without motion, for Maria Mouse is not in the house! 10:10, how can five minutes pass in five seconds, and an hour and a half take half a lifetime? Take half a lifetime away.

I wish Dougie were here. He should be here right now. I can lean on Dougie. He makes everything okay, or at least seem okay even when it's not. Dougie, you're so strong and I'm so weak. Is it fair that you always have to take care of me…us…me? Broad shouldered over-burdened Dougie. Happy. Dougie makes me happy. Whenever I look at the photo on the fridge door I feel happy. Happy, happy, happy. The three of us together, smiling together, happy together. Together forever. On the fridge door. Forever on photographic paper…together safe and secure in the rigid enclosure of the magnetic plastic photo frame. A little present from me to Mouse for 'Delightful Daughter Day'. We have lots of those. We'll have another tomorrow.... … …

"He's looking at you."

"No, he's looking at you…I think."

"Well, I have to admit it's rather hard to tell exactly who he's looking at with those eyes."

"What do you mean?"

"Well, he's got one eye in the spit and the other up the chimney!"

I choke on my drink. "Eva…for goodness sake! I don't believe you sometimes," But I think he's delicious. Tall and blond. Muscled and tanned. Yes, he does have one dodgy eye;

it's darker than the other and tends to go off a little in its own direction. This gives him a certain air, no not exactly an air, but it does something for him, makes him look…interesting, sexy even. Yet, now that he's talking to me, I'm not exactly sure which eye to look at. Later, he tells me that he'd actually been eyeing up my friend. What irony, I think. And I don't mind, we laugh, we're in love and I'm expecting twins. Life is marvellous.

Mouse looks like Dougie. She's blonde and tans easily. She has a feminine version of his strong chin and cheekbones, and she has his bright blue eye, well Mouse has two bright blue eyes. Beautiful with full long lashes. She laughs easily, and seeing good in people comes naturally to her. People love her for it, she makes them become good. She's a good girl. Everyone loves her. Loved by all at school…she will be sorely missed…stop it, she's coming, she'll be home soon. Make it rhyme, she'll come home on time…count to ten 1,2,3,4,5,6,7,8,9,10, then do it again 1,2,3,4,5,6,7,8,9,10. She'll put her key in the door, just like before…

The kitchen window. So dark outside. One large blind eye that throws the face of a hag back at me. Desperate, crazed…aged. Is that how Dougie sees me too?

Don't be gone! Sigh, cry, die – but don't lie!
All in the bedroom is clean, scrubbed and new,
except there's only one cot where there used to be two.

Don't die, be strong: grow big and sleep and eat and breathe. Grow strong, don't die, keep breathing. Are you still breathing? Breathe. Mm, baby smell. New skin, baby skin, talc. Mm. Hold her tight, breathe in deeply. An innocent smell, pure, new…love. Love me and I'll love you. Soft downy hair. Baby soft skin. Hold her tight…not too tight. Breathe her in. Mm. Is she still breathing? Soft breath, baby breath. Soft sweet. Baby murmurs. Tiny sounds. Sweet sounds. Touch her small round head. Watch her tiny chest. In, out, in, out. Mm. Baby smell. Breathe her in, is she still breathing?

Scary. First night home. So small...so scary. I understand the night, so full of shadows and dark corners – so long. Her corner is light, baby light, night light, pull the string, stars and light and music and light – twinkle, twinkle little star, how I wonder what you are. Big cot. Dougie made the cots...Dougie made two cots. Big cot, too big, and such a small baby. Big cot, rocking cot, wooden cot – cot death. No! Stop it! Touch her head, softly. Ssh don't wake the baby! Ssh brush her forehead softly with my finger. Soft, soft...soft, soft. Four sets of four and she'll make it until morning. No, not enough, four times four sets of four. Brush one, brush two, brush three, brush four, br...

"What are you doing?"

"Nothing."

"Come to bed, she'll be fine. She's okay, relax."

"Okay," I'm smiling. But it's not okay. I have to finish my four times four sets of four; she won't be fine if I don't do the fours. Got to get out of bed – Dougie hugs me, strokes my hair. Go to sleep Dougie. Sleep, Dougie, sleep, then out of the bed I'll creep. Four times four sets of four – stoke her head, that's better. Dougie sleeps like a baby – I don't. Leave her alone now; come on back to bed...Okay sorry, I'm coming. Sleep Dougie, dream Dougie, sleep.

10:11. Seven, Devon, eleven, seven, heaven... hell...bloody hell...living hell. Are you alive? Are you okay? Please ring me to let me know you are safe. Please come home Mouse, I can't wait any longer. Where are you? Why don't you call? Please come home Mouse... please...Watch the hag in the window because she watches you. You watch me and I watch you, watch and wait what else to do?

The hag in the window smiles at me,
"I'd like to invite you in to tea.
I have a special delicacy
something we'll share just you and me.
Perhaps a bit bloody.
Perhaps a bit blue.
There's a hole in her thigh
where a fox had a chew.
Her dead eyes are fixed
A death mask of fright.
She's been taunted, used, beaten
for most of the night.
You stared out of the window.
You drank lots of wine.
Whilst your poor little mouse
had a really bad time."

She's missed the bus or fallen asleep at a friend's house. She'll come home in a minute, her face full of concern for me: "I'm so sorry Mummy, I forgot the time." I won't be angry. My relief will be too great for anger. In fact, I could never be angry with Mouse. Well, except for that one time.

I'll hug her so tight, and she'll hug me back. Mummy and Mouse. I love you Mummy, I love you too Mouse. Breathe her in. Breathe, breathe. Such soft hair. Soft baby hair…breathe, breathe, watch and check every five minutes that her little chest is going up and down…that she's still breathing…

Count to ten 1,2,3,4,5,6,7,8,9,10, then do it again 1,2,3,4,5,6,7,8,9,10.

Ten Possible Reasons Why Mouse is Late

1. She's missed the bus.
2. She's fallen asleep at a friend's house.

3. She has simply forgotten the time.

4. She has lost her mobile and is looking for it now.

5. She's talking outside with friends.

6. She has a secret boyfriend and is with him. *Shudder.* (I'll forgive her if she has, although this isn't a possibility as we don't have secrets.)

7. One of her friends is in trouble and she's helping them.

8. She's in trouble.... ....

9. Can't think anymore.

10. Can't think anymore.

Where is she? Mouse where are you?

"You think that you're such a good mother – but you don't even know where your daughter is!" The hag in the black window wags a finger at me.

"Sorry?"

"Naughty, naughty, naughty…did you ask your fifteen year old daughter where she was going before she left the house?" I hate the hag.

"No, but…"

"But what? What possible excuse can you have?" I really hate the hag.

"We're best friends. Love, trust, that sort of thing…I trust her and I know that she is honest with me. She has never given me any reason to mistrust her." The hag makes me fume. My heart. It pumps and runs the blood through my vein and into my brain – implode – explode. I loathe the hag, I want to pick up the toaster, the kettle, something, and throw it through her face – smashing her into a million pieces.

"I'd still be here though." She smiles. "Shall we have another glass of wine?"

Sip it slowly. Slow, slow, little sips. Not too quickly, no. This bottle must last until Mouse comes home. This bottle will last – mm, I think…I can just…get…one more glass out of it.... there we are. Now, four sets of four – but tiny, tiny sips. Count to ten 1,2,3,4,5,6,7,8,9,10, then do it again 1,2,3,4,5,6,7,8,9,10. Have a drink it will help me think.

<u>Ten Places Mouse Could Be</u>

1. Tara's house. (No. Tara's mum said that she wasn't there, and if she turns up she'll ring me.)
2. The youth club. (I know she sometimes goes there.)
3. The park. (I hope not.)
4. Possibly the cinema. (She had some money.)
5. Ice-skating. (Her new hobby and latest dream. She wants to be a professional figure skater; I think she's starting a bit late, but what do I know? No, she can't be there, she didn't take her skates out with her.)
6. A different friend's house. (Possible, she's a popular girl.)
7. A secret boyfriend's house. *Shudder.* (Not possible, we don't have secrets.)
8. At the shopping centre. (Possible, it's late night closing on Saturdays.)
9. In the town centre. (No, she doesn't go there in the evenings.)
10. In danger. (No…no…no…I refuse to let my imagination go there… I try not to go there…)

Tara's house…no, youth club…maybe…could… possibly be. *The Yellow Pages*. Yes, run to find it. Excitement, activity, adrenalin…I can do something! In the lounge, here we are, in the cupboard under the phone. Got to catch a mouse…no, find my baby. Okay, let's go. Recreational centres and youth clubs. Gottcha. S. Follow my fingernail down the S column. Long, strong fingernail. Okay, here we have it. Stour Street Youth Club: 413920. Four sets of four, damn, don't want to do it, but have to, and have to do it well. Put the receiver down quickly before it connects. Have to make it okay. Four sets of four and she'll be there:

413920 413920 413920 413920
413920 413920 413920 413920
413920 413920 413920 413920
413920 413920 413920 413920. *Connect…*

"Yeah?"

"Good evening. Is this the Stour Street Youth Club?"

"Yeah." Not helpful – let's see if we can elicit any words with more than one syllable. "I'm looking for someone and I was wondering if you could help me."

"Um, dunno," A sentence would be good. "We're closing soon."

"Is it possible to speak to someone in charge, please?"

"Like who?" Please. Why this torture? I just want my Mouse. Deep breath. Breathe, breathe…just keep breathing. Is Maria still breathing?

"I don't know, a youth worker, someone responsible – the person who locks up!"

"Oh, that'll be Andy."

"Well, can I speak to Andy please?"

"He's just popped out for a bag of chips." Great! Try anyway, keep trying.

"Well, maybe you can help me. Do you know Maria Taylor? I'm her mother and I really need to speak with her."

"Ma-ria Tay-lor…" Could he say the name more slowly? "Umm, let me think." This boy's mental process – it grinds and grates on me – such unused cogs turning slowly for lack of practice. Cogs turning slowly, cogs inside a clock. The clock on the wall opposite me ticks 10:22 and I need to find you. The second hand moves on…tick, tock…and on…tick, tock…no tick brings Maria closer to me…

"Yes. Maria Taylor." Must I really repeat everything? "She's petite, pretty, with long blonde hair."

"Oh, there are lots of those here – curvy, yeah lovely, what's petite?"

"She's small. Look...is Maria Taylor there?" No, I just can't stand this anymore – she could be trying to get through while I'm wasting my time with this oaf. I resist the impulse to smash down the phone. Tick, tock, tick, tock.

"Yeah, hang on...I think she's here. Yo! Jake, is that Maria over there? Eh? Wait a mo." Come on, come on...

"Maria. That's Maria over there right? Maria!" He shouts, he calls her. She's there! Oh my God. Relief. What relief. My little Mouse is there. Thank God. Thank you! Relief. My baby, my Mouse, I've found her. She's alive – she's okay. "Yo! Maria. Ya mum's on the phone." My baby, my baby – my small, small Mouse. She's safe...she'll soon be back in the house. Thank you, thank you. I'll go and get her straight away; I don't want her walking the streets now, not at this time, not in the dark. Hang on. I've drunk too much. I'll call for a taxi to pick her up – I'll pay when it arrives. I won't be angry with her I'll-

"What do you want? Why the hell are you ringing me here? Has dad gone off on one again....?"

"Maria? I wanted to speak to Maria."

"I am Maria – who are you?" Spinning, spinning, spinning...out of control – no control. All black – falling can't breathe. 1,2,3,4, 1,2,3,4, 1,2,3,4, 1,2,3,4.

"Maria Taylor." Gasping. Can't breathe. "I want to speak to Maria Taylor." My voice sounds frantic, strange – not me. I'm screaming – am I screaming? Hysterical.

"Sorry Mrs. I don't know her." *Disconnect.*

Maria Mouse, Maria Mouse. Hickory dickory, hickory dickory. Where's my Mouse – she's not in the house. Make it rhyme and she'll come home on time. Count to ten 1,2,3,4,5,6,7,8,9,10, and then do it again 1,2,3,4,5,6,7,8,9,10. Wine, wine, have some wine and then I'll feel fine.

In the kitchen, we all pitch in. Dougie do the dishes, Maria you can dry. I spy a broken glass. Who did it? Come on – own up! "I did it, Mum." I know that it was Dougie – but Mouse loves her dad. Dougie carries me; Maria carries Dougie – who carries Maria? I know that they know that I know that no one is angry and no one is guilty – it's only a wine glass. Secretly I'm am a little irritated as it's one of four, a special collection. They won't be in the shops again. I don't mention it. Worse things happen... ... ...

Is the glass empty already? Maria's not home and I've finished the bottle. Not good, not good. A Merlot. Another bottle of the same. So it doesn't count, it's like drinking one big bottle.

"Liar."

Should I close the kitchen blinds? Block out the hag. "No, you shouldn't. One should never drink on one's own." She's right.

"Cheers hag!"

"Cheers to you too, hag!"

"Oh, by the way, I've got something to say, something I should mention – well really a question."

"What's that?"

"Where is Mouse?"

Look at the clock, dickory dock. 10:23. Oh, where could she be? She could be at the park, but it's ever so dark.

"You could drive down and take a look."

"Yes, I'll do that, good idea."

"But you've had too much to drink. You can't drive in that condition you silly thing." She's right...she's always right. And I'm always wrong.

"Yes...such a shame that you can't drive down there. After all, there's that scary wood behind the park too. If it's scary by day, I can't imagine what it must be like at night. Oh, but I can. Wouldn't want to be a young girl alone in there. If you hadn't drunk so much, you could have gone down there and saved her, no, I mean looked for her."

"I'm not drunk." Just guilty. "Anyway, Mouse isn't stupid; she'd never go into those woods."

"Well no – not willingly…"

Chills, down my spine, all of the time. Can't feel my hands, can't feel my feet. Feeling so sick – quick, quick, run – bathroom quick.

"… … … Dear God!" It drips from my lips. Red, red like life's blood. Pale red, watery red, red on white – acid, acrid – blood wine, stomach wine. Wine from my gut, gut feeling, gut instinct, mother's instinct.

Red: passion, sex, danger, depression…blood.

Red on red on white. It drips from my lips…Where's the towel? Wipe my face. Can't clean my teeth, have to do it four times four, takes too long. The hag in the bathroom mirror looks at me – she smiles, a thin empty smile, which doesn't reach her eyes.

"Well, that got rid of some of it! Ready for a top-up?" Feel ill, feel bad. Water…cool, clear.

10:26. The clock in the kitchen blinks at me – it's blinking and flashing furiously. Wake up. Move. Do something. But what can I do? Water, cool, clear my head. Drink…

(A typical child's bedroom. Pink. There's a soft glow, a mother is bending over a child who is lying in a bed in the centre of the room.)

CHILD: Mummy, can I have some water please?

MUMMY: Yes, here you are darling, little sips, that's right. How are you feeling?

CHILD: A bit better now.

MUMMY: Here let me straighten your covers. Chicken pox eh?

CHILD: I'm so spotty.

MUMMY: You're so beautiful. Now sleepy-bye, apple pie. Night, night Mouse.

CHILD: Mummy?

MUMMY: Yes darling?

CHILD: Tell me a story first.
MUMMY: Okay, which story would you like?
CHILD: My favourite; the one about my name.
MUMMY: Maria?
CHILD: No silly Mummy. You always tease. The one
           about the mouse, and how I got my name.
MUMMY: Okay then.

(The mother sits down on the bed, whilst the child wriggles into a comfortable position for the story.)

You were only a little baby. Tiny. You came into the world a little bit too early. You weren't really ready for the world, but it was ready for you. There were many doctors and nurses waiting to look after you, and a mummy and daddy already full of love. You stayed in hospital for a long time while the doctors made you strong and ready to come home.

(Pause. The mother strokes the child's hair tenderly as the child fidgets in anticipation of the rest of the story.)

You were so, so small. So fragile. We had to look after you very carefully. But your mummy and daddy were worried. We kept hearing a squeak; this squeaking noise that wouldn't go away. So we thought that there was a mouse in the house, and we kept looking and looking, high and low and low and high until…*(mother smiles lovingly at child),* we realised that it had been you making the squeaking sound all the time. You see, you were so teeny, so small and you weren't very strong. Instead of crying like a baby does, when you wanted your milk or a cuddle from your mummy, you made a little squeak like a mouse. So, we started calling you Mouse, because you had been that little mouse squeaking in the house.

CHILD: Squeak, squeak.
(The mother hugs the child and they laugh together.)
CHILD: Night night Mummy.

TOGETHER: Night night, sleep tight, don't let the bed
                     bugs bite; dream about the fairies.
CHILD: I love you Mummy.
MUMMY: I love you too Mouse.

(The mother leans over the child, kisses her on the forehead, and exits. Lights dim.)

Her legs and her arms are somehow skewiff.
She's bent at odd angles,
she's somehow adrift.
Adrift, but a gift would perhaps compensate,
for making Maria so dreadfully late.
What gift do we get after passionate hours?
A phone number, some chocolates, a large bunch of
flowers.
A small diamond ring would suit many young girls
but Maria's new beau left a choker of pearls.
A choker of black pearls embraces her throat,
but this type of gift would not make a girl gloat.
A host of these gems left this generous lover,
her stomach, chest, limbs have this bluish-black cover.
But mostly it's blood, thick red on her thighs.
It's matted her hair and it's dripped from her eyes.
Small gifts from the choker who really did choke-her.
Whose monstrous embrace, mangled, mauled and then
broke her.

Damned imagination…source of dark creation. Broke her?
Broke me – *is* breaking me. The clock in the kitchen blinks at
me – it's blinking and flashing furiously. Wake up. Move. Do
something. But what can I do?

"We'll wait as one, you and I, if we whisper together we
won't hear her cry…Another drink?"

"Okay, just a small one."… … …It's breaking me. Beating

me, breaking me. Break, break, break. Something is breaking in my brain. Breaking me, beating me. Am I going insane? "Ring...ring..." break...break..."ring...ring"...break... break "ring...ring". What? The phone...it's Mouse...it's Mouse. Mouse. Run, run. "Ring, ring". Quick, run ring run ring run.

"Mouse?"

"No love, it's Dougie. What's going on?" Dougie? What? I was sure it was Mouse. Can't be Dougie, he's working.

"Dougie? I thought you were Mouse. Oh Dougie, Dougie, it's Mouse, she hasn't come home, she's ever so late Dougie. I've been waiting for ages and I'm so worried about her. She hasn't rung. Nothing! Dougie, what shall we do? This isn't like her. Dougie what shall we do? Nearly two hours late. Dougie, shall I call the police?"

"Slow down babes, slow down. Don't do anything – just sit tight and I'll be home in about ten minutes. Okay?" Oh Dougie, I love you. Here we are again. You take over, you make it all okay. My poor Dougie. Broad shouldered over-burdened Dougie. I already feel better. Okay now...I can think.

"But how come you're on your way home? I thought you were working late tonight."

"I was love, but Tara's mum called and..."

"Tara's mum? Is Mouse there?" Mouse is at Tara's house!

"No love, she's not. Now, slow down. She rang because she was worried about you. Now relax, make a cup of tea and I'll be home in ten minutes. Sit tight and wait for me. Okay?"

"Okay...love you, Dougie."

"Love you too, babes."

Okay. Good. Dougie is on his way and everything will be okay. Back in ten minutes. Good, good. What's the time? 10:30. Already 10:30. Mouse, you're two hours late. I said half past eight! You are ever so late. But this isn't like you, Mouse, you're never late. Never ever late! That's why I'm so worried. That's why I'm going crazy. This is not like you. Did someone prevent you coming home?

Call her again: just in case she picks up. Ring her phone. Yes, try again. Four sets of four. If I do this thing her phone will ring…and this time she'll answer…

07741017811 07741017811 07741017811 07741017811

07741017811 07741017811 07741017811 07741017811

07741017811 07741017811 07741017811 07741017811

07741017811 07741017811 07741017811 07741017811

Connect… "Hi. You've got through to Maria. Sorry I can't take your call at the moment, but I'm obviously having too much fun to answer. If you'd like to leave a message after the tone, I'll get back to you when the fun's finished. Bye!" *Bleep*.

"Maria, it's Mum again. Please, please pick up, I'm so very worried about you darling. I hope everything's alright. Please, please call me. I'm waiting, Maria. Call me. I love you."

I tell her all the time to keep her mobile close by, to keep it switched on, and to keep it where she can hear it. I'm always telling her. So why is it turned off? I don't understand. Maybe the battery is dead. I don't know. I don't really understand mobiles. Maria does all the settings on my phone. I was embarrassed the other day in Tesco when my phone rang with the music from *Star Wars*. Yes, that's it. It's her phone. It's broken, something's wrong with it. She'd have called by now otherwise; she wouldn't make me suffer. But then why doesn't she call me on a friend's mobile? Don't think. Don't worry. Don't think. Dougie will be home soon. Ten minutes he said. Just ten minutes to wait and all will be fine. Dougie will do something to make it right.

Make a cup of tea. Kitchen, cups…cups for tea. I get two mugs not three.

"That's his way of saying stop drinking," the hag tells me.

"I know that!"

"But you could still fit in one more before he comes." She's looking at me. Tempting me. Trying to tempt me.

That's it; I've had enough of you. Blinds down; clack, clack, clack – shut the hag out. "But you know I'll come back," her voice rings in my head.

Kettle on. Mugs ready. I'll drink tea for you Dougie. Kettle on, mugs, sugar…one for me, two for you. Tea bags, where are you? There you are, in the pot – the way Dougie likes it. Mouse isn't fussy – she puts the teabag straight into the mug, milk and sugar too. Milk, sugar, water, and teabag, she mixes it all together– "It tastes the same," she says.

Yes, feeling better, much better. Dougie will come, and then Mouse will come and all will be fine again. Have a nice cup of tea. Milk, fridge, fridge…photo!

"You know I'm still here," she whispers softly in my ear. "I still can't believe that you still can't see, that you'll never, ever be rid of me."

Mummy and Daddy sitting in a tree,
K – I – S – S – I – N – G

Three in the family, as happy as can be,
Mummy, Daddy and Mouse makes three.

A small but cheery family, nestled in a frame,
sunshine and light: then darkness came.

This bright little group, a sunny solid crew,
a dark cloud passed and then there were two.

A Mummy and a Daddy sitting in a tree,
but the kids are in the cemetery.

"Is that all you've got, hag? Tut, tut. It's not very good is it? I thought you could do much better than that!" I'm okay, I'm strong. Dougie will be home soon. "Ha, and then what you will do? Nothing I suspect." Silence. "You don't like it when Dougie's around do you?" Silence. 10:34. Dougie will come soon, and then Mouse, and then we'll all be safe and happy together inside our photo frame, no, house. Tick, tock, tick, tock, tick, tock. Click. Kettle. I won't pour yet. Wait for Dougie, don't want it to stew. If I wait Mouse will come and then I can put in a teabag for her too.

"Hi Mum, I'm back. Gosh, I'm starving!" She throws her bag and coat on the sofa. "What's to eat?"

"Bacon sandwich?" I pick up her things, and put them where they should be.

"Mm. Sounds good...there wouldn't be a nice cup of tea going with that too?"

"Oh, I think I can rustle you one up."

"Thanks Mum, you're a star!"

Fridge, photo. Let's have a look. There's bacon, good. I've got some fresh bread. All set for when she comes. She does like to be spoilt...

(A typical teenage girl's room. Pink. There are posters of pop stars and ice-skaters on the walls. There's a soft glow in the room. A young girl is sitting up in bed. The mother is standing next to the bed, hands on hips in mock anger.)

YOUNG GIRL: *(Licking her fingers.)* Mm Mum...that was just so good!

MOTHER: I spoil you too much Maria.

YOUNG GIRL: Oh, don't call me Maria; it sounds like you're angry with me.

MOTHER: I'm ruining you…Mouse.

YOUNG GIRL: You don't believe that for a second.

MOTHER: No, you're right, I don't. You're my baby and I love you; you deserve spoiling…you're a good mouse.

YOUNG GIRL: So it's supper in bed tomorrow then?

MOTHER: Don't push your luck!

YOUNG GIRL: I know I'm lucky; there aren't many mothers who would make breakfast in bed for their daughters at 9 o'clock at night.

MOTHER: Half-past nine! And, there aren't many mothers who still tuck their fifteen year old daughters into bed at night.

YOUNG GIRL: (Giggling.) Ssh…that's our secret. But you love it as much as I do.

MOTHER: Ssh…that's our secret too!

(Both laugh, whilst the mother straightens the covers and tucks the sheets in.)

YOUNG GIRL: Night night Mum.

MOTHER: Night my love.

TOGETHER: Night night, sleep tight, don't let the bed bugs bite; dream about the fairies.

YOUNG GIRL: I love you Mum.

MUMMY: I love you too Mouse.

(The mother leans over the young girl, kisses her on the forehead, takes the empty cup and plate then exits. Lights dim.)

"Mm this is so cosy." Mm yes…snuggled up with Dougie on the sofa in front of the TV. We never seem to have a lot of time together recently, him and me, not quality time anyway. Passing, pausing for a quick kiss, he's on his way out – I'm on my way in. He often comes home late from work; it appears that everybody in the world needs a carpenter at the moment. So cosy here with Dougie – good telly tonight too. But where's Mouse?

"Dougie...where's Mouse?" He's watching telly, only half listening.

"Dunno babes." I feel a little anxious.

"I haven't seen her for ages Dougie! Where can she be?"

"She's probably in the kitchen getting the milk and biscuits ready for Rudolph." Yes, maybe he's right.

"I'll just go and check."

"No you don't." Dougie pulls me back down into the sofa and his arms. "Leave her alone for five minutes babe – give her a bit of space." What does he mean by that? Who am I kidding? I know exactly what he means. Sit back, relax – telly's good tonight...I wonder where she is though, just can't help myself. She's taking a long time to pour a bit of milk into a saucer and select a couple of biscuits. Must get up and check. I can't relax anymore, useless even trying.

"I'm just going to the loo." Dougie raises an eyebrow. I pretend not to see.

"Mouse?" She's not in the kitchen.

"Mouse?" The toilet is free.

"Mouse?" She's not in her bedroom either. Panic is beginning to bunch in my stomach. Where is she? There's only our room – and she's got no reason to be in there...or has she?

"Maria!" She turns – caught in the act; her small face is a picture of guilt and horror. Discarded wrapping paper, boxes and toys surround her; a Barbie doll is in her arms. How did she find those? Oh Maria how could you? You've ruined everything! I cross the room in two strides, *crack*, my hand slaps her, too hard, across the face. Oh my God! We stare at each other. Both in shock. Neither of us can believe what has just happened...what I've just done. I can already see the impression of my hand, angry, furious, bright red, bright red on white. Her bottom lip begins to tremble and tears spill silently from her eyes. "Mouse,"…there's no words, what can I say? "Mouse, I'm so sorry!" How can I even begin to explain myself? I didn't want Christmas ruined for her; for her to find the presents before Father Christmas could have delivered them. I want her to still believe in the magic of Christmas…of Father Christmas. I wanted to watch her face as she opened all of her carefully chosen presents – see the excitement, hear her squeals of pleasure. How can I explain this to a six year old? I want, I want, I want. I'm on my knees and crying, begging her "Mouse…I'm so, so sorry." In silence she pushes past me, running full speed into the lounge and into Dougie's ever ready embrace.

Dougie's furious with me. He's going to talk to me later, when Mouse is asleep. He'll reprimand me, parent to child. He's very angry…but he won't slap me across the face, not like I did to Mouse. For now, neither acknowledges my presence. Exiled I tidy the bedroom, re-wrap the presents, cry…guilt ridden and rejected I sit on the bed…cry. Happy Christmas!

MOTHER: I'm so sorry Mouse. I really am.

CHILD: Mummy, don't worry. It doesn't matter anymore.

MOTHER: I still feel so awful. Mouse…

CHILD: Mummy, it was two Christmases ago. Now forget about it. Come on. *(Pulling the mother into the kitchen.)* Let's get Rudolph's supper ready.

I've told you a million times, and if you come through the door now, I'll tell you a million times more how sorry I am. I know that it irritates you; I know you've forgiven me…but I haven't forgiven myself.

Did I pour the water? Hope not, the tea will stew. No, pot

empty all okay. 10:38 I hope that Dougie won't be late. Okay. Everything ready for tea, Dougie, me and Mouse makes three.

"I'd like to invite you in for tea

I have a special delicacy."

"No you don't!" I'm strong, I'm okay. Dougie's coming now. Into the lounge, sit on the sofa. No, not on the edge! Sit back, look around. Breathe slowly; try to calm down before he comes. I love it, my lounge, so sunny, warm, pastel colours. I'm smiling down at myself from every available space on the wall. Above the televison I smile down at me, my arms linked with Mouse and Mickey Mouse at Euro Disney. Dougie, Mouse and me, happy, looking so smart at a cousin's wedding. Dougie and Mouse; even blonder, even browner, even happier lounging by the pool in Tenerife. From every wall and every shelf, we look down at me. We smile out happily at anyone who cares to look in. Look at us, the perfect family. Put in a frame to show you how happy we are; put in a frame to remember. Picture this, picture this family, we make such a pretty picture, picture perfect. We are happy. Many families pretend they get along, because they have to. We don't, we are a happy family. We don't have to pretend at anything. Come on, try not to be smug; but it's difficult not to be. I'm a very lucky woman. So lucky…I hope I'm still lucky. Why hasn't Mouse rung? Where is she? Where are you Mouse? In a frame we are always happy. There are only good pictures in a frame…The bad ones stay inside, hidden within. Those pictures aren't taken with a camera – snapshots, memories we don't want to remember.

"If you'd like to take a picture, cut a wisp of hair – I'm afraid she hasn't got long. I'll leave you alone with her now. Please…take your time." The nurse pauses, I think she wants to say something; she raises her hands slightly, but then drops them. There's nothing left to say. Oh Dougie, don't let go of my hand. But I suppose you must, to take the picture, cut a wisp of hair…No, I can't watch you lean over the incubator…turn away…can't turn away…careful, don't lean too heavily, you'll tip it up…turn away…flash, snip. Put it all away – somewhere safe, but out of sight – like her baby body. The only picture not to make it into a frame. It's ironic that I look at this picture the most; a daily resurrection from its well thumbed, well worn plastic envelope.

It's okay…I'm okay, Dougie's coming. I feel strong. When Dougie comes we'll find Mouse, Dougie always knows what to do. 10:39. I know he'll come on time. Crunch, scrunch, crunch, scrunch. "Do you hear it?" It's heavy, it's brisk, it's Dougie.

"Dougie!" run to him, rush to him, run rush run rush. "Oh, Dougie," hold him tight, tight, tight.

"Hey, slow down love, you nearly knocked me flying!" Tell him all, explain everything, he'll sort it out, he'll make it fine, he'll find Mouse, and bring her home.

"Dougie – Mouse is so, so late, over two hours, I said half past eight Dougie – but she's ever so late. Why hasn't she called me? Dougie this isn't like her, something bad has happened, I just know it. Dougie, what shall we do?"

"Okay, love, okay." Such a gentle voice Dougie – gentle voice, gentle face. "Here, sit on the sofa, that's right, sit down and slow down." Dougie, I know you'll make it right. But why are you kneeling down like that. You can't be proposing – we're already married. This is not the time Dougie!"

"Dougie?"

"Ssh." His finger against my lips, ssh, be quiet, ssh. I'll be silent Dougie. Just take charge, and I'll do what you say. Make it better, Dougie. He's on his knee in front of me holding my hands as if in prayer. He can't be proposing. Now? At this moment? Too bizarre. I don't understand or like this situation…I really don't think I like it. "You have to listen to me love," nod, listen, keep nodding, keep listening, "you have to listen really well…can you do that for me?" Nod, yes okay, keep nodding, yes I can do that for you Dougie.

"Yes Dougie." What's going on, is it Mouse? Something has happened. He's not smiling. "What is it Dougie? When is Mouse coming?" Dougie, please answer me. Something is hurting you. Your face – I don't like it. Dougie tell me, "Dougie?"

"Maria isn't coming home love." Sorry? What? What does that mean? Maria always comes home.

"I, I don't understand, what? Is she staying at Tara's house?" I know she's not; his face, it's too serious, I really don't like it!

"No love…Maria…she's…she's not coming home anymore."

What?

"What do you mean? Tell me now! What do you mean she's not coming home anymore?" Dougie's face is broken, beaten and broken – a special delicacy…

"Babes, love…Maria died nearly three years ago." 1,2,3,4, 1,2,3,4, 1,2,3,4, 1,2,3,4. Count to ten 1,2,3,4,5,6,7,8,9,10, then do it again 1,2,3,4,5,6,7,8,9,10. Hickory, dickory, dock. Hickory, dickory, dock.

"Dougie? Why are you saying this? I don't understand. Why would you say this to me? Dougie?" Why? Why? Why? Why? *She tried hard to scream, she tried hard to fight*…Um mm, mm, mm, I don't understand…

"Love, come on, calm down. Maria was…Maria died three years ago. You're having a bad night. It's nearly the anniversary of her…death…I should have…I should have realised…I've just been so busy…I…"

"What do you mean I'm having a bad night?"

"Sometimes you…Oh, love..." What? What? Tell me! "Sometimes you do this. You see, you waited for her that night and she didn't come…and sometimes you, sort of…wait again."

"No, no, that's not possible – I rang her – her phone?"

"You keep it charged babes – you like to listen to her

192

voice." No, not possible, I don't…do I? Dougie, don't hang your head Dougie, I can't see your face…is this the truth? Dougie, show me the truth in your face.

"Dougie look at me!" Oh God!… … …"Mouse, Mouse she's not in the house, I told her half past eight now she's really so late. She's really so late, so late, so late, so late…"

"Ssh…come on love, come on babes, relax, calm down." No! No! 10:48 – she's late – just late!

"But Tara's mum?"

"She didn't know what to say love, she feels so bad…" No! No! No! Nononono! Can't be true, isn't true. Can't be real, isn't real…isn't real…orange peel, orange peel. Make it rhyme she'll come on time. Mouse is dead? My baby Maria is dead? Maria is dead? Maria is dead.

"If it's true, how did it happen?"

"Oh love, I can't do this!" He's breaking. Dougie's breaking. My poor Dougie. Broad shouldered over-burdened Dougie. Don't cry Dougie! Why are you crying? Dougie doesn't cry. Maria doesn't die…cry, die, cry, die, cry, die, cry, die.

"Dougie?" Don't breathe. "How did it happen?" You look like a puppy, be strong for me Dougie.

"She was…" Please don't cry Dougie. I don't like it. "She…she…"

She was used and abused by a drunk with the horn.

"It's okay Dougie…you don't have to say it.

His calloused crude hands stank of fags and beer
as he wrung out the life of the one you hold dear.

You don't have to say it…I know…But…but…where did it happen?"

"In the woods, behind the park…She'd been at the park with some friends and on the way home realised she'd left her mobile there, she ran back to get it and…" Oh no, no, no "Babes?" Four sets of four: 1,2,3,4, 1,2,3,4, 1,2,3,4, 1,2,3,4. Count to ten 1,2,3,4,5,6,7,8,9,10, then do it again 1,2,3,4,5,6,7,8,9,10. Hickory, dickory, dock. Hickory, dickory, dock. 1,2,3,4, 1,2,3,4, 1,2,3,4, 1,2,3,4. Count to ten 1,2,3,4,5,6,7,8,9,10, then do it again 1,2,3,4,5,6,7,8,9,10. Hickory, dickory, dock. Hickory, dickory, dock. 1,2,3,4, 1,2,3,4, 1,2,3,4, 1,2,3,4. Count to ten 1,2,3,4,5,6,7,8,9,10, then do it again 1,2,3,4,5,6,7,8,9,10. Hickory, dickory, dock. Hickory, dickory, dock. 1,2,3,4, 1,2,3,4, 1,2,3,4, 1,2,3,4. Count to ten 1,2,3,4,5,6,7,8,9,10, then do it again 1,2,3,4,5,6,7,8,9,10. Hickory, dickory, dock. Hickory, dickory, dock.

Hickory, hickory, dock, rock, rock, rock.

Hickory, dickory, dock, rock, rock, rock.

Hickory, hickory, dock, rock, rock, rock.

Hickory, hickory, dock, rock, rock, rock.

Rock. "Love – babes?" Rock. "Love!" What? "Stop it. Stop rocking. Sit still. Stop!" Rock, rock. What? Dougie sounds cross. Sorry Dougie, can't help it Dougie. Dougie, smell. Mm, smell Dougie. Dougie still crying? Dougie crying…don't like it. Dougie you're strong. Broad shouldered over-burdened Dougie. Hold me tight, yes that right Dougie. Dougie smell…smell Dougie. Don't cry Dougie…it frightens me. Stroke my hair, yes that's right. Make me calm…calm me down…calm sea…an ocean without motion. Dougie will know what to do; he always knows what to do. Calm me down. Hold me tight. Mm, smell of wood shavings and sweat. A Dougie combination, he smells of man. Bury my face deep in his chest, deep, mm, don't even come up for air, it's so safe there. Hide in Dougie, in Dougie I'm safe, Dougie's my frame. Let's just sit. Hold each other and sit. Yes, like this...Tick tock, tick tock. 10:58. Tick tock, tick tock. Lean on Dougie, he sorts me out, picks up the pieces – my pieces.

"I'm sorry."

"Why?" Gentle face – gentle voice.

"Because you always have to carry me."

"You're as light as a feather. Anyway, after all these years

I'm used to us. Me, you…if I didn't have you to carry I'd lose my balance and topple over." I love you so much Dougie.

"I love you so much Dougie."

"I love you too babes."

"She's not on her own is she?"

"No, they're resting together – side by side." Yes…I remember…

"Yes that's right."

"We can take some flowers there tomorrow if you like."

"Yes, I'd like that." Sunday, the family all together.

"Hold me tight Dougie – let's stay like this for a while."

10:59. Mm yes…snuggled up with Dougie on the sofa in front of the television. But it isn't on, and Mouse isn't secretly opening her Christmas presents in the bedroom… Dougie hold me tight. Let's just stay like this for a while. Let's just sit for a while… let's not move…Ssh…still…so still…so still…

So here we sit as still as stone,
two statues now at peace.
Two living headstones
of flesh and bone,
alive but yet deceased.

Under creeping moss our bones may groan. The night is often dark. But together in grief we are never alone, and our love for each other has proven – has shown, that death cannot stunt all, for in each other we've grown. There's a glimmer of light in the dark. So tomorrow morning with the sun, we'll rise to do the day. When Dougie and I live, love, breathe as one, we can almost feel that we've just begun to see the light of the day not the set of the sun. And make some sense in this strange, fickle world.

Some sense in this strange, fickle world. Sense… light…Dougie and I…we'll rise. Hold me tight, Dougie, tight.

Sometimes, alone, I can't fight the night, but together we can make it light – if only a little. A glimmer of light in the dark. Hold on tight. When we're together there is always hope, so we won't let go, we'll hold each other, and just sit for a while. Let's just sit for while…

Tick tock, tick tock, tick tock, tick tock. It's 11 o'clock.

"I love you Mummy."

"I love you too Mouse."

1am

A Thousand Dreams

By Daniel Gothard

I don't have much time. Things keep coming back to me. I have to think, use this space and find a way out. I'm back at the house and I can smell her perfume. I can see her everywhere. She hasn't taken down the photographs of us yet. She must feel stunned and lifeless – I know I do. I feel as if she is dead, as if I have ended her.

She'd wanted the keys back. A clean break, as if there could ever be such a thing when love dies screaming, prematurely ripped apart. She'd asked me three times in as many days. What was the rush, I was still paying half the mortgage and the utility bills – didn't that entitle me to a key? I'd avoided giving them to her, changed the subject and made some excuse or other about needing to collect the last of my possessions. I was flippant, ignoring the pain in her eyes and the way she continually scratched her arm. I wanted to pretend everything was normal, would be normal, and that what I was doing could in no way be thought of as callous. I was a good person. I had to be, otherwise everything I had done could be seen as wrong – my entire existence gone mouldy and I would be nowhere.

The gradual collection of my property could be made endless by my fiddle-faddling with lost photographs or LPs caught behind loft insulation – the final minute remnants turning into an excruciatingly drawn-out process, stretching out over days and weeks. Would I collect motes of dust from the top of the wardrobe before I was finally gone? No, to save this kind of prolonged and agonising break up I'd decided to go back to the house one last time, just for an hour or so, and pick up the rest of my things.

She had telephoned me at work on a daily basis during the first week of separation, asking me why and how we could have come to such a place, such an expiration of desire – still in our twenties and without the heart to go on and through the wall of emotionless days and nights. Surely we could have tried again, failing better each time? She said we had become like brother and sister – but that was a nasty oversimplification and its cold core of enmity made me dislike her, although my guilt only allowed the negative feelings towards her to last for a few hours. Later, compassion and the weight of my own inhumanity returned to bury any self-righteousness. Like a reverse palliative.

We had been planning our marriage for six months and were three months away from the date when I walked out. So much effort had gone into the *perfect* day – I had never felt a burning wish to stay or go during that time, although I always harboured a strange ambiguity whenever we visited a possible reception venue or looked at wedding cake designs, as if my involvement wasn't *that* important. I was the mainstay helper rather than a participant. One of the last things I remember about our life together, before I closed the front door, was the sight of her pouring the contents of her wedding folder into the kitchen bin, like supper leftovers. Jesus, what a tragic sight that was – photographs of wedding dresses, seating plans, civil ceremony location options; all the artificial trappings of happiness. It was the thing we had shared in the pretence that we would be okay. I was supposed to be her rock but I had become the tumbling boulder that squashed her love – a Sisyphus who let go. A crappy metaphor, I know, but the situation calls for it.

"Don't torture me with lies. Just be honest, if that's possible. That's all I ask. Let's move on," she'd said, two nights before, the last time I saw her. It was immediately before she went to visit her sister (who, incidentally, had also taken to phoning me and yelling that I wasn't good enough to be with Louise anyway, and I should leave her alone). I'd returned to collect my jacket and had, rather tactlessly, taken an overnight bag with me. I think her first thought was that I might be expecting to stay with her and then it had dawned on her that I was already staying in someone else's bed. I suppose I should have thought about the ramifications of the bag and what it signalled – it was like tipping a bucket of ice-cold water over her head and then whacking the empty bucket into her teeth. A clear sign that I was moving on. In hindsight I had probably wanted to show her that I wasn't ever coming back. It was a subconscious move – and obviously not the best thing to have done. Like most men I'm never that good at reading women's feelings, in fact I'm useless. I used to think I had a talent for it.

I had remained technically faithful to Louise in the early days of my romance with Sophia, in the sense that I never slept with Sophia or even as much as kissed her. It had been quickly obvious to me that Sophia and I felt the same way about each other – work suddenly became a pleasure instead of the usual bore, and I made sure I organised my day around when I could spend time with her. She has a daughter, a beautiful little girl called Lily. On the day we first made love we had just collected Lily from school – Sophia worked part-time and I'd ducked out of work early, pretending illness. We had gone to a fast food place and eaten afternoon burgers – like a family, but not quite. It was a deception and Sophia kept glancing at me with a strained expression. She was probably worried about her child and thinking that Lily might begin to see her mother in a different way. But I also believe she was waiting for me to spring to my feet and, realising my mistake, run back home to my future wife and the 'wonderful life' I had with her.

But I couldn't leave. I felt like I never wanted to be without

Sophia again. She seemed the epitome of what I had dreamed of through the years listening to my parents' marriage fall apart, sitting alone in my box bedroom, playing David Sylvian, Roxy Music and Suzanne Vega to drown out the arguments. She seemed to be the one God had sent to me. I treasured every second with her as if it were more than a lifetime.

The main reason I'd chosen tonight for my last visit to the house was that I knew Louise wouldn't be there and, even better, that the neighbours would be looking after our cats – her cats. I hated the bloody things and they didn't like me either. I was allergic to their fur, their stinking litter tray and the sight of their fat bellies dragging along the carpets. She loved them more than she did me, or so I often thought. They would always get a goodnight kiss after she had finished her nightly bath routine. I would be left on my own watching a film or whatever was on the television, and be the one expected to make the effort to go upstairs to seek a lip smacker from her – knowing she still had cat fur on her mouth.

I conducted an experiment once when I decided not to initiate any physical contact with her, waiting to see how long it took for her to notice and redress the balance. After three weeks of nothing I confronted her during an episode of *Heartbeat* – she threw wine in my face and ran away crying. I can't hear Buddy Holly without thinking of that moment. There were so many moments of ire in that house. Our responsibilities were limited to the cats and a mortgage, so what was the problem? We both had good jobs but she seemed to be permanently on edge and imagining the worst about me – I was a spendthrift to her, unreliable, a difficult character. Maybe I was, I hadn't been through a particularly well-governed childhood and I think I do live in a perma-dysfunctional state, but we could have worked on that together and I had loved her *so* much. She had been my true love. I had felt it deeply and completely with her. True love is a corny expression, I know, but I believe in it.

She and Sophia are exact opposites. Sophia is from a Russian background, a broken family. She lost her mother when she was ten through breast cancer and, when she was seventeen, watched her father go to prison for fraud. Then three years later her brother, her only remaining family, was killed in a motorbike accident. But despite all this, she had somehow found a way to appreciate life and love more – where I am sure I would have *hated* more – and to cherish every day of calm and give her daughter everything she needed to be happy.

We'd made love for the first time on that afternoon, after the burger place, back at Sophia's flat when Lily had fallen asleep in front of a Disney film. I watched Sophia cry with passion on top of me. She whispered how much she loved me and how she had waited for me. After the sex we had dressed and made some coffee. Sophia's hands trembled as she stroked my arms and told me her life story. She said she had never told anybody else about her father's imprisonment – she had been ashamed and then forgiven him. I had touched her cheek and thought of Barber's *Adagio For Strings*. When Lily woke, Sophia drove me to the railway station and I made my way home. That was to be the evening I left Louise to go and live with Sophia. My decision had been made that afternoon in the first moments of lovemaking, perhaps I had been waiting to see whether she would be as perfect as I imagined. I was happy to give up everything to be with her.

The short span of time it took me to arrive back at the house that day has come, I can already tell, to be a marker in my life – a point when I will always remember how I was waiting for my heart to start beating again – as if I was being carried along by fate and circumstance and the emotional drive that says *everything will be okay*.

I'd watched the rain on the windows as the train pulled

away, Sophia and Lily waving me off as if I was going to war. I suppose I *was* beginning my own kind of conflict and destruction. I'd felt a numbness all the way home. I knew what was coming, as if someone, a seer perhaps, had told me my life would be ending shortly and time had been slowed to a series of essential movements and thoughts. Travelling home the glow of a signal light to the right side of the track had been like the green beacon Gatsby seized upon as his sign that Daisy could be his again if he made enough money and proved his place in Society.

During tonight's journey I have felt just as numb. As the train pulled into the station my stomach dropped and my body felt cold. I waited for a bus to take me to the house – her house, I supposed I could not call it 'my house' for much longer. I'd had to deal with many hours either on, or waiting for, public transport during the affair with Sophia – it would probably amount to whole days. It had given me time to think and plan what to say to each of the people I'd inadvertently involved in the separation, and tonight it had given me chance to prepare myself for my last ever visit to the house. I held myself together by listening to music – the Sylvian I had listened to in my youth, and on which I was still hooked, crooned in my ears, "... *upon the wave of summer, a hilltop paved with gold. We shut our eyes and make the promises we hold...*"

The bus was damp and steamy. I couldn't see out of the windows without using my sleeve to repeatedly rub a circular clear patch. And then I walked from the bus-stop towards to the house – *our house* – as I was still drawn to think of it, despite efforts to force myself to do otherwise. I walked past the park and the memories of laughter when we tried to get fit and jog the perimeter twice a day, and the time we went to a steam fair and I became nauseous; past the church which we had visited twice, pretending goodness and reaching out towards something Holy; around the corner we had excitedly turned the first time we went to view the house; and onto the road where we had planned to live as husband and wife, attempting to carve out a good life, a rich and happy existence. Now she is away for a short while, I want to reclaim all this, if only for a short while, just some time to try to say goodbye to my memories. There is so much to say and do. I have to commune with regions of the past where the recollections stored in the four walls of the house can reach me and expose my fragility as a human being; as a man who has committed many sins.

The day before I left her we tried to brave-face another twenty-four hours and work on our problems. Over breakfast Louise begged me not to go, and I agreed to a trip to Oxford for the day. The journey was silent and the tension was enough to drown hope.

The last film she and I saw together, on that day in Oxford, was *Mission Impossible*. The following evening my mother made a joke about the aptness of the title. I didn't laugh. It was one of the worst days of my life.

Sophia never knew Louise and I had tried to find a compromise. As soon as we had returned home, Louise went to bed crying and I phoned Sophia to tell her I loved her and would be leaving the house, and my life, soon. I was attempting the impossible – three-sided honour and decency in a perfidious state. Sophia told me she understood why I had to give my dying life one last kiss. She told me she would be waiting and I didn't sleep that night. I couldn't wait for the end to come – it is only now, as I approach the house, that I realise what an awful person I am for doing what I have done.

I knew she wouldn't be there as she'd gone to be with her family – first her sister's and then to her Mum and Dad's for a bit. She'd said she was telling me in case I wanted to get in touch with her. She was keeping the couple-like farce going out of habit and I was grateful to her – it eased the rush in separating and that was what I needed.

Her dad must have been overjoyed that his daughter was finally losing the baggage (me) and running back to him and her mother. He'd always hated me; he thought I was fey and a waster. I didn't have the type of *right stuff* for him. I wasn't an athlete or a doctor, niether did I have a reliable Civil Service job like the one he had been constrained by for thirty years. I was the guy women usually loved to spend time with – the good-looking, funny charmer. He hadn't been to university and I had, which I think was another reason why he tried to belittle me. He imagined he could buy intellectual credibility by investing in leather-bound editions of classic novels and reading *The Daily Telegraph* instead of *The Daily Mail*. For Louise's sake we had tried to bond on numerous occasions – playing golf, seeing Nanci Griffith in concert as a foursome and changing the tyres on his Ford Cortina. But it was forced and useless. Eventually he had been proven right; I had been the guy to screw his daughter over, and she had run home to him. Perhaps, to open his eyes, I should send him some of the pornographic photographs I took of his 'little girl'. I would pay a fortune to watch as he opened the envelope and see his features lock into a deathly grimace. I would have the satisfaction that the rest of his life would be an endless replay of *that* moment.

I glance at my watch as I get nearer and nearer the house, my pace slowing with each section of pavement. It's now just past 1am. I've left Sophia in bed, curled up and fast asleep. I planned the night, and didn't leave until I knew she was asleep, hoping that she wouldn't realise I'd gone. Sophia is the *other woman*. It isn't her fault I have fallen in love with her; I couldn't have done anything else. She looks like Grace Kelly and is everything I could ever have imagined in a dream. As I left her I could see sweat still clinging to her contented face, and smell sex in the bedsheets.

Sex seems a completely new experience with her – I am still in the first throws of lust. When it's that good it's hard to summon guilt, but still I have, I am, over and over. I should have been a Catholic – I have the contrition chops and then some.

I promised Sophia earlier at dinner that I wouldn't re-visit the house again, not for any reason. I had to tell her something and I figured that, since I was up to my neck in lies, one more wouldn't hurt.

"I know it's painful, but we have to start from somewhere. You have to make a clean break from her," she'd said, stroking my right forearm. She meant it kindly and was probably worried about her situation, but it felt patronising (or perhaps matronising?) and only served to galvanise my spirit of purpose and intent for the night ahead. As I think of this I wonder how, when, and whether, our love affair will end. Will she become weary of me and my ways, or will I meet another Grace Kelly or perhaps an Audrey Hepburn? But such pointless conjecture can wait.

I feel strange that now, after my long journey of a taxi, two trains and a bus, I am finally approaching the house for what will be the last time. This is the place I've lived for three quick-fire years of my life; three years of IKEA weekends, leaving spare rooms full of moving-in junk and attempts at domestic bliss. This is the residence I'd walked away from just over a week ago, willingly dislocating myself from my past. I come from divorced, adulterous parents so treachery and separation seem normal to a dysfunction-junkie like me.

This journey has been a test of my will and resolve. I have been trying to ignore the real reasons I've been drawn back to the house. Sure, I know I love the building and it harbours grand memories but part of me wonders if my motivation is to show her that I can return whenever I want to, or, being more honest still, to show *myself* that I can. I admit to myself that it must be the latter as I feel strongly that I don't want her to know I've been there. In the space of a few days I've gone from being an equal member of the household to a creeping figure of secrecy. The thing that nags at me most is that maybe, despite having left of my own free will, I want the chance to change my mind if things don't work out with Sophia. Caddish, I know, but honest...

Before I even reach the front door I start to wonder how long I should stay. I'd previously told myself that I only wanted to stay an hour, but suddenly I'm tempted to think that overnight would be more logical. Or maybe not logical, maybe I just want more time here before it ceases to be half mine.

But what if she comes back? I could say that I had wanted to collect some CDs and thought it best to do it when she wasn't around. No, I know she would instantly see through that line of bullshit and kick me out – probably change the locks too. In fact I wonder whether she hasn't done that anyway? Surely it was obvious I might try to let myself in? I let myself wonder if this is perhaps what she wants? Unbidden comes a strong feeling that I miss my old life. The house and her. I miss the reliability of it all. The safety and satisfaction we created together. That kitchen table with croissant crumbs ingrained in the cracks and the chair with the loose leg. Weekend sex and forgetting the working week. We *did* things together. I used to lament the lack of free time and the way she would organise us into dinners and charity walks, helping feed the poor at New Year and many other good works. All of that had become my life. And I had willingly disengaged from it, floated off into the atmosphere of grass-is-greener-land only to realise now that most of it is dead from the roots up. I am starting to be aware that I am not the sort of person who welcomes change and emotional upheaval.

Sophia is exciting and new and I genuinely believe in her and her goodness, the greatness of what she represents has changed my whole world. But it also unnerves me to think that I might not have given myself a chance to evolve my *own* life. Am I, and had I, been living for another person?

I need to feel emotion again. Perhaps this is the real reason I've returned to the house. I need time to stop feeling as if I would stop breathing every time the telephone rang at work or I had to look at mortgage statements and the value of the endowment policy. I need some warmth back in my stomach, like a child at Christmas when his parents are happy just because he is happy. It dawns on me that I used to have this sort of warmth from the complacency that came with my long-term relationship – maybe complacency isn't that bad. We all get psychologically and emotionally flabby when love mutates into domesticity. Perhaps being back at the house will make life and its wonder seem tangible again.

In the early stages of the affair with Sophia everything seemed to be spinning away and back at me, as though a door into my soul had been taken off at the hinges and the wind was howling through. The times when I wasn't with Sophia, like when I was at work or the supermarket, or on a train, I felt threatened and lonely. I felt as if I was being judged and those around me would read my thoughts and guess my past, chase me to the edge of the nearest town and stone me to death. I read a lot – Graham Greene, Anthony Powell and Julian Maclaren-Ross – as a way to draw (male-centred) empathy and experience to my plight. It usually worked for the length of the book, but the frozen agony returned moments after my bookmark had been placed in the front cover flyleaf. I felt as if I might evaporate or become condemned by the silence in my head. And the voice of so-called inner reason just made everything that bit worse. I used every penny I had, and more, to keep Louise and Sophia apart from each other and happy. I think it worked with Sophia, but to Louise, I guess, my continued monthly pay-outs must have looked as gullible and guilt-ridden as they actually were. I was the saturnine man – gone into a night-world of emotional voids and meaningless efforts to please. She had always berated me for spending money unnecessarily and would have been happier, superficially, if I had spent more time expanding my clothing collection than increasing the weight of LPs on the loft conversion floor. I must have been a drawn-out disappointment to her and, by the way she begged me to stay one minute then told me she would find someone else to marry her the next, I never knew how much she loved me, or whether she was just hanging onto our relationship because it was better than nothing – *I was better than nothing*.

The rain is still hammering down, as it has done for the entire journey back. It seems fitting for the night that I am going home for the last time. I am soaked as I finally arrive at the front door. I don't care and breath deeply, savouring the first, vital moments. The *spirit* of home is a hard thing to define, but I feel it is where part of your soul resides and, when you leave for good, a small element of you is gone for ever.

I can't find my front door key. I find I am crying, weeping against the door. I am distraught at not being able to get in. I have earned the right for this last visit, planned it, balanced everything required and put it in the right order – and here I am, potentially thwarted at the very last second by a stupid oversight. A torrent of sadness washes over me and I let it. Then I remember that we had decided to place spare keys under one of the recently laid front garden paving slabs. Would she have had the thought or time to move them? I dab my eyes, feeling pathetic, and laugh nervously with hope. I lean down and study the red slab I had put the front door key under just a month before. I look into the small puddle on top of the slab, see my reflection and wipe it away, then dry the back of my hand on my jacket imagining my face gone forever with that simple act. I reach down, lift the slab and see the key glinting up at me. I take it from its earthy spot. Have I just become a burglar? I feel like a criminal, but content myself that my name is still on the mortgage and I *do* have a key somewhere. I have the right to enter.

I sit on the white wall outside the house for a few minutes and smoke a cigarette to regain my composure. I am back where I belong, it feels right – the location, the proximity to my parents and my job. Maybe Louise should be the one to give up living here. I could wrestle the house back! But immediately I know that my new friend Mr. Guilt would prevent me from doing it.

As a distraction from the unwanted guilt I begin to think back, remembering another time I forgot my house key and, after telephoning her at work, waited for two hours before she came home to let me in. It had rained hard on that occasion too, and I had been desperate to use the toilet, but she kept me hanging on. She'd said she was in a meeting and couldn't possibly fit in the ten minute drive home. The memory acts as a stark reminder of the worst parts of our previous life. We had both been selfish but, while I sit here, I don't want to admit that. Right now I am only interested in her failings.

We had fought hard to buy the house. The guy who owned the property was also an estate agent and builder – he had renovated the place not long before we made an offer. He pitched us against another buyer and told us the first to come up with the money would get the house. It was a gruelling month whilst we pestered solicitors and pushed for a firm mortgage offer. We won eventually, but it was on the verge of becoming a pyrrhic victory. She cried all the time and I developed a nasty facial rash due to stress. How could we ever rest easy with an accumulation of anxiety like that in our lives?

Looking around me, and up at the half-moon, I watch fat, silvery clouds speed by. I feel numb with indecision. The Clash pounds in my skull – "*Should I stay or should I go?*" I have always used songs as reference points and to activate purpose and motivation. Simple and perhaps undignified, but it usually works.

There is a sticky film of rainwater on the road, but I notice a dry rectangle in front of the house where Louise's car must have been parked earlier. The weather turned ugly only two hours ago after three days of unbroken sunshine. Has she only recently departed? My nerves rise and jangle at the thought that I could have walked in on her. How awful that would have been, me as the slippery interloper.

The pale orange light cast by the street lamps makes the moment seem less desolate – as if there might be a chance for redemption. But I am not naïve enough to believe in such an enigmatic sign. I have watched those same lights from our bedroom window in every season – watched rain and snow, my life passing by in the process.

I open the front door slowly, as if some elaborate booby-trap might spear me to the walls, and I stroke the blue frame of the doorway as I enter. We did some decorating a few months ago. The gloss is still shining around the bronze keyhole. It was supposed to be a new beginning – but was a metaphor for superficiality too. I had spent all the time I wielded a sponge and paintbrush thinking of Sophia. I shut the door carefully – only the click of the catch on the lock registering. Should I switch on the main hallway light? No, I'll feel my way to the lounge. I pass the Art Deco mirror we bought at Camden market. I look at my reflection again and immediately look away; the sight of my fear and anguish is repulsive.

There's a dull light coming from underneath the lounge door, at the end of the hall. I remember how she always checked and double-checked the timer switch whenever we went away. We'd been burgled twice in under eighteen months. She'd had hysterics one night as we returned from the cinema to see *The Truth About Cats And Dogs*, a howling turkey of a film, and saw the curtains moving in the front bay window. She'd torn me to pieces when I insisted on going into the house to investigate. What else could I do, I had argued, wait for the burglars to escape with our belongings again? It turned out to be just our cats fighting and, still angry, she had run to our bedroom screaming at me and crying, hurling her car keys at my head, grazing my right eyebrow and making me trip over a wicker chair. I had tried, and failed, to reassure her. I told her everything was okay and we need not be scared any more but as usual I handled the male-female-interaction divide badly and fluffed my chance at making amends. We didn't talk for two days so I found solace at work with Sophia, and after work with thoughts of Sophia.

For a moment I fool myself into believing that she's left the light on for me as a *Welcome Home*. I walk into the lounge and immediately feel as if I never want to leave again. The sadness is almost unbelievable, like misery I've never known before. Returning from work, the cinema, a holiday, I have walked into that room so many times and it suddenly strikes me, like a heart attack, that I will never have that with her again. And I have done it to myself. One of the things that has sickened me most since I walked out on her was friends and relatives 'enlightening' me of their negative feelings towards her. Some I had been made aware of before, but the way and the detail of what and how they told me broke my heart all over again. She and I had been *there* – a place where lovers gain and regain something about themselves, their personalities and qualities in life, something which adds to them as humans. I didn't want to hear the opinions of people who should have empathised with me and protected me. I was too stunned to defend her at the time and I deeply regret that too.

Everything about the room is perfect and seemingly unchanged, as if I have just been out for a while, on a whimsical flight like ol' George Bailey from *It's A Wonderful Life*, seeing another side of my life and what it would be like without her. I am home and she will be back soon. We can begin again. I try to stay in this fake reverie, forcing the fantasy to hold. But it slips away.

I notice that the reproduction Cezanne painting we'd bought together from the Tate is missing. It had been given to us as a present from her parents after a day out with them. I wonder if she has given it back to them. Is it too much to hope that she partially blames her dad for driving me away and therefore doesn't want the reminder of his gift hanging on the wall?

The photograph on the shelving unit by the television is face down. I pick it up and look at us standing in front of the leaning tower of Pisa. Memories of that holiday come flooding back. Pisa then Florence.

It was our first foreign holiday together and we had been full of excitement. We had landed in Pisa at night and she used the Italian she'd learned at night school to issue orders to the taxi driver – asking him to take us to a hotel we had hastily booked the day before. She did her best with the accent and turned to me, smiling and confident, as the taxi drove away from the airport.

The next morning she tried to find out how far from the leaning tower we were. The hotel proprietor laughed and waved her arms – she kept repeating three words that neither of us understood. And then, as we left the hotel, we realised why she had laughed so hard. The top of the tower was visible from the doorway – approximately five hundred metres from where we stood.

I turn on a table lamp and look closely at our faces in the photo which I remember was taken by a fellow English tourist. We looked so happy. That was a good day.

I recall that when we reached Florence I had felt as Stendhal must have – overwhelmed by the beauty of the city, by the location and the way the environment began to nudge romance towards us. There is a celestial wonder to Florence, and although it has crime, high prices and many other negatives of life, it also has enough glory to make you never want to leave. The Medici's, the Renaissance and a total appreciation of the metaphor for heaven on earth has been attempted in the architecture. We walked miles, looked in awe at churches paintings and sculpture – topped by Michelangelo's *David* – and climbed Il Duomo and saw what Brunelleschi intended The sight of the city and its grace.

I read *Room With A View* and she *Nights At The Circus* as we sat each morning, after breakfast, near the Uffizi, under a bright red parasol. It felt like a life worth living. And when we eventually made our way back to Pisa to catch the plane home, she said to me, "I adore you beyond any words. I want to spend my life with you. I'm pregnant."

Within a month she'd had a miscarriage and decided to take a sabbatical from work to stay with her parents. She was gone for three weeks, and even though we had tried as hard as we could to revive the energy, love and hope for the future which had come from the Tuscan holiday, we couldn't make it happen. The spectre of the unborn child hung above us like the sword of Damocles and little by little killed our love.

I look around the lounge and see memories everywhere. I decide I won't stay the night after all, just for a while longer I have made Sophia a promise and, even though I have already broken my word by coming to the house at all, I will try not to let her down further. But, however much I shouldn't be here, I know that I have to stay long enough to do the thing I most want, collect memories. Clothes, records, photographs and all the other items aren't important but what I can store away in my mind is worth everything.

I go into the kitchen for something to drink. Something to dull my nerves and soak the stress. The fridge is full of the things she's always condemned. Junk food lines the white shelves. The only nod to healthy living is bio-yogurts. Whenever we went to the supermarket she used to put back anything I placed in the trolley she considered unhealthy, or too expensive.

"Yes, I know it might seem like fun-food now, but just

think about the cholesterol and your health," she would say, like a brainwashing mantra. I usually complied, and kept my resentment hidden. It makes me smile now to see the wealth of fatty indulgence in the fridge, then I realise that I am the reason she is punishing herself and my smile fades.

I pull a bottle of vodka from the freezer compartment and a large bar of chocolate from the fridge. White chocolate. Her favourite. But then I put it back. If I eat the chocolate she will realise I've been in the house. It has come to this triviality – confectionary is the line I can't cross. I get a tall glass from a wall cupboard, and some ice, then fill the tray with water and put it back in the freezer. I take the bottle and glass back to the lounge and sit in the armchair I always used to sit in. I stare around. I see her everywhere. On the sofa, where we made love three weeks before, and by the window near the kitchen, where she stood as I walked into the room on the evening I'd asked her to marry me.

"I will, you know I will," she'd said. My hand was in hers; a tear had rolled across her cheek and settled on her lip. I'd kissed it away. The taste of the tear comes back to me. I pour a hefty measure of vodka and down it like a drunk on his first round. Then another and a quick refill. Will the pain in my gut ever lessen? Is this official heartbreak?

I remember her standing in front of me, as I slumped forward in the same seat, on that evening, a few days ago – when I'd arrived home smelling of first-time sex with Sophia.

"No, that isn't fair, it isn't fair, please," she'd screamed when I said I was leaving that night. Her face was red, her hand held across her open mouth as if I had slapped her.

I look behind me, through the bay window to the front garden. I'd stood out there, two years before, and watched her nervously play with her new hairstyle. I'd only ever known her with long hair and she'd decided to have it bobbed. I'd arrived home late from work, the curtains were open and the lights shone out to the middle of the street.

There I'd stood, watching that woman touch her hair, look at her watch and then smile to herself, perhaps hoping for words of approval from me.

I am overcome with love as I recall that moment. That was her essence, her goodness. Why have I done what I have to her? That same evening we had played badminton as part of our weekly routine and I watched her more than I did the shuttlecocks. I was seeing her anew; shouldn't I have tried to get back that same feeling again and not have walked away so fast – just because another beautiful woman had caught my attention?

I reach above my head and pull down four photograph albums. I slowly turn the pages. There is a shot of me and two friends, on location in London. I had produced a short film a year before and we had managed to persuade a well-known British actress to star. The work was long and hard and I used a lot of my own money, which hadn't gone down too well. But the experience had felt like the best thing I had ever done in my personal struggle to get somewhere. I'm certain the film production, and its necessary workload, acted as a wedge between Louise and me, particularly since I had ignored her pleading and spent a lot of time away from her.

I suppose I am looking for as many reasons to blame myself as possible and also find reasons for feeling the way I did when I left. Surely I wasn't *so* male, *so* obvious and such a cliché that I would walk away just for lust?

I carry on turning the pages. The rest of the first album is family event shots. Christmas, birthdays, and other boring images of obligation.

The second set of photographs were taken at various gigs, including Bowie at Milton Keynes – a total waste of time; we had arrived in the midday sun, he came on stage at 9pm, only played for an hour and didn't come back for an encore. We then had a three hour journey home. The best gig memory was Lloyd Cole at what used to be the Hammersmith Odeon.

It was Louise's birthday present that year – she had been a huge Cole fan since university, and the elation on her face from the moment I gave her the tickets, in a restaurant in Central London, to the end of the show made me as happy as I feel I ever could be. *That* was the point – I had known *real* happiness with her. Would I ever know it again?

We had stayed with my cousin in her plush Barbican apartment at the end of that night. As we made love I had felt wonderfully free, and afterwards, looking from the large window by the bed I saw London lit up – St. Paul's Cathedral in the middle distance had reminded me of Florence – and I know I would have been even sanguine with the idea of death in those minutes of *our* life together. She slept beside me like a vision of love and I had intended, I had prayed, that we would be together for the rest of our lives. If I can confess these things to myself now and whatever deity may or may not be listening, then perhaps there might be some hope for me.

I flick past many pages of times spent with friends at dinner parties or by the river and at some indistinguishable place for a weekend break – we went on lots of those. And then I come upon a telling collection from just a few weeks earlier. We had spent a Sunday travelling around the county looking at civil ceremony venues for the wedding. By late-afternoon we had ended up at my mother's house. Louise and my mum disliked each other, but made the effort to appear friendly. My grandmother had come down from Edinburgh for the week and I had promised I would visit her.

I study each of the five photographs hard, trying to pick out signs of disintegration in my psyche. I looked confident and happy, even though Sophia and I were already at the point of taking up our life together. What a sham it all was – the fake grinning, the sun washing the garden and creating such a glorious scene of the family ideal. And there we were, she and I holding each other, planning a marriage, talking about the struggle of planning and finding the time for it all. All that time, all those words, and I was planning a future without her. My mother had sent us the photographs of that day and I know they will be thrown away in time, so I take them out and put them in my jacket pocket. I realise how little I have of Louise – how few keepsakes. I have a few letters from our early days, but that's about it. Most of the photographs we'd taken are in the albums I have in my hand. That is our past – on a shelf.

I look at a last photograph – an image of her taken in Florence. She was reading at the time and I had called softly to her a second before I took the shot. She was smiling and holding her book aloft, in a fake 'no photos, please' pose. I looked at her face – her eyes, her nose, the mouth I had kissed so many times. Her hands were slender and lovely. Before I met her I would never have imagined I would notice a woman's hands, but hers were perfect, like a Rodin creation.

I take the vodka back to the kitchen and, in a moment of paranoia, put water in the bottle to the approximate level it had been before my indulgence.

There is a crack in the window above the sink from where I'd tried to swipe a mosquito last summer. I stare at it for a moment, touch the glass and think of her requests for me to repair it. She'd *requested* a lot from me – always wanting instant perfection, sometimes doubting her own abilities but constantly forgetting mine.

"Please find the time, it really does look awful, don't you think?" she'd said. It did, that was true, but I wasn't a glazier and the net curtain covered it up nicely.

The air bubbles in the linoleum by the bathroom door are still there and I begin to notice other things I'd ignored requests to rectify. If I had attended to the domestic chores more expediently would I have known more happiness?

The vodka had felt cool and clean in my mouth at first, but now makes me gag as I swallow and burns my throat as it goes down. I run the cold tap and put my face under it to lose the bitter aftertaste. The water flows into my mouth, then onto my chin and onto my shirt, soaking it through.

I walk into the bathroom, take Louise's towel from the back of the door and begin to dry my chest. I hold the towel to my nose. The aroma from her shower gel is heavy. I bury my face into the material. I want to take it with me. But I'm not supposed to be here. I don't live here anymore.

My head feels light, I lose my footing and almost fall backwards into the bath. I sit on the floor for a few moments and rest my head on the toilet seat, listening to my breathing and whispering her name.

I must have drifted off. I wake up with a start and look at my watch – it's just after 1.40. Only a few minutes have passed since I came into the bathroom, but I'm aware that the single hour I have given myself here is fast being used up. I think I can hear a voice, her voice. It must have been from the street, someone walking by, perhaps on their way home from a late night drinking session. I go into the kitchen, open the backdoor and step out into the garden. The new patio slabs seem to stretch out further than I remember. I go over and lie down on them, looking up at the star speckled sky. I try to feel contemplative, as if nothing really matters set against such a cosmic vision of things. I try to tell myself that we are all so inconsequential compared to the planets but my thoughts tail off uncertainly.

The fact is it all feels fake and uncomfortable and my back on the cold patio slabs is beginning to ache. There are times you have to allow yourself to feel whatever comes your way, good or bad. I feel bad.

I stand up again and turn back to look at the house. My eyes trail off to the right towards the new trellis fencing, the creosote still fresh. I spent three hours, just a week and a half ago, slapping the sticky liquid on and I will never watch it fade.

I wonder about Sophia. Will she have woken up, wondered what I was doing, suspecting the worst? After all, she already knows I am a liar. But then, we all tell lies, and no doubt she in turn will tell me her own. I rip up some grass and put it in my pocket – as a keepsake, surely Louise won't miss that?

I walk back to the house and go in. I lock the back door and check the window locks downstairs. I don't want to leave the house unsecured. I re-open the freezer and take a swig of vodka. It tastes like vodka and water. Should I try to replace it tomorrow morning? I decide to risk it being undetected and put the bottle back. I know I should leave now, but feel compelled to go upstairs. Only *then* can I leave.

The stairs creak and groan at all the familiar points and I smile at the predictability. We hadn't bothered to repair the wood – she said the creaking would act as an alarm if we were asleep and being burgled again.

I see two boxes that have been put into the spare room at the top of the stairs. They are both old and tatty. One looks like it has been in water. The bottom is crinkled and soft. Great – what is left of mine in the house is boxed in soggy cardboard ready to be sent away. I start to resent her again, but crush the ill feeling, knowing that she is merely trying to survive.

I walk slowly along the landing towards our bedroom. I pass by the second spare room and it brings back a memory of the time a sparrow got trapped in the chimney, on the other side of the air-vent in the stack at the centre of the room. We had both been scared for some reason, perhaps because of the Hitchcock film. I had eventually plucked up the courage to loosen the screws on the vent cover.

"Don't forget it's more scared of you," she had called to me from behind the door, and, "be careful, I love you. " As I pulled the cover off, I had run screaming towards the door. She had slammed it shut behind me and, as we waited for the sound of wings, or a thud if the bird panicked and flew into the wall, we were giggling like children. The bird must have flown through the open window. We never bothered to check.

We laughed a lot that day, she phoned me at work and it became a catalyst to talk about things we had done together, as if she was trying to tell me we were good together. In the evening as we recounted the story to friends, the details became more preposterous as the wine flowed. That was the day before I asked her to marry me.

I walk into our bedroom and close the door. The telephone rings downstairs.   Four rings, and then the machine picks up the call. She hasn't bothered to change the message yet. *"Sorry we're not here to take your call, please leave a message after the beep."* My voice sounded clear and happy. I had managed to record the outgoing words on the fifth attempt – she kept pulling silly faces to make me laugh. We'd had the machine from the day we moved in. It seemed like a symbol – *"…we're not here…"*

Whoever the caller is they don't leave a message. I run downstairs and play the tape back hearing some breathing before it cuts out. Was it Louise? Or was it Sophia?

I go back to the bedroom and close the door again. I'm fearful she'll come back early – give up on pretending she's okay being away from home. She might say she wanted to be surrounded by her things. Her sister would understand, or at least pretend she did.

What would I say if she *did* walk in and find me in the bedroom?

Would she be happy? Would I have to make excuses? After all, the house is still half mine. *What a fool I've been.* She would almost certainly scream and shout and throw things, maybe call the police. And I wouldn't blame her. I deserve all the anger and hatred she must be feeling.

I go to the bedroom window, pull the curtains back and look out. Still no sign of the car. It's nearly two in the morning, she won't be back now.

I walk across the room to the dressing table. We'd bought it at a house clearance place. She had loved it.

"It's like us; it belongs in this house."

I run my fingers across the wooden surface, the dust is thick. The way it was when I left. She's taken most of her toiletries – her talcum powder, her perfume, make-up bag and some jewellery. But, her handcream is still there.

I lift it up carefully, unscrew the lid and pour some of the cream onto my left hand. I rub both hands together, then put them to my nose and draw in deeply the rich, musky smell. Its familiarity makes my stomach drop.

I go to the bed and lie down on the side she's always slept on. I rest my head on her pillow. Some of her hairs are clinging to it. I pick them off and put them in my pocket, along with the grass.

She hasn't changed the tumbler on her bedside table. It's still half-full of water. I can see her fingerprints smudged on the side. The room feels airless so I open the window by the bed. The curtain lifts from the windowsill with a rush of cool breeze. I turn away and look at a blouse hanging on the wardrobe door.

I wish many things about my life. I wish I had more self-belief. I wish I were more sensitive to other people's feelings and also didn't place so much faith and trust in those close to me. I wish I had a plan – something to live by and for. And, most of all I wish I had *never* left her – ignored all new desires and the urge to break out.

I have lost her. I have lost my life.

Legend Press
Independent Book Publisher

This book has been published by vibrant publishing company Legend Press. If you enjoyed reading it then you can help make it a major hit. Just follow these three easy steps:

1. Recommend it
Pass it onto a friend to spread word-of-mouth or, if now you've got your hands on this copy you don't want to let it go, just tell your friend to buy their own or maybe get it for them as a gift. Copies are available with special deals and discounts from our own website and from all good bookshops and online outlets.

2. Review it
It's never been easier to write an online review of a book you love and can be done on Amazon, Waterstones.com, WHSmith.co.uk and many more. You could also talk about it or link to it on your own blog or social networking site.

3. Read another of our great titles
We've got a wide range of diverse modern fiction and it's all waiting to be read by fresh-thinking readers like you! Come to us direct at www.legendpress.co.uk to take advantage of our superb discounts. (Plus, if you email info@legendpress.co.uk just after placing your order and quote 'WORD OF MOUTH', we will send another book with your order absolutely free!)

Thank you for being part of our word of mouth campaign.

info@legendpress.co.uk
www.legendpress.co.uk